# Bonaventure

A Prose Pastoral of Acadian Louisiana

George W. Cable

**Bonaventure: A Prose Pastoral of Acadian Louisiana**

Copyright © 2020 Bibliotech Press
All rights reserved

ISBN: 978-1-64799-392-4

# CONTENTS

## CARANCRO

# CARANCRO

## CHAPTER I

## SOSTHÈNE

Bayou Teche is the dividing line. On its left is the land of bayous, lakes, and swamps; on its right, the beautiful short-turfed prairies of Western Louisiana. The Vermilion River divides the vast prairie into the countries of Attakapas on the east and Opelousas on the west. On its west bank, at its head of navigation, lies the sorry little town of Vermilionville, near about which on the north and east the prairie rises and falls with a gentle swell, from whose crests one may, as from the top of a wave, somewhat overlook the surrounding regions.

Until a few years ago, stand on whichever one you might, the prospect stretched away, fair and distant, in broad level or gently undulating expanses of crisp, compact turf, dotted at remote intervals by farms, each with its low-roofed house nestled in a planted grove of oaks, or, oftener, Pride of China trees. Far and near herds of horses and cattle roamed at will over the plain. If for a moment, as you passed from one point of view to another, the eye was shut in, it was only where in some lane you were walled in by fields of dense tall sugar-cane or cotton, or by huge green Chickasaw hedges, studded with their white-petalled, golden-centred roses. Eastward the plain broke into slight ridges, which, by comparison with the general level, were called hills; while toward the north it spread away in quieter swells, with more frequent fields and larger houses.

North, south, east, and west, far beyond the circle of these horizons, not this parish of Lafayette only, but St. Landry, St. Martin, Iberia, St. Mary's, Vermilion,—all are the land of the Acadians. This quarter off here to northward was named by the Nova-Scotian exiles, in memory of the land from which they were driven, the Beau Bassin. These small homestead groves that dot the plain far and wide are the homes of their children. Here is this one on a smooth green billow of the land, just without the town. It is not like the rest,—a large brick house, its Greek porch half hid in a grove of oaks. On that dreadful day, more than a century ago, when the

1

British in far-off Acadie shut into the chapel the villagers of Grand Pré, a certain widow fled with her children to the woods, and there subsisted for ten days on roots and berries, until finally, the standing crops as well as the houses being destroyed, she was compelled to accept exile, and in time found her way, with others, to these prairies. Her son founded Vermilionville. Her grandson rose to power,—sat in the Senate of the United States. From early manhood to hale gray age, the people of his State were pleased to hold him, now in one capacity, now in another, in their honored service; they made him Senator, Governor, President of Convention, what you will. I have seen the portrait for which he sat in early manhood to a noted English court painter: dark waving locks; strong, well-chiselled features; fine clear eyes; an air of warm, steady-glowing intellectual energy. It hangs still in the home of which I speak. And I have seen an old ambrotype of him, taken in the days of this story: hair short-cropped, gray; eyes thoughtful, courageous; mouth firm, kind, and ready to smile.

It must have been some years before this picture was taken, that, as he issued from his stately porch,—which the oaks, young then, did not hide from view as they do now,—coming forth to mount for his regular morning ride, a weary-faced woman stood before him, holding by the hand a little toddling boy. She was sick; the child was hungry. He listened to her tale. Their conversation was in French.

"Widow, are you? And your husband was a Frenchman: yes, I see. Are you an Acadian? You haven't the accent."

"I am a Creole," she said, with a perceptible flush of resentment. So that he responded amiably:—

"Yes, and, like all Creoles, proud of it, as you are right to be. But I am an Acadian of the Acadians, and never wished I was any thing else."

He found her a haven a good half-day's ride out across the prairies north-westward, in the home of his long-time acquaintance, Sosthène Gradnego, who had no more heart than his wife had to say No to either their eminent friend or a houseless widow; and, as to children, had so many already, that one more was nothing. They did not feel the burden of her, she died so soon; but they soon found she had left with them a positive quantity in her little prattling, restless, high-tempered Bonaventure. Bonaventure Deschamps: he was just two years younger than their own little Zoséphine.

Sosthène was already a man of some note in this region,—a region named after a bird. Why would it not often be well so to name places,—for the bird that most frequents the surrounding woods or fields? How pleasant to have one's hamlet called

2

Nightingale, or Whippoorwill, or Goldfinch, or Oriole! The home of Zoséphine and Bonaventure's childhood was in the district known as Carancro; in bluff English, Carrion Crow.

## CHAPTER II

## BONAVENTURE AND ZOSÉPHINE

They did not live à la chapelle; that is, in the village of six or eight houses clustered about the small wooden spire and cross of the mission chapel. Sosthène's small ground-story cottage, with garret stairs outside in front on the veranda and its five-acre farm behind, was not even on a highway nor on the edge of any rich bas fond,—creek-bottom. It was au large,—far out across the smooth, unscarred turf of the immense prairie, conveniently near one of the clear circular ponds—maraises—which one sees of every size and in every direction on the seemingly level land. Here it sat, as still as a picture, within its hollow square of China-trees, which every third year yielded their limbs for fuel; as easy to overlook the first time— as easy to see the next time—as a bird sitting on her eggs. Only the practised eye could read aright the infrequent obscure signs of previous travel that showed the way to it,—sometimes no more than the occasional soilure of the short turf by a few wheels or hoofs where the route led into or across the coolées—rivulets—that from marais to marais slipped southward toward the great marshes of the distant, unseen Gulf.

When I say the parent of one of these two children and guardian of the other was a man of note, I mean, for one thing, his house was painted. That he was the owner of thousands of cattle, one need not mention, for so were others who were quite inconspicuous, living in unpainted houses, rarely seeing milk, never tasting butter; men who at call of their baptismal names would come forth from these houses barefooted and bareheaded in any weather, and, while their numerous progeny grouped themselves in the doorway one behind another in inverse order of age and stature, would either point out your lost way, or, quite as readily as Sosthène, ask you in beneath a roof where the coffee-pot never

3

went dry or grew cold by day. Nor would it distinguish him from them to say he had many horses or was always well mounted. It was a land of horsemen. One met them incessantly; men in broad hats and dull homespun, with thin, soft, untrimmed brown beards, astride of small but handsome animals, in Mexican saddles, the girths and bridles of plaited hair, sometimes a pialle or arriatte—lasso, lariat—of plaited rawhide coiled at the saddle-bow. "Adieu, Onesime"—always adieu at meeting, the same as at parting. "Adieu, François; adieu, Christophe; adieu, Lazare;" and they with their gentle, brown-eyed, wild-animal gaze, "Adjieu."

What did make Sosthène notable was the quiet thing we call thrift, made graceful by certain rudiments of taste. To say Sosthène, means Madame Sosthène as well; and this is how it was that Zoséphine Gradnego and Bonaventure Deschamps, though they went not to school, nevertheless had "advantages." For instance, the clean, hard-scrubbed cypress floors beneath their pattering feet; the neat round parti-colored mats at the doors that served them for towns and villages; the strips of home-woven carpet that stood for roads—this one to Mermentau, that one to Côte Gelée, a third à la chapelle; the walls of unpainted pine; the beaded joists under the ceiling; the home-made furniture, bedsteads and wardrobes of stained woods, and hickory chairs with rawhide seats, hair uppermost; the white fringed counterpanes on the high featherbeds; especially, in the principal room, the house's one mantelpiece, of wood showily stained in three  colors and surmounted by a pair of gorgeous vases, beneath which the two children used to stand and feast their eyes, worth fifty cents if they were worth one,—these were as books to them indoors; and out in the tiny garden, where they played wild horse and wild cow, and lay in ambush for butterflies, they came under the spell of marigolds, prince's-feathers, lady-slippers, immortelles, portulaca, jonquil, lavender, althæa, love-apples, sage, violets, amaryllis, and that grass ribbon they call jarretière de la vierge,—the virgin's garter.

Time passed; the children grew. The children older than they in the same house became less and less like children, and began to disappear from the family board and roof by a mysterious process called marrying, which greatly mystified Zoséphine, but equally pleased her by the festive and jocund character of the occasions, times when there was a ravishing abundance of fried rice-cakes and boulettes—beef-balls.

To Bonaventure these affairs brought less mystery and less unalloyed pleasure. He understood them better. Some boys are born lovers. From the time they can reach out from the nurse's arms, they must be billing and cooing and choosing a mate. Such was ardent little Bonaventure; and none of the Gradnego weddings ever got quite through its ceremony without his big blue eyes being found full of tears—tears of mingled anger and desolation—because by some unpardonable oversight he and Zoséphine were still left unmarried. So that the pretty damsel would have to take him aside, and kiss him as they clasped, and promise him, "Next time—next time, without fail!"

Nevertheless, he always reaped two proud delights from these events. For one, Sosthène always took him upon his lap and introduced him as his little Creole. And the other, the ex-governor came to these demonstrations—the great governor! who lifted him to his knee and told him of those wonderful things called cities, full of people that could read and write; and about steamboats and steam-cars.

At length one day, when weddings had now pretty well thinned out the ranks of Sosthène's family, the ex-governor made his appearance though no marriage was impending. Bonaventure, sitting on his knee, asked why he had come, and the ex-governor told him there was war.

"Do you not want to make haste and grow up and be a dragoon?"

The child was silent, and Sosthène laughed a little as he said privately in English, which tongue his exceptional thrift had put him in possession of:

"Aw, naw!"—he shook his head amusedly—"he dawn't like hoss. Go to put him on hoss, he kick like a frog. Yass; squeal wuss'n a pig. But still, sem time, you know, he ain't no coward; git mad in minute; fight like little ole ram. Dawn't ondstand dat little fellah; he love flower' like he was a gal."

"He ought to go to school," said the ex-governor. And Sosthène, half to himself, responded in a hopeless tone:

"Yass." Neither Sosthène nor any of his children had ever done that.

# CHAPTER III

## ATHANASIUS

War it was. The horsemen grew scarce on the wide prairies of Opelousas. Far away in Virginia, Tennessee, Georgia, on bloody fields, many an Acadian volunteer and many a poor conscript fought and fell for a cause that was really none of theirs, simple, non-slaveholding peasants; and many died in camp and hospital—often of wounds, often of fevers, often of mere longing for home. Bonaventure and Zoséphine learned this much of war: that it was a state of affairs in which dear faces went away, and strange ones came back with tidings that brought bitter wailings from mothers and wives, and made les vieux—the old fathers—sit very silent. Three times over that was the way of it in Sosthène's house.

It was also a condition of things that somehow changed boys into men very young. A great distance away, but still in sight south-westward across the prairie, a dot of dark green showed where dwelt a sister and brother-in-law of Sosthène's vieille,—wife. There was not the same domestic excellence there as at Sosthène's; yet the dooryard was very populous with fowls; within the house was always heard the hard thump, thump, of the loom, or the loud moan of the spinning-wheel; and the children were many. The eldest was Athanase. Though but fifteen he was already stalwart, and showed that intelligent  sympathy in the family cares that makes such offspring the mother's comfort and the father's hope. At that age he had done but one thing to diminish that comfort or that hope. One would have supposed an ambitious chap like him would have spent his first earnings, as other ambitious ones did, for a saddle; but 'Thanase Beausoleil had bought a fiddle.

He had hardly got it before he knew how to play it. Yet, to the father's most welcome surprise, he remained just as bold a rider and as skilful a thrower of the arriatte as ever. He came into great demand for the Saturday-night balls. When the courier with a red kerchief on a wand came galloping round, the day before, from île to île,—for these descendants of a maritime race call their homestead groves islands,—to tell where the ball was to be, he would assert, if there was even a hope of it, that 'Thanase was to be the fiddler.

In this way 'Thanase and his pretty little jarmaine—first cousin—Zoséphine, now in her fourteenth year, grew to be well acquainted. For at thirteen, of course, she began to move in society, which meant to join in the contra-dance. 'Thanase did not dance with her, or with any one. She wondered why he did not; but many other girls had similar thoughts about themselves. He only played, his playing growing better and better, finer and finer, every time he was heard anew. As to the few other cavaliers, very willing were they to have it so. The music could not be too good, and if 'Thanase was already perceptibly a rival when hoisted up in a chair on top of a table, fiddle and bow in hand, "twisting," to borrow their own phrase—"twisting the ears of that little red beast and rubbing his abdomen with a stick," it was just as well not to urge him to come down into the lists upon the dancing-floor. But they found one night, at length, that the music could be too good—when 'Thanase struck up something that was not a dance, and lads and damsels crowded around standing and listening and asking ever for more, and the ball turned out a failure because the concert was such a success.

The memory of that night was of course still vivid next day, Sunday, and Zoséphine's memory was as good as any one's. I wish you might have seen her in those days of the early bud. The time had returned when Sosthène could once more get all his household—so had marriages decimated it—into one vehicle, a thing he had not been able to do for almost these twenty years. Zoséphine and Bonaventure sat on a back seat contrived for them in the family calèche. In front were the broad-brimmed Campeachy hat of Sosthène and the meek, limp sunbonnet of la vieille. About the small figure of the daughter there was always something distinguishing, even if you rode up from behind, that told of youth, of mettle, of self-regard; a neatness of fit in the dress, a firm erectness in the little slim back, a faint proudness of neck, a glimpse of ribbon at the throat, another at the waist; a something of assertion in the slight crispness of her homespun sunbonnet, and a ravishing glint of two sparks inside it as you got one glance within— no more. And as you rode on, if you were a young blade, you would be—as the soldier lads used to say—all curled up; but if you were an old mustache, you would smile inwardly and say to yourself, "She will have her way; she will make all winds blow in her chosen direction; she will please herself; she will be her own good luck and her own commander-in-chief, and, withal, nobody's misery or humiliation, unless you count the swain after swain that will sigh in vain." As for Bonaventure, sitting beside her, you could just see his bare feet limply pendulous under his wide palm-leaf hat. And yet he was a very real personage.

"Bonaventure," said Zoséphine,—this was as they were returning from church, the wide rawhide straps of their huge wooden two-wheeled vehicle creaking as a new saddle would if a

7

new saddle were as big as a house,—"Bonaventure, I wish you could learn how to dance. I am tired trying to teach you." (This and most of the unbroken English of this story stands for Acadian French.)

Bonaventure looked meek for a moment, and then resentful as he said:

"'Thanase does not dance."

"'Thanase! Bah! What has 'Thanase to do with it? Who was even thinking of 'Thanase? Was he there last night? Ah yes! I just remember now he was. But even he could dance if he chose; while you—you can't learn! You vex me. 'Thanase! What do you always bring him up for? I wish you would have the kindness just not to remind me of him! Why does not some one tell him how he looks, hoisted up with his feet in our faces, scratching his fiddle? Now, the fiddle, Bonaventure—the fiddle would just suit you. Ah, if you could play!" But the boy's quick anger so flashed from his blue eyes that she checked herself and with contemplative serenity added:

"Pity nobody else can play so well as that tiresome fellow. It was positively silly, the way some girls stood listening to him last night. I'd be ashamed, or, rather, too proud, to flatter such a high-headed care-for-nobody. I wish he wasn't my cousin!"

Bonaventure, still incensed, remarked with quiet intensity that he knew why she wished 'Thanase was not a cousin.

"It's no such a thing!" exclaimed Zoséphine so forcibly that Madame Sosthène's sunbonnet turned around, and a murmur of admonition came from it. But the maiden was smiling and saying blithely to Bonaventure:

"Oh, you—you can't even guess well." She was about to say more, but suddenly hushed. Behind them a galloping horse drew near, softly pattering along the turfy road. As he came abreast, he dropped into a quiet trot.

The rider was a boyish yet manly figure in a new suit of gray home-made linsey, the pantaloons thrust into the tops of his sturdy russet boots, and the jacket ending underneath a broad leather belt that carried a heavy revolver in its holster at one hip. A Campeachy hat shaded his face and shoulders, and a pair of Mexican spurs tinkled their little steel bells against their huge five-spiked rowels on his heels. He scarcely sat in the saddle-tree—from hat to spurs you might have drawn a perpendicular line. It would have taken in shoulders, thighs, and all.

"Adjieu," said the young centaur; and Sosthène replied from the creaking calèche, "Adjieu, 'Thanase," while the rider bestowed his rustic smile upon the group. Madame Sosthène's eyes met his, and her lips moved in an inaudible greeting; but the eyes of her little daughter were in her lap. Bonaventure's gaze was hostile. A word or two passed between uncle and nephew, including a remark and admission that the cattle-thieves were getting worse than ever; and with a touch of the spur, the young horseman galloped on.

It seems enough to admit that Zoséphine's further remarks were silly without reporting them in full.

"Look at his back! What airs! If I had looked up I should have laughed in his face!" etc. "Well," she concluded, after much such chirruping, "there's one comfort—he doesn't care a cent for me. If I should die to-morrow, he would forget to come to the funeral. And you think I wouldn't be glad? Well, you're mistaken, as usual. I hate him, and I just know he hates me! Everybody hates me!"

The eyes of her worshipper turned upon her. But she only turned her own away across the great plain to the vast arching sky, and patted the calèche with a little foot that ached for deliverance from its Sunday shoe. Then her glance returned, and all the rest of the way home she was as sweet as the last dip of cane-juice from the boiling battery.

# CHAPTER IV

## THE CONSCRIPT OFFICER

By and by 'Thanase was sixteen. Eighteen was the lowest age for conscription, yet he was in the Confederate uniform. But then so was his uncle Sosthène; so was his father. It signified merely that he had been received into the home guard. The times were sadly unsettled. Every horseman, and how much more every group of horsemen, that one saw coming across the prairie, was watched by anxious eyes, from the moment they were visible specks, to see whether the uniform would turn out to be the blue or the gray. Which was the more unwelcome I shall not say, but this I can, that the blue meant invasion and the gray meant conscription. Sosthène was just beyond the limit of age, and 'Thanase two years below it; but 'Thanase's father kept a horse saddled all the time, and slept indoors only on stormy nights.

Do not be misled: he was neither deserter nor coward; else the nickname which had quite blotted out his real name would not have been Chaouache—savage, Indian. He was needed at home, and—it

9

was not his war. His war was against cattle-thieves and like marauders, and there was no other man in all Carancro whom these would not have had on their track rather than him. But one gray dawn they found there was another not unlike him. They had made an attempt upon Sosthène's cattle one night; had found themselves watched and discovered; had turned and fled westward half the night, and had then camped in the damp woods of a bas fond; when, just as day was breaking and they were looking to their saddles about to mount—there were seven of them—just then—listen!—a sound of hoofs!

Instantly every left foot is in stirrup; but before they can swing into the saddle a joyous cry is in their ears, and pop! pop! pop! pop! ring the revolvers as, with the glad, fierce cry still resounding, three horsemen launch in upon them—only three, but those three a whirlwind. See that riderless horse, and this one, and that one! And now for it—three honest men against four remaining thieves! Pop! pop! dodge, and fire as you dodge! Pop! pop! pop! down he goes; well done, gray-bearded Sosthène! Shoot there! Wheel here! Wounded? Never mind—ora! Another rogue reels! Collar him, Chaouache! drag him from the saddle—down he goes! What, again? Shoot there! Look out, that fellow's getting away! Ah! down goes Sosthène's horse, breaking his strong neck in the tumble. Up, bleeding old man—bang! bang! Ha, ha, ora! that finishes—ora! 'Twas the boy saved your life with that last shot, Sosthène, and the boy—the youth is 'Thanase.

He has not stopped to talk; he and his father are catching the horses of the dead and dying jayhawkers. Now bind up Sosthène's head, and now 'Thanase's hip. Now strip the dead beasts, and take the dead men's weapons, boots, and spurs. Lift this one moaning villain into his saddle and take him along, though he is going to die before ten miles are gone over. So they turn homeward, leaving high revel for the carrion-crows.

Think of Bonaventure, the slender, the intense, the reticent—with 'Thanase limping on rude but glorious crutches for four consecutive Saturdays and Sundays up and down in full sight of Zoséphine, savior of her mother from widowhood, owner of two fine captured horses, and rewarded by Sosthène with five acres of virgin prairie. If the young fiddler's music was an attraction before, fancy its power now, when the musician had to be lifted to his chair on top of the table!

Bonaventure sought comfort of Zoséphine, and she gave it, tittering at 'Thanase behind his back, giving Bonaventure knowing looks, and sticking her sunbonnet in her mouth.

"Oh, if the bullet had only gone into the dandy's fiddle-bow arm!" she whispered gleefully.

"I wish he might never get well!" said the boy.

The girl's smile vanished; her eyes flashed lightning for an instant; the blood flew to her cheeks, and she bit her lip.

"Why don't you, now while he cannot help himself—why don't you go to him and hit him square in the face, like"—her arm flew up, and she smote him with her sunbonnet full between the eyes—"like that!" She ran away, laughing joyously, while Bonaventure sat down and wept with rage and shame.

Day by day he went about his trivial tasks and efforts at pastime with the one great longing that Zoséphine would more kindly let him be her slave, and something—any thing—take 'Thanase beyond reach.

Instead of this 'Thanase got well, and began to have a perceptible down on his cheek and upper lip, to the great amusement of Zoséphine.

"He had better take care," she said one day to Bonaventure, her eyes leaving their mirth and expanding with sudden seriousness, "or the conscript officer will be after him, though he is but sixteen."

Unlucky word! Bonaventure's bruised spirit seized upon the thought. They were on their way even then à la chapelle; and when they got there he knelt before Mary's shrine and offered the longest and most earnest prayer, thus far, of his life, and rose to his feet under a burden of guilt he had never known before.

It was November. The next day the wind came hurtling over the plains out of the north-west, bitter cold. The sky was all one dark gray. At evening it was raining. Sosthène said, as he sat down to supper, that it was going to pour and blow all night. Chaouache said much the same thing to his wife as they lay down to rest. Farther away from Carancro than many of Carancro's people had ever wandered, in the fire-lighted public room of a village tavern, twelve or fifteen men were tramping busily about, in muddy boots and big clanking spurs, looking to pistols and carbines of miscellaneous patterns, and securing them against weather under their as yet only damp and slightly bespattered great-coats, no two of which were alike. They spoke to each other sometimes in French, sometimes in English that betrayed a Creole rather than an Acadian accent. A young man with a neat kepi tipped on one side of his handsome head stood with his back to the fire, a sabre dangling to the floor from beneath a captured Federal overcoat. A larger man was telling him a good story. He listened smilingly, dropped the remnant of an exhausted cigarette to the floor, put his small, neatly

11

booted foot upon it, drew from his bosom one of those silken tobacco-bags that our sisters in war-time used to make for all the soldier boys, made a new cigarette, lighted it with the flint and tinder for which the Creole smokers have such a predilection, and put away his appliances, still hearkening to the story. He nodded his head in hearty approval as the tale was finished. It was the story of Sosthène, Chaouache, 'Thanase, and the jayhawkers. He gathered up his sabre and walked out, followed by the rest. A rattle of saddles, a splashing of hoofs, and then no sound was heard but the wind and the pouring rain. The short column went out of the village at full gallop.

Day was fully come when Chaouache rose and stepped out upon his galérie. He had thought he could venture to sleep in bed such a night; and, sure enough, here morning came, and there had been no intrusion. 'Thanase, too, was up. It was raining and blowing still. Across the prairie, as far as the eye could reach, not a movement of human life could be seen. They went in again, made a fire of a few fagots and an armful of cotton-seed, hung the kettle, and emptied the old coffee from the coffee-pot.

The mother and children rose and dressed. The whole family huddled around the good, hot, cotton-seed fire. No one looked out of window or door; in such wind and rain, where was the need? In the little log stable hard by, the two favorite saddle-horses remained unsaddled and unbridled. The father's and son's pistol-belts, with revolvers buttoned in their holsters, hung on the bedposts by the headboards of their beds. A long sporting rifle leaned in a corner near the chimney.

Chaouache and 'Thanase got very busy plaiting a horse-hair halter, and let time go by faster than they knew. Madame Chaouache, so to call her, prepared breakfast. The children played with the dog and cat. Thus it happened that still nobody looked out into the swirling rain. Why should they? Only to see the wide deluged plain, the round drenched groves, the maraises and sinuous coolées shining with their floods, and long lines of benumbed, wet cattle seeking in patient, silent Indian file for warmer pastures. They knew it all by heart.

Yonder farthest île is Sosthène's. The falling flood makes it almost undiscernible. Even if one looked, he would not see that a number of horsemen have come softly plashing up to Sosthène's front fence, for Sosthène's house and grove are themselves in the way. They spy Bonaventure. He is just going in upon the galérie with an armful of China-tree fagots. Through their guide and spokesman they utter, not the usual halloo, but a quieter hail, with a friendly beckon.

12

"Adjieu." The men were bedraggled, and so wet one could not make out the color of the dress. One could hardly call it a uniform, and pretty certainly it was not blue.

"Adjieu," responded Bonaventure, with some alarm; but the spokesman smiled re-assuringly. He pointed far away south-westward, and asked if a certain green spot glimmering faintly through the rain was not Chaouache's île; and Bonaventure, dumb in the sight of his prayer's answer, nodded.

"And how do you get there?" the man asks, still in Acadian French; for he is well enough acquainted with prairies to be aware that one needs to know the road even to a place in full view across the plain. Bonaventure, with riot in his heart, and feeling himself drifting over the cataract of the sinfullest thing that ever in his young life he has had the chance to do, softly lays down his wood, and comes to the corner of the galérie.

It is awful to him, even while he is doing it, the ease with which he does it. If, he says, they find it troublesome crossing the marshy place by Numa's farm,—le platin à coté d' l'habitation à Numa,—then it will be well to virer de bord—go about, et naviguer au large—sail across the open prairie. "Adjieu." He takes up his fagots again, and watches the spattering squad trot away in the storm, wondering why there is no storm in his own heart.

They are gone. Sosthène, inside the house, has heard nothing. The tempest suffocates all sounds not its own, and the wind is the wrong way anyhow. Now they are far out in the open. Chaouache's île still glimmers to them far ahead in the distance, but if some one should only look from the front window of its dwelling, he could see them coming. And that would spoil the fun. So they get it into line with another man's grove nearer by, and under that cover quicken to a gallop. Away, away; splash, splash, through the coolées, around the maraises, clouds of wild fowl that there is no time to shoot into rising now on this side, now on that; snipe without number, gray as the sky, with flashes of white, trilling petulantly as they flee; giant snowy cranes lifting and floating away on waving pinions, and myriads of ducks in great eruptions of hurtling, whistling wings. On they gallop; on they splash; heads down; water pouring from soaked hats and caps; cold hands beating upon wet breasts; horses throwing steaming muzzles down to their muddy knees, and shaking the rain from their worried ears; so on and on and on.

The horse-hair halter was nearly done. The breakfast was smoking on the board. The eyes of the family group were just turning toward it with glances of placid content, when a knock sounded on the door, and almost before father or son could rise or astonishment dart from eye to eye, the door swung open, and a man

13

stood on the threshold, all mud and water and weapons, touching the side of his cap with the edge of his palm and asking in French, with an amused smile forcing its way about his lips:—

"Can fifteen of us get something to eat, and feed our horses?"

Chaouache gave a vacant stare, and silently started toward the holsters that hung from the bedpost; but the stranger's right hand flashed around to his own belt, and, with a repeater half drawn, he cried:

"Halt!" And then, more quietly, "Look out of the door, look out the window."

Father and son looked. The house was surrounded.

Chaouache turned upon his wife one look of silent despair. Wife and children threw themselves upon his neck, weeping and wailing. 'Thanase bore the sight a moment, maybe a full minute; then drew near, pressed the children with kind firmness aside, pushed between his father and mother, took her tenderly by the shoulders, and said in their antique dialect, with his own eyes brimming:—

"Hush! hush! he will not have to go."

At a gentle trot the short column of horsemen moves again, but with its head the other way. The wind and rain buffet and pelt horse and rider from behind. Chaouache's door is still open. He stands in it with his red-eyed wife beside him and the children around them, all gazing mutely, with drooping heads and many a slow tear, after the departing cavalcade.

None of the horsemen look back. Why should they? To see a barefoot man beside a woman in dingy volante and casaquin, with two or three lads of ten or twelve in front, whose feet have known sunburn and frost but never a shoe, and a damsel or two in cotton homespun dress made of one piece from collar to hem, and pantalettes of the same reaching to the ankles—all standing and looking the picture of witless  incapacity, and making no plea against tyranny! Is that a thing worth while to turn and look back upon? If the blow fell upon ourselves or our set, that would be different; but these illiterate and lowly ones—they are—you don't know—so dull and insensible. Yes, it may be true that it is only some of them who feel less acutely than some of us—we admit that generously; but when you insinuate that when we overlook parental and fraternal anguish tearing at such hearts the dulness and insensibility are ours, you make those people extremely offensive to us, whereas you should not estrange them from our tolerance.

Ah, poor unpitied mother! go back to your toils; they are lightened now—a little; the cooking, the washing, the scrubbing. Spread, day by day, the smoking board, and call your spared

14

husband and your little ones to partake; but you—your tears shall be your meat day and night, while underneath your breath you moan, "'Thanase! 'Thanase!"

# CHAPTER V

## THE CURÉ OF CARANCRO

It was an unexpected and capital exchange. They had gone for a conscript; they came away with a volunteer.

Bonaventure sat by the fire in Sosthène's cottage, silent and heavy, holding his small knees in his knit hands and gazing into the flames. Zoséphine was washing the household's few breakfast dishes. La vieille—the mother—was spinning cotton. Le vieux—Sosthène—sat sewing up a rent in a rawhide chair-bottom. He paused by and by, stretched, and went to the window. His wife caught the same spirit of relaxation, stopped her wheel, looked at the boy moping in the chimney-corner, and, passing over to his side, laid a hand upon his temple to see if he might have fever.

The lad's eyes did not respond to her; they were following Sosthène. The husband stood gazing out through the glass for a moment, and then, without moving, swore a long, slow execration. The wife and daughter pressed quickly to his either side and looked forth.

There they came, the number increased to eighteen now, trotting leisurely through the subsiding storm. The wife asked what they were, but Sosthène made no reply; he was counting them: twelve, thirteen, fourteen—fourteen with short guns, another one who seemed to wear a sword, and three, that must be—

"Cawnscreep," growled Sosthène, without turning his eyes. But the next moment an unusual sound at his elbow drew his glance upon Zoséphine. "Diable!" He glared at her weeping eyes, his manner demanding of her instant explanation. She retreated a step, moved her hand toward the approaching troop, and cried distressfully:

"Tu va oère!"—"You will see!"

His glance was drawn to Bonaventure. The lad had turned toward them, and was sitting upright, his blue eyes widened, his

15

face pale, and his lips apart; but ere Sosthène could speak his wife claimed his attention.

"Sosthène!" she exclaimed, pressing against the window-pane, "ah, Sosthène! Ah, ah! they have got 'Thanase!"

Father, mother, and daughter crowded against the window and one another, watching the body of horse as it drew nigh. Bonaventure went slowly and lay face downward on the bed.

Now the dripping procession is at hand. They pass along the dooryard fence. At the little garden gate they halt. Only 'Thanase dismounts. The commander exchanges a smiling word or two with him, and the youth passes through the gate, and, while his companions throw each a tired leg over the pommel and sit watching him, comes up the short, flowery walk and in at the opening door.

There is nothing to explain, the family have guessed it; he goes in his father's stead. There is but a moment for farewells.

"Adjieu, Bonaventure."

The prostrate boy does not move. 'Thanase strides up to the bed and looks at one burning cheek, then turns to his aunt.

"Li malade?"—"Is he ill?"

"Sa l'air a ca," said the aunt. (Il a l'air—he seems so.)

"Bien, n'onc' Sosthène, adjieu." Uncle and nephew shake hands stoutly. "Adjieu," says the young soldier again to his aunt. She gives her hand and turns to hide a tear. The youth takes one step toward Zoséphine. She stands dry-eyed, smiling on her father. As the youth comes her eyes, without turning to him, fill. He puts out his hand. She lays her own on it. He gazes at her for a moment, with beseeching eye—"Adjieu." Her eyes meet his one instant—she leaps upon his neck—his strong arms press her to his bosom—her lifted face lights up—his kiss is on her lips—it was there just now, and now—'Thanase is gone, and she has fled to an inner room.

Bonaventure stood in the middle of the floor. Why should the boy look so strange? Was it anger, or fever, or joy? He started out.

"A ou-ce-tu va Bonaventure?"—"Whereabouts are you going?"

"Va crier les vaches."—"Going to call the cows."

"At this time of day?" demanded la vieille, still in the same tongue. "Are you crazy?"

"Oh!—no!" the boy replied, looking dazed. "No," he said; "I was going for some more wood." He went out, passed the woodpile by, got round behind a corn-crib, and stood in the cold, wet gale watching the distant company lessening on the view. It was but a short, dim, dark streak, creeping across the field of vision like some slow insect on a window-glass. A spot just beyond it was a grove that would presently shut the creeping line finally from sight. They

16

reached it, passed beyond, and disappeared; and then Bonaventure took off the small, soft-brimmed hat that hung about his eyes, and, safe from the sight and hearing of all his tiny world, lifted his voice, and with face kindling with delight swung the sorry covering about his head and cried three times:

"Ora! Or-r-ra! Ora-a-a-a!"

But away in the night Madame Sosthène, hearing an unwonted noise, went to Bonaventure's bedside and found him sobbing as if his heart had broken.

"He has had a bad dream," she said; for he would not say a word.

The curé of Vermilionville and Carancro was a Creole gentleman who looked burly and hard when in meditation; but all that vanished when he spoke and smiled. In the pocket of his cassock there was always a deck of cards, but that was only for the game of solitaire. You have your pipe or cigar, your flute or violoncello; he had his little table under the orange-tree and his game of solitaire.

He was much loved. To see him beyond earshot talking to other men you would say he was by nature a man of affairs, whereas, when you came to hear him speak you find him quite another sort: one of the Elisha kind, as against the Elijahs; a man of the domestic sympathies, whose influence on man was personal and familiar; one of the sort that heal bitter waters with a handful of salt, make poisonous pottage wholesome with a little meal, and find easy, quiet ways to deliver poor widows from their creditors with no loss to either; a man whom men reverenced, while women loved and children trusted him.

The ex-governor was fond of his company, although the curé only smiled at politics and turned the conversation back to family matters. He had a natural gift for divining men's, women's, children's personal wants, and every one's distinctively from every other one's. So that to everybody he was an actual personal friend. He had been a long time in this region. It was he who buried Bonaventure's mother. He was the connecting link between Bonaventure and the ex-governor. Whenever the curé met this man of worldly power, there were questions asked and answered about the lad.

A little after 'Thanase's enlistment the priest and the ex-governor, who, if I remember right, was home only transiently from camp, met on the court-house square of Vermilionville, and stood to chat a bit, while others contemplated from across the deep mud of the street these two interesting representatives of sword and gown. Two such men standing at that time must naturally, one would say,

17

have been talking of the strength of the defences around Richmond, or the Emperor Maximilian's operations in Mexico, or Kirby Smith's movements, hardly far enough away to make it seem comfortable. But in reality they were talking about 'Thanase.

"He cannot write," said the curé; "and if he could, no one at home could read his letters."

The ex-governor promised to look after him.

"And how," he asked, "does Sosthène's little orphan get on?"

The curé smiled. "He is well—physically. A queer, high-strung child; so old, yet so young. In some things he will be an infant as long as he lives; in others, he has been old from the cradle. He takes every thing in as much earnest as a man of fifty. What is to become of him?"

"Oh! he will come out all right," said the ex-governor.

"That depends. Some children are born with fixed characters: you can tell almost from the start what they are going to be. Be they much or little, they are complete in themselves, and it makes comparatively little difference into what sort of a world you drop them."

"'Thanase, for instance," said the ex-governor.

"Yes, you might say 'Thanase; but never Bonaventure. He is the other type; just as marked and positive traits, but those traits not yet builded into character: a loose mass of building-material, and the beauty or ugliness to which such a nature may arrive depends on who and what has the building of it into form. What he may turn out to be at last will be no mere product of circumstances; he is too original for that. Oh, he's a study! Another boy under the same circumstances might turn out entirely different; and yet it will make an immense difference how his experiences are allowed to combine with his nature." The speaker paused a moment, while Bonaventure's other friend stood smiling with interest; then the priest added, "He is just now struggling with his first great experience."

"What is that?"

"It belongs," replied the curé, smiling in his turn, "to the confidences of the confessional. But," he added, with a little anxious look, "I can tell you what it will do; it will either sweeten his whole nature more and more, or else make it more and more bitter, from this time forth. And that is no trifle to you or me; for whether for good or bad, in a large way or in a small way, he is going to make himself felt."

The ex-governor mused. "I'm glad the little fellow has you for a friend, father.—I'll tell you; if Sosthène and his wife will part with him, and you will take him to live with you, and, mark you, not try too hard to make a priest of him, I will bear his expenses."

"I will do it," said the curé.

It required much ingenuity of argument to make the Gradnego pair see the matter in the desired light; but when the curé promised Sosthène that he would teach the lad to read and write, and then promised la vieille that Zoséphine should share this educational privilege with him, they let him go.

Zoséphine was not merely willing, but eager, to see the arrangements made. She beckoned the boy aside and spoke to him alone.

"You must go, Bonaventure. You will go, will you not—when I ask you? Think how fine that will be—to be educated! For me, I cannot endure an uneducated person. But—ah! ca sré vaillant, pour savoir lire. [It will be bully to know how to read. Aie ya yaie!"—she stretched her eyes and bit her lip with delight—"C'est t'y gai, pour savoir écrire! [That's fine to know how to write. I will tell you a secret, dear Bonaventure. Any girl of sense is bound to think it much greater and finer for a man to read books than to ride horses. She may not want to, but she has to do it; she can't help herself!"

Still Bonaventure looked at her mournfully. She tried again.

"When I say any girl of sense I include myself—of course! I think more of a boy—or man, either—who can write letters than of one who can play the fiddle. There, now, I have told you! And when you have learned those things, I will be proud of you! And besides, you know, if you don't go, you make me lose my chance of learning the same things; but if you go, we will learn them together."

He consented. She could not understand the expression of his face. She had expected gleams of delight. There were none. He went with silent docility, and without a tear; but also without a smile. When in his new home the curé from time to time stole glances at his face fixed in unconscious revery, it was full of a grim, unhappy satisfaction.

"Self is winning, or dying hard. I wish no ill to 'Thanase; but if there is to be any bad news of him, I hope, for the sake of this boy's soul, it will come quickly." So spoke the curé alone, to his cards.

# CHAPTER VI

## MISSING

The war was in its last throes even when 'Thanase enlisted. Weeks and months passed. Then a soldier coming home to Carancro—home-comers were growing plentiful—brought the first news of him. An officer making up a force of picked men for an expedition to carry important despatches eastward across the Mississippi and far away into Virginia had chosen 'Thanase. The evening the speaker left for home on his leave of absence 'Thanase was still in camp, but was to start the next morning. It was just after Sunday morning mass that Sosthène and Chaouache, with their families and friends, crowded around this bearer of tidings.

"Had 'Thanase been in any battles?"

"Yes, two or three."

"And had not been wounded?"

"No, although he was the bravest fellow in his company."

Sosthène and Chaouache looked at each other triumphantly, smiled, and swore two simultaneous oaths of admiration. Zoséphine softly pinched her mother, and whispered something. Madame Sosthène addressed the home-comer aloud:

"Did 'Thanase send no other message except that mere 'How-d'ye all do?'"

"No."

Zoséphine leaned upon her mother's shoulder, and softly breathed:

"He is lying."

The mother looked around upon her daughter in astonishment. The flash of scorn was just disappearing from the girl's eyes. She gave a little smile and chuckle, and murmured, with her glance upon the man:

"He has no leave of absence. He is a deserter."

Then Madame Sosthène saw two things at once: that the guess was a good one, and that Zoséphine had bidden childhood a final "adjieu."

The daughter felt Bonaventure's eyes upon her. He was standing only a step or two away. She gave him a quick, tender look that thrilled him from head to foot, then lifted her brows and made a grimace of pretended weariness. She was growing prettier almost from day to day.

And Bonaventure, he had no playmates—no comrades—no

20

amusements. This one thing, which no one knew but the curé, had taken possession of him. The priest sometimes seemed to himself cruel, so well did it please him to observe the magnitude Bonaventure plainly attributed to the matter. The boy seemed almost physically to bow under the burden of his sense of guilt.

"It is quickening all his faculties," said the curé to himself. Zoséphine had hardly yet learned to read without stammering, when Bonaventure was already devouring the few French works of the curé's small bookshelf. Silent on other subjects, on one he would talk till a pink spot glowed on either cheek-bone and his blue eyes shone like a hot noon sky;—casuistry. He would debate the right and wrong of any thing, every thing, and the rights and wrongs of men in every relation of life.

Blessed was it for him then that the tactful curé was his father and mother in one, and the surgeon and physician of his mind. Thus the struggle brought him light. To the boy's own eyes it seemed to be bringing him only darkness, but the priest saw better.

"That is but his shadow; he is standing in it; it is deepening; that shows the light is increasing." Thus spake the curé to himself as he sat at solitaire under his orange-tree one afternoon.

The boy passed out of sight, and the curé's eyes returned to his game of solitaire; but as he slowly laid one card upon another, now here, now there, he still thought of Bonaventure.

"There will be no peace for him, no sweetness of nature, no green pastures and still waters, within or without, while he seeks life's adjustments through definitions of mere right and rights. No, boy; you will ever be a restless captive, pacing round and round those limits of your enclosure. Worse still if you seek those definitions only to justify your overriding another's happiness in pursuit of your own." The boy was not in hearing; this was apostrophe.

"Bonaventure," he said, as the lad came by again; and Bonaventure stopped. The player pushed the cards from him, pile by pile, leaned back, ran his fingers slowly through his thin gray hair, and smiled.

"Bonaventure, I have a riddle for you. It came to me as I was playing here just now. If everybody could do just as he pleased; if he had, as the governor would say, all his rights,—life, liberty, pursuit of happiness,—if everybody had this, I say, why should we still be unhappy?"

The boy was silent.

"Well, I did not suppose you would know. Would you like me to tell you? It is because happiness pursued is never overtaken. And can you guess why that is? Well, never mind, my son. But—would you like to do something for me?"

Bonaventure nodded. The curé rose, taking from his bosom as he left his chair a red silk handkerchief and 'a pocket-worn note-book. He laid the note-book on the table, and drawing back with a smile said:

"Here, sit down in my place, and write what I tell you, while I stretch my legs. So; never mind whether you understand or not. I am saying it for myself: it helps me to understand it better. Now, as I walk, you write. 'Happiness pursued is never overtaken, because'—have you written that?—'because, little as we are, God's image makes us so large that we cannot live within ourselves, nor even for ourselves, and be satisfied.' Have you got that down? Very well—yes—the spelling could be improved, but that is no matter. Now wait a moment; let me walk some more. Now write: 'It is not good for man to be alone, because'—because—let me see; where—ah, yes!—'because rightly self is the'—Ah! no, no, my boy; not a capital S for 'self'—ah! that's the very point,—small s,—'because rightly self is the smallest part of us. Even God found it good not to be alone, but to create'—got that?—'to create objects for His love and benevolence.' Yes—'And because in my poor, small way I am made like Him, the whole world becomes a part of me'—small m, yes, that is right!" From bending a moment over the writer, the priest straightened up and took a step backward. The boy lifted his glance to where the sunlight and leaf-shadows were playing on his guardian's face. The curé answered with a warm smile, saying:

"My boy, God is a very practical God—no, you need not write it; just listen a moment. Yes; and so when He gave us natures like His, He gave men not wives only, but brethren and sisters and companions and strangers, in order that benevolence, yes, and even self-sacrifice,—mistakenly so called,—might have no lack of direction and occupation; and then bound the whole human family together by putting every one's happiness into some other one's hands. I see you do not understand: never mind; it will come to you little by little. It was a long time coming to me. Let us go in to supper."

The good man had little hope of such words taking hold. At school next day there was Zoséphine with her soft electric glances to make the boy forget all; and at the Saturday-night balls there she was again.

"Bonaventure," her manner plainly said, "did you ever see any thing else in this wide world so tiresome as these boys about here? Stay with me; it keeps them away." She never put such thoughts into words. With an Acadian girl such a thing was impossible But girls do not need words. She drew as potently, and to all appearances as impassively, as a loadstone. All others than Bonaventure she repelled. If now and then she toyed with a heart, it was but to see her image in it once or twice and toss it aside. All got one treatment in the main. Any one of them might gallop by her father's veranda seven times a day, but not once in all the seven would she be seen at the window glancing up at the weather or down at her flowers; nor on the veranda hanging up fresh hanks of yarn; nor at the well with the drinking-pail, getting fresh water, as she might so easily have been, had she so chosen. Yonder was Sosthène hoeing leisurely in the little garden, and possibly the sunbonnet of la vieille half seen and half hidden among her lima-beans; but for the rest there was only the house, silent at best, or, worse, sending out through its half-open door the long, scornful No-o-o! of the maiden's unseen spinning-wheel. No matter the fame or grace of the rider. All in vain, my lad: pirouette as you will; sit your gallantest; let your hat blow off, and turn back, and at full speed lean down from the saddle, and snatch it airily from the ground, and turn again and gallop away; all is in vain. For by her estimate either you are living in fear of the conscript officer; or, if you are in the service, and here only transiently on leave of absence, your stay seems long, and it is rumored your leave has expired; or, worse, you cannot read; or, worst, your age, for all your manly airs, is so near Zoséphine's as to give your attentions strong savor of presumption. But let any fortune bring Bonaventure in any guise—sorriest horseman of all, youngest, slenderest, and stranger to all the ways that youth loves—and at once she is visible; nay, more, accessible; and he, welcome. So accessible she, so welcome he, that more than once she has to waft aside her mother's criticisms by pleading Bonaventure's foster-brotherhood and her one or two superior years.

"Poor 'Thanase!" said the youths and maidens.

And now the war came to an end. Bonaventure was glad. 'Thanase was expected home, but—let him come. If the absent soldier knew what the young folks at the balls knew, he would not make haste in his return. And he did not, as it seemed. Day after day, in group after group, without shouting and without banners, with wounds and scars and tattered garments, some on horses, but many more on foot, the loved ones—the spared ones, remnants of this command and that command and 'Thanase's command—came home. But day by day brought no 'Thanase.

Bonaventure began to wish for him anxiously. He wanted him back so that this load might be lifted. Thus the bitter would pass out of the sweet; the haunting fear of evil tidings from the absent rival would haunt no more. Life would be what it was to other lads, and Zoséphine one day fall to his share by a better title than he could ever make with 'Thanase in exile. Come, 'Thanase, come, come!

More weeks passed. The youth's returned comrades were all back at their ploughs again and among their herds. 'Thanase would be along by and by, they said; he could not come with them, for he had not been paroled with them; he had been missing—taken prisoner, no doubt—in the very last fight. But presently they who had been prisoners were home also, and still 'Thanase had not come. And then, instead of 'Thanase coming, Chaouache died.

A terror took up its home in the heart of Bonaventure. Every thing he looked upon, every creature that looked upon him, seemed to offer an unuttered accusation. Least of all could he bear the glance of Zoséphine. He did not have to bear it. She kept at home now closely. She had learned to read, and Sosthène and his vieille had pronounced her education completed.

In one direction only could the eyes of Bonaventure go, and meet nothing that accused him: that was into the face of the curé. And lest accusation should spring up there, he had omitted his confession for weeks. He was still child enough not to see that the priest was watching him narrowly and tenderly.

One night, away in the small hours, the curé was aroused by the presence of some one in his room.

"Who is that?" He rose from his pillow.

"It is I, father," said a low voice, and against the darkness of an inner door he saw dimly the small, long nightdress of the boy he loved.

"What gets you up, Bonaventure? Come here. What troubles you?"

"I cannot sleep," murmured the lad, noiselessly moving near. The priest stroked the lad's brow.

"Have you not been asleep at all?"

"Yes."

"But you have had bad dreams that woke you?"

"Only one."

"And what was that?"

There was a silence.

"Did you dream about—'Thanase, for example?"

"Yes."

The priest reached out and took the boy's small, slender hands in his. They were moist and cold.

"And did you dream"—

"I dreamed he was dead. I dream it every night."

"But, my child, that does not make it so. Would you like to get

24

into bed here with me? No?—or to go back now to your own bed? No? What, then?"

"I do not want to go back to bed any more. I want to go and find 'Thanase."

"Why, my child, you are not thoroughly awake, are you?"

"Yes, I want to go and find 'Thanase. I have been thinking to-night of all you have told me—of all you said that day in the garden,—and—I want to go and find 'Thanase."

"My boy," said the priest, drawing the lad with gentle force to his bosom, "my little old man, does this mean that you have come to the end of all self-service?—that self is never going to be spelt with a capital S any more? Will it be that way if I let you go?"

"Yes."

"Well, then, my son—God only knows whether I am wise or foolish, but—you may go."

The boy smiled for the first time in weeks, then climbed half upon the bed, buried his face in the priest's bosom, and sobbed as though his heart had broken.

"It has broken," said the curé to himself as he clasped him tightly. "It has broken—thank God!"

# CHAPTER VII

## A NEEDLE IN A HAYSTACK

In such and such a battle, in the last charge across a certain cornfield, or in the hurried falling back through a certain wood, with the murderous lead singing and hitting from yonder dark mass descending on the flank, and the air full of imperious calls, "Halt!"— "Surrender!" a man disappeared. He was not with those who escaped, nor with the dead when they were buried, nor among the wounded anywhere, nor in any group of prisoners. But long after the war was over, another man, swinging a bush scythe among the overgrown corners of a worm fence, found the poor remnant of him, put it scarcely underground, and that was the end. How many times that happened!

Was it so with 'Thanase? No. For Sosthène's sake the ex-governor had taken much pains to correspond with officials

25

concerning the missing youth, and had secured some slender re-assurances. 'Thanase, though captured, had not been taken to prison. Tidings of general surrender had overhauled him on the way to it, near, I think, the city of Baltimore—somewhere in that region, at any rate; and he had been paroled and liberated, and had started penniless and on foot, south-westward along the railway-tracks.

To find him, Bonaventure must set out, like him on foot, south-eastward over some fifty miles of wagon-road to the nearest railway; eastward again over its cross-ties eighty miles to la ville, the great New Orleans, there to cross the Mississippi. Then away northward, through the deep, trestled swamps, leagues and leagues, across Bayou La Branche and Bayou Desair, and Pass Manchac and North Manchac, and Pontchatoula River two or three times; and out of the swamps and pine barrens into the sweet pine hills, with their great resinous boles rising one hundred—two hundred feet overhead; over meadows and fields and many and many a beautiful clear creek, and ten or more times over the winding Tangipahoa, by narrow clearings, and the old tracks of forgotten hurricanes, and many a wide plantation; until more than two hundred miles from the great city, still northward across the sinking and swelling fields, the low, dark dome of another State's Capitol must rise amid spires and trees into the blue, and the green ruins of fortifications be passed, and the iron roads be found branching west, north, and east.

Thence all was one wide sea of improbability. Even before a quarter of that distance should have been covered, how many chances of every sort there were against the success of such a search!

"It is impossible that he should find him," said the ex-governor.

"Well,"—the curé shrugged,—"if he finds no one, yet he may succeed in losing himself." But in order that Bonaventure in losing himself should not be lost, the priest gave him pens and paper, and took his promise to write back as he went step by step out into the world.

"And learn English, my boy; learn it with all speed; you will find it vastly, no telling how vastly, to your interest—I should say your usefulness. I am sorry I could not teach it to you myself. Here is a little spelling-book and reader for you to commence with. Make haste to know English; in America we should be Americans; would that I could say it to all our Acadian people! but I say it to you, learn English. It may be that by not knowing it you may fail, or by knowing it succeed, in this errand. And every step of your way let your first business be the welfare of others. Hundreds will laugh at

26

you for it: never mind; it will bring you through. Yes, I will tell Sosthène and the others good-by for you. I will tell them you had a dream that compelled you to go at once. Adieu." And just as the rising sun's first beam smote the curé's brimming eyes, his "little old man" turned his face toward a new life, and set forward to enter it.

"Have you seen anywhere, coming back from the war, a young man named 'Thanase Beausoleil?"—This question to every one met, day in, day out, in early morning lights, in noonday heats, under sunset glows, by a light figure in thin, clean clothing, dusty shoes, and with limp straw hat lowered from the head. By and by, as first the land of the Acadians and then the land of the Creoles was left behind, a man every now and then would smile and shake his head to mean he did not understand—for the question was in French. But then very soon it began to be in English too, and by and by not in French at all.

"Sir, have you seen anywhere, coming back from the war, a young man named 'Thanase Beausoleil?"

But no one had seen him.

Travel was very slow. Not only because it was done afoot. Many a day he had to tarry to earn bread, for he asked no alms. But after a while he passed eastward into a third State, and at length into the mountains of a fourth.

Meantime the weeks were lengthening into months; the year was in its decline. Might not 'Thanase be even then at home? No. Every week Bonaventure wrote back, "Has he come?" and the answer came back, "He is not here."

But one evening, as he paced the cross-ties of a railway that hugged a huge forest-clad mountain-side, with the valley a thousand feet below, its stony river shining like a silken fabric in the sunset lights, the great hillsides clad in crimson, green, and gold, and the long, trailing smoke of the last train—a rare, motionless blue gauze—gone to rest in the chill mid-air, he met a man who suddenly descended upon the track in front of him from higher up the mountain,—a great, lank mountaineer. And when Bonaventure asked the apparition the untiring question to which so many hundreds had answered No, the tall man looked down upon the questioner, a bright smile suddenly lighting up the unlovely chin-whiskered face, and asked:

"Makes a fiddle thess talk an' cry?"

"Yes."

"Well, he hain't been gone from hyer two weeks."

It was true. Only a few weeks before, gaunt, footsore, and ragged, tramping the cross-ties yonder where the railway comes from the eastward, curving into view out of that deep green and gray

27

defile, 'Thanase had come into this valley. So short a time before, because almost on his start homeward illness had halted him by the way and held him long in arrest. But at length he had reached the valley, and had lingered here for days; for it happened that a man in bought clothing was there just then, roaming around and hammering pieces off the rocks, who gave 'Thanase the chance to earn a little something from him, with which the hard-marched wanderer might take the train instead of the cross-ties for as far as the pittance would carry him.

# CHAPTER VIII

## THE QUEST ENDED

The next sunrise saw Bonaventure, with a new energy in his step, journeying back the way he had come. And so anew the weeks wore by. Once more the streams ran southward, and the landscapes opened wide and fertile.

"Sir,—pardon your stopping,—in what State should I find myself at the present?"

The person inquired of looked blank, examined the questioner from head to foot, and replied:

"In what—oh! I understand; yes. What State—Alabama, yes, Alabama. You must excuse me, I didn't understand you at first. Yes, this is Alabama."

"Thank you, sir. Have you seen anywhere, coming back from the war, a young man named 'Thanase Beausoleil?"

"Back from the war! Why, everybody done got back from the war long ago." "Lawng ago-o-o," the speaker pronounced it, but the pronunciation could not be as untrue as the careless assertion.

A second time, and again a third, Bonaventure fell upon the trail. But each time it was colder than before. And yet he was pushing on as fast as he dared. Many a kind man's invitation to tarry and rest was gratefully declined. Once, where two railways parted, one leading south, the other west, he followed the southern for days, and then came back to the point of separation, and by and by found the lost thread again on the more westward road. But the time since 'Thanase had passed was the longest yet. Was it certainly

'Thanase? Yes; the fiddle always settled that question. And had he not got home? He had not come. Somewhere in the long stretch between Bonaventure and Carancro there must be strange tidings.

On the first New Year's eve after the war, as the sun was sinking upon the year's end, Bonaventure turned that last long curve of the New Orleans, Jackson, and Great Northern Railroad, through the rushes, flags, willows, and cypress-stumps of the cleared swamp behind the city of the Creoles, and, passing around the poor shed called the depot, paused at the intersection of Calliope and Magnolia Streets, waiting the turn of chance.

Trace of the lost 'Thanase had brought him at length to this point. The word of a fellow-tramp, pledged on the honor of his guild, gave assurance that thus far the wanted man had come in strength and hope—but more than a month before.

The necessity of moving on presently carried Bonaventure aimlessly into the city along the banks of the New Canal. The lad had shot up in these few months into the full stature, without the breadth, of manhood. The first soft, uneven curls of a light-brown beard were on his thin cheek and chin. Patient weariness and humble perseverance were in his eyes. His coarse, ill-matched attire was whole and, but for the soilure  of foot-travel, clean. Companioning with nature had browned his skin, and dried his straight fine hair. Any reader of faces would have seen the lines of unselfish purpose about his lips, and, when they parted nervously for speech, the earnest glow of that purpose in a countenance that neither smiled nor frowned, and, though it was shaded, cast no shadow.

The police very soon knew him. They smiled at one another and tapped the forehead with one finger, as he turned away with his question answered by a shake of the head. It became their habit. They would jerk a thumb over a shoulder after him facetiously.

"Goes to see every unknown white man found dead or drowned. And yet, you know, he's happy. He's a heap sight"— sometimes they used other adjectives—"a heap sight happier than us, with his trampin' around all day and his French and English books at night, as old Tony says. He bunks with old Tony, you know, what keeps that little grocery in Solidelle Street. Tony says his candles comes to more than his bread and meat, or, rather, his rice and crawfish. He's the funniest crazy I ever see. All the crazies I ever see is got some grind for pleasing number one; but this chap is everlastin'ly a-lookin' out for everybody but number one. Oh, yes, the candles and books,—I reckon they are for number one,—that's so; but anyhow, that's what I hear Madame Tony allow."

The short, wet winter passed. The search stretched on into the

29

spring. It did not, by far, take up the seeker's whole daily life. Only it was a thread that ran all through it, a dye that colored it. Many other factors—observations, occupations, experiences—were helping to make up that life, and to make it, with all its pathetic slenderness, far more than it was likely ever to have been made at Carancro. Through hundreds of miles of tramping the lad had seen, in a singularly complete yet inhostile disentanglement from it, the world of men; glimpses of the rich man's world with its strivings, steadier views of the poor man's world with its struggles. The times were strong and rude. Every step of his way had been through a land whose whole civil order had been condemned, shattered, and cast into the mill of revolution for a total remoulding. Every day came like the discharge of a great double-shotted gun. It could not but be that, humble as his walk was, and his years so few, his fevered mind should leap into the questions of the hour like a naked boy into the surf. He made mistakes, sometimes in a childish, sometimes in an older way, some against most worthy things. But withal he managed to keep the main direction of truth, after his own young way of thinking and telling it. He had no such power to formulate his large conclusions as you or even I have; but whatever wrought to enlighten the unlettered, whatever cherished manhood's rights alike in lofty and lowly, whatever worked the betterment of the poor, whatever made man not too much and not too little his brother's keeper,—his keeper not by mastery, but by fraternal service,—whatever did these things was to him good religion, good politics. So, at least, the curé told the ex-governor, as from time to time they talked of the absent Bonaventure and of his letters. However, they had to admit one thing: all this did not find 'Thanase.

And why, now, should 'Thanase longer be sought? Was there any thing to gain by finding him dead? Not for Bonaventure; he felt, as plainly as though he had seen an angel write the decree, that to Bonaventure Deschamps no kind of profit or advantage under the sun must come by such a way. But was there any thing to be gained in finding that 'Thanase still lived? The police will tell you, as they told Bonaventure, that in these days of steam and steel and yoked lightning a man may get lost and be found again; but that when he stays lost, and is neither dead nor mad, it is because he wants to be lost. So where was to be the gain in finding 'Thanase alive? Oh, much, indeed, to Bonaventure! The star of a new hope shot up into his starless sky when that thought came, and in that star trembled that which he had not all these weary months of search dared see even with fancy's eye,—the image of Zoséphine! This—this! that he had never set out to achieve—this! if he could but stand face to face with evidence that 'Thanase could have reached home and would not.

This thought was making new lines in the young care-struck face, when—

"See here," said a voice one day. Bonaventure's sleeve was caught by the thumb and forefinger of a man to whom, in passing, he had touched his hat. The speaker was a police captain.

"Come with me." They turned and walked, Bonaventure saying not a word. They passed a corner, turned to the right, passed two more, turned to the left,—high brick walls on either side, damp, ill-smelling pavements under foot,—and still strode on in silence. As they turned once more to the right in a dim, narrow way, the captain patted the youth softly on the back, and said:

"Ask me no questions, and I'll tell you no lies."

So Bonaventure asked none. But presently, in one of those dens called sailors' boarding-houses, somewhere down on the water-front near the Mint, he was brought face to face with a stranger whose manner seemed to offer the reverse proposition. Of him the youth asked questions and got answers.

'Thanase Beausoleil still lived, far beyond seas. How? why? If this man spake truly, because here in New Orleans, at the last turn in the long, weary journey that was to have brought the young volunteer home, he had asked and got the aid of this informant to ship—before the mast—for foreign parts. But why? Because his ambition and pride, explained the informant, had outgrown Carancro, and his heart had tired of the diminished memory of the little Zoséphine.

Bonaventure hurried away. What storms buffeted one another in his bosom!

Night had fallen upon the great city. Long stretches of street lay now between high walls, and now between low-hanging eaves, empty of human feet and rife with solitude. Through long distances he could run and leap, and make soft, mild pretence of shouting and smiting hands. The quest was ended! rivalry gone of its own choice, guilt washed from the hands, love returned to her nest. Zoséphine! Zoséphine! Away now, away to the reward of penance, patience, and loyalty! Unsought, unhoped-for reward! As he ran, the crescent moon ran before him in the sky, and one glowing star, dipping low, beckoned him into the west.

And yet that night a great riot broke out in his heart; and in the morning there was a look on his face as though in that tumult conscience had been drugged, beaten, stoned, and left for dead outside the gate of his soul.

There was something of defiance in his eye, not good to see, as

31

he started down the track of the old Opelousas Railroad, with the city and the Mississippi at his back. When he had sent a letter ahead of him, he had no money left to pay for railway passage. Should he delay for that or aught else, he might never start; for already the ghost of conscience was whispering in at the barred windows of his heart:

"It is not true. The man has told you falsely. It is not true."

And so he was tramping once more—toward Carancro. And never before with such determined eagerness. Nothing could turn him about now. Once a train came in sight in front of him just as he had started across a trestle-work; but he ran forward across the open ties, and leaped clear of the track on the farther side, just when another instant would have been too late. He stood a moment, only half-pausing among the palmettos and rushes as the hurtling mass thundered by; then pushed quickly into the whirling dust of the track and hurried on between the clicking rails, not knowing that yonder dark, dwindling speck behind was bearing away from him strange tidings from the curé.

The summer was coming on; the suns were hot. There were leagues on leagues of unbroken shaking prairie with never a hand-breadth of shade, but only the glowing upper blue, with huge dazzling clouds moving, like herds of white elephants pasturing across heavenly fields, too slowly for the eye to note their motion; and below, the far-reaching, tremulous sheen of reed and bulrush, the wet lair of serpent, wild-cat, and alligator. Now and then there was the cool blue of sunny, wind-swept waters winding hither and thither toward the sea, and sometimes miles of deep forest swamp through which the railroad went by broad, frowzy, treeless clearings flanked with impassable oozy ditches; but shade there was none.

Nor was there peace. Always as he strode along, something he could not outgo was at his side, gaunt, wounded, soiled, whispering: "Turn back; turn back, and settle with me," and ever put off with promises—after that fashion as old as the world—to do no end of good things if only the one right thing might be left undone.

And so because there were no shade, no peace, and no turning back, no one day's march made him stronger for the next; and at length, when he came to the low thatch of a negro-cabin, under the shadow of its bananas he sank down in its doorway, red with fever.

There he had to stay many days; but in the end he was up and on his way again. He left the Atchafalaya behind him. It was easier going now. There was shade. Under his trudging feet was the wagon-road along the farther levee of the Teche. Above him great live-oaks stretched their arms clad in green vestments and gray drapings, the bright sugar-cane fields were on his left, and on his right the beautiful winding bayou. In his face, not joy, only pallid eagerness, desire fixed upon fulfilment, and knowledge that happiness was something else; a young, worn face, with hard lines about the mouth and neck; the face of one who had thought self to be dead and buried, and had seen it rise to life again, and fallen captive to it. So he was drawing near to Carancro. Make haste, Bonaventure!

# CHAPTER IX

# THE WEDDING

A horse and buggy have this moment been stopped and are standing on a faint rise of ground seven miles out beyond the south-western outskirt of Carancro. The two male occupants of the vehicle are lifting their heads, and looking with well-pleased faces at something out over the plain. You know the curé?—and the ex-governor.

In the far distance, across the vast level, something that looks hardly so large on the plain as an ant on the floor, is moving this way across it. This is what the curé and his friend are watching. Open in the curé's hand, as if he had just read it aloud again, is that last letter of Bonaventure's, sent ahead of him from New Orleans and received some days ago. The governor holds the reins.

What do they see? Some traveller afoot? Can it be that Bonaventure is in sight? That is not even the direction from which Bonaventure, when he comes, will appear. No, speck though it is, the object they are looking at is far larger than a man afoot, or any horse, or horse and calèche. It is a house. It is on wheels, and is drawn by many yoke of oxen. From what the curé is saying we gather that Sosthène has bought this very small dwelling from a neighbor, and is moving it to land of his own. Two great beams have been drawn under the sills at each end, the running gear of two heavy ox-wagons is made to bear up the four ends of these beams, all is lashed firmly into place, the oxen are slowly pulling, the long whips are cracking, the house is answering the gentle traction, and, already several miles away from its first site, it will to-morrow settle down upon new foundations, a homely type of one whose wreath will soon be a-making, and who will soon after come to be the little house's mistress.

But what have we done—let time slip backward? A little; not much; for just then, as the ex-governor said, "And where is Bonaventure by this time?" Bonaventure had been only an hour or two in the negro-cabin where fever had dragged him down.

Since then the house had not only settled safely upon its new foundations, but Sosthène, in the good, thorough way that was his own, had carried renovation to a point that made the cottage to all intents and purposes a new house. And the curé had looked upon it again, much nearer by; for before a bride dared enter a house so nearly new, it had been deemed necessary for him to come and, before a temporary altar within the dwelling, to say mass in the time of full moon. But not yet was the house really a dwelling; it, and all Carancro, were waiting for the wedding. Make haste, Bonaventure!

He had left the Teche behind him on the east. And now a day breaks whose sunset finds him beyond the Vermilion River. He cannot go aside to the ex-governor's, over yonder on the right. He is making haste. This day his journey will end. His heart is light; he has thought out the whole matter now; he makes no doubt any longer that the story told him is true. And he knows now just what to do: this very sunset he will reach his goal; he goes to fill 'Thanase's voided place; to lay his own filial service at the feet of the widowed mother; to be a brother in the lost brother's place; and Zoséphine?—why, she shall be her daughter, the same as though 'Thanase, not he, had won her. And thus, too, Zoséphine shall have her own sweet preference—that preference which she had so often whispered to him—for a scholar rather than a soldier. Such is the plan, and Conscience has given her consent.

The sun soars far overhead. It, too, makes haste. But the wasted, flushed, hungry-eyed traveller is putting the miles behind him. He questions none to-day that pass him or whom he overtakes; only bows, wipes his warm brow, and presses on across the prairie. Straight before him, though still far away, a small, white, wooden steeple rises from out a tuft of trees. It is la chapelle!

The distance gets less and less. See! the afternoon sunlight strikes the roofs of a few unpainted cottages that have begun to show themselves at right and left of the chapel. And now he sees the green window-shutters of such as are not without them, and their copperas or indigo-dyed curtains blowing in and out. Nearer; nearer; here is a house, and yonder another, newly built. Carancro is reached.

He enters a turfy, cattle-haunted lane between rose-hedges. In a garden on one side, and presently in another over the way, children whom he remembers—but grown like weeds since he saw them last—are at play; but when they stop and gaze at him, it is without a sign of recognition. Now he walks down the village street. How empty it seems! was it really always so? Still, yonder is a man he knows—and yonder a woman—but they disappear without seeing him.

How familiar every thing is! There are the two shops abreast of the chapel, Marx's on this side, Lichtenstein's on that, their dingy false fronts covered with their same old huge rain-faded words of promise. Yonder, too, behind the blacksmith's shop, is the little schoolhouse, dirty, half-ruined, and closed—that is, wide-open and empty—it may be for lack of a teacher, or funds, or even of scholars.

"It shall not be so," said the traveller to himself, "when she and I"—

His steps grow slow. Yet here, not twenty paces before him, is the home of the curé. Ah! that is just the trouble. Shall he go here first? May he not push on and out once more upon the prairie and make himself known first of all to her? Stopping here first, will not the curé say tarry till to-morrow? His steps grow slower still.

And see, now. One of the Jews in the shop across the street has observed him. Now two stand together and scrutinize him; and now there are three, looking and smiling. Plainly, they recognize him. One starts to come across, but on that instant the quiet of the hamlet is broken by a sound of galloping hoofs.

Bonaventure stands still. How sudden is this change! He is not noticed now; every thing is in the highest animation. There are loud calls and outcries; children are shouting and running, and women's heads are thrust out of doors and windows. Horsemen come dashing into the village around through the lanes and up the street. Look! they wheel, they rein up, they throw themselves from the rattling saddles; they leave the big wooden stirrups swinging and the little unkempt ponies shaking themselves, and rush into the boutique de Monsieur Lichtenstein, and are talking like mad and decking themselves out on hats and shoulders with ribbons in all colors of the rainbow!

Suddenly they shout, all together, in answer to a shout outside. More horsemen appear. Lichtenstein's store belches all its population.

"La calége! La calége!" The calèche is coming!

Something, he knows not what, makes Bonaventure tremble.

"Madame," he says in French to a chattering woman who has just run out of her door, and is standing near him tying a red Madras kerchief on her head as she prattles to a girl,—"madame, what wedding is this?"

"C'est la noce à Zoséphine," she replies, without looking at him, and goes straight on telling her companion how fifty dollars has been paid for the Pope's dispensation, because the bridal pair are first cousins.

Bonaventure moves back and leans against a paling fence, pallid and faint. But there is no time to notice him—look, look!

Some women on horseback come trotting into the street. Cheers! cheers! and in a moment louder cheers yet—the calèche with the bride and groom and another with the parents have come.

Throw open the church door!

Horsemen alight, horsewomen descend; down, also, come they that were in the calèche. Look, Bonaventure! They form by twos—forward—in they go. "Hats off, gentlemen! Don't forget the rule!—Now—silence! softly, softly; speak low—or speak not at all; sh-sh! Silence! The pair are kneeling. Hush-sh! Frown down that little buzz about the door! Sh-sh!"

Bonaventure has rushed in with the crowd. He cannot see the kneeling pair; but there is the curé standing over them and performing the holy rite. The priest stops—he has seen Bonaventure! He stammers, and then he goes on. Here beside Bonaventure is a girl so absorbed in the scene that she thinks she is speaking to her brother, when presently she says to the haggard young stranger, letting herself down from her tiptoes and drawing a long breath:

"La sarimonie est fait."

It is true; the ceremony is ended. She rises on tiptoe again to see the new couple sign the papers.

Slowly! The bridegroom first, his mark. Step back. Now the little bride—steady! Zoséphine, sa marque. She turns; see her, everybody; see her! brown and pretty as a doe! They are kissing her. Hail, Madame 'Thanase!

"Make way, make way!" The man and wife come forth.—Ah! 'Thanase Beausoleil, so tall and strong, so happy and hale, you do not look to-day like the poor decoyed, drugged victim that woke up one morning out in the Gulf of Mexico to find yourself, without fore-intent or knowledge, one of a ship's crew bound for Brazil and thence to the Mediterranean!—"Make way, make way!" They mount the calèches, Sosthène after Madame Sosthène; 'Thanase after Madame 'Thanase. "To horse, ladies and gentlemen!" Never mind now about the youth who has been taken ill in the chapel, and whom the curé has borne almost bodily in his arms to his own house. "Mount! Mount! Move aside for the wedding singers!"—The wedding singers take their places, one on this side the bridal calèche, the other on that, and away it starts, creaking and groaning.

"Mais, arretez!—Stop, stop! Before going, passez le 'nisette!—pass the anisette!" May the New-Orleans compounder be forgiven the iniquitous mixture! "Boir les dames avant!—Let the ladies drink first!" Aham! straight from the bottle.

Now, go. The calèche moves. Other calèches bearing parental and grandparental couples follow. And now the young men and maidens gallop after; the cavalcade stretches out like the afternoon shadows, and with shout and song and waving of hats and kerchiefs, away they go! while from window and door and village street follows the wedding cry:

"Adjieu, la calége! Adjieu, la calége!—God speed the wedding pair!"

Coming at first from the villagers, it is continued at length, faint and far, by the attending cavaliers. As mile by mile they drop aside, singly or in pairs, toward their homes, they rise in their stirrups, and lifting high their ribbon-decked hats, they shout and curvette and curvette and shout until the eye loses them, and the ear can barely catch the faint farewell:

"Adjieu, la calége! Adjieu, les mariées!"

# CHAPTER X

# AFTER ALL

Adieu; but only till the fall of night shall bring the wedding ball.

One little tune—and every Acadian fiddler in Louisiana knows it—always brings back to Zoséphine the opening scene of that festive and jocund convocation. She sees again the great clean-swept seed-cotton room of a cotton-gin house belonging to a cousin of the ex-governor, lighted with many candles stuck into a perfect wealth of black bottles ranged along the beams of the walls. The fiddler's seat is mounted on a table in the corner, the fiddler is in it, each beau has led a maiden into the floor, the sets are made for the contra-dance, the young men stand expectant, their partners wait with downcast eyes and mute lips as Acadian damsels should, the music strikes up, and away they go.

Yes, Zoséphine sees the whole bright scene over again whenever that strain sounds.

It was fine from first to last! The ball closed with the bride's dance. Many a daughter Madame Sosthène had waltzed that farewell measure with, and now Zoséphine was the last. So they danced it, they two, all the crowd looking on: the one so young and lost in self, the other so full of years and lost to self; eddying round and round each other in this last bright embrace before they part, the mother to swing back into still water, the child to enter the current of a new life.

And then came the wedding supper! At one end of the long table the bride and groom sat side by side, and at their left and right the wedding singers stood and sang. In each corner of the room there was a barrel of roasted sweet potatoes. How everybody ate, that night! Rice! beef-balls! pass them here! pass them there! help yourself! reach them with a fork! des riz! des boulettes! more down this way! pass them over heads! des riz! des boulettes! And the anisette!—bad whiskey and oil of anise—never mind that; pour, fill, empty, fill again! Don't take too much—and make sure not to take too little! How merrily all went on! How gay was Zoséphine!

"Does she know that Bonaventure, too, has come back?" the young maidens whisper, one to another; for the news was afloat.

"Oh, yes, of course; some one had to let it slip. But if it makes any difference, she is only brighter and prettier than before. I tell you—it seems strange, but I believe, now, she never cared for anybody but 'Thanase. When she heard Bonaventure had come back, she only let one little flash out of her eyes at the fool who told her, then said it was the best news that could be, and has been as serene as the picture of a saint ever since."

The serenity of the bride might have been less perfect, and the one flash of her eyes might have been two, had she known what the curé was that minute saying to the returned wanderer, with the youth's head pressed upon his bosom, in the seclusion of his own chamber:

"It is all for the best, Bonaventure. It is not possible that thou shouldst see it so now, but thou shalt hereafter. It is best this way." And the tears rolled silently down his cheek as the weary head in his bosom murmured back:

"It is best. It is best."

The curé could only press him closer then. It was much more than a year afterward when he for the first time ventured to add:

"I never wanted you to get her, my dear boy; she is not your kind at all—nay, now, let me say it, since I have kept it unsaid so long and patiently. Do you imagine she could ever understand an unselfish life, or even one that tried to be unselfish? She makes an excellent Madame 'Thanase. 'Thanase is a good, vigorous, faithful, gentle animal, that knows how to graze and lie in the shade and get up and graze again. But you—it is not in you to know how poor a Madame Bonaventure she would have been; not now merely, but poorer and poorer as the years go by.

"And so I say, do not go away. I know why you want to go; you want to run away from a haunting thought that some unlikely accident or other may leave Madame 'Thanase a widow, and you step into his big shoes. They would not fit. Do not go. That thing is not going to happen; and the way to get rid of the troublesome notion is to stay and see yourself outgrow it—and her."

Bonaventure shook his head mournfully, but staid. From time to time Madame 'Thanase passed before his view in pursuit of her outdoor and indoor cares. But even when he came under her galérie roof he could see that she never doubted she had made the very best choice in all Carancro.

And yet people knew—she knew—that Bonaventure not only enjoyed the acquaintance, but sometimes actually went from one place to another on the business, of the great ex-governor. Small matters they may have been, but, anyhow, just think!

Sometimes as he so went or came he saw her squatting on a board at the edge of a coolée, her petticoat wrapped snugly around her limbs, and a limp sunbonnet hiding her nut-brown face, pounding her washing with a wooden paddle. She was her own housekeeper, chambermaid, cook, washerwoman, gooseherd, seamstress, nurse, and all the rest. Her floors, they said, were always bien fourbis (well scrubbed); her beds were high, soft, snug, and covered with the white mesh of her own crochet-needle.

He saw her the oftener because she worked much out on her low veranda. From that place she had a broad outlook upon the world, with 'Thanase in the foreground, at his toil, sometimes at his sport. His cares as a herder, vacheur,—vaché, he called it,—were wherever his slender-horned herds might roam or his stallions lead their mares in search of the sweetest herbage; and when rains filled the maraises, and the cold nor'westers blew from Texas and the sod was spongy with much water, and he went out for feathered game, the numberless mallards, black ducks, gray ducks, teal—with sometimes the canvas-back—and the poules-d'eau—the water-hens and the rails, and the cache-cache—the snipe—were as likely to settle or rise just before his own house as elsewhere, and the most devastating shot that hurtled through those feathered multitudes was that sent by her husband—hers—her own—possessive case—belonging to her. She was proud of her property.

Sometimes la vieille—for she was la vieille from the very day that she counted her wedding presents, mostly chickens, and turned them loose in the dooryard—sometimes she enjoyed the fine excitement of seeing her vieux catching and branding his yearling colts. Small but not uncomely they were: tougher, stronger, better when broken, than the mustang, though, like the mustang, begotten and foaled on the open prairie. Often she saw him catch two for the plough in the morning, turn them loose at noon to find their own food and drink, and catch and work another pair through the afternoon. So what did not give her pride gave her quiet comfort. Sometimes she looked forth with an anxious eye, when a colt was to be broken for the saddle; for as its legs were untied, and it sprang to its feet with 'Thanase in the saddle, and the blindfold was removed from its eyes, the strain on the young wife's nerves was as much as was good, to see the creature's tremendous leaps in air and not tremble for its superb, unmovable rider.

Could scholarship be finer than—or as fine as—such horsemanship? And yet, somehow, as time ran on, Zoséphine, like all the rest of Carancro, began to look up with a certain deference, half-conscious, half-unconscious, to the needy young man who was nobody's love or lover, and yet, in a gentle, unimpassioned way, everybody's; landless, penniless, artless Bonaventure, who honestly thought there was no girl in Carancro who was not much too good for him, and of whom there was not one who did not think him much too good for her. He was quite outside of all their gossip. How could they know that with all his learning—for he could read and write in two languages and took the Vermilionville newspaper—and with all his books, almost an entire mantel-shelf full—he was feeling heart-hunger the same as any ordinary lad or lass unmated? Zoséphine found her eyes, so to speak, lifting, lifting, more and more as from time to time she looked upon the inoffensive Bonaventure. But so her satisfaction in her own husband was all the more emphatic. If she had ever caught a real impulse toward any thing that even Carancro would have called culture, she had cast it aside now—as to herself; her children—oh! yes; but that would be by and by.

Even of pastimes and sports she saw almost none. For 'Thanase there was, first of all, his fiddle; then la chasse, the chase; the papegaie, or, as he called it, pad-go—the shooting-match; la galloche, pitch-farthing; the cock-fight; the five-arpent pony-race; and too often, also, chin-chin, twenty-five-cent poker, and the gossip and glass of the roadside "store." But for Madame 'Thanase there was only a seat against the wall at the Saturday-night dance, and mass à la chapelle once in two or three weeks; these, and infant baptisms. These showed how fast time and life were hurrying along. The wedding seemed but yesterday, and yet here was little Sosthène, and tiny Marguerite, and cooing Zoséphine the younger—how fast history repeats itself!

But one day, one Sunday, it repeated itself in a different way. 'Thanase was in gay humor that morning. He kissed his wife, tossed his children, played on his fiddle that tune they all liked best, and, while Zoséphine looked after him with young zest in her eye, sprang into the saddle and galloped across the prairie à la chapelle to pass a jolly forenoon at chin-chin in the village grocery.

Since the war almost every one went armed—not for attack, of course; for defence. 'Thanase was an exception.

"My fists," he said, in the good old drawling Acadian dialect and with his accustomed smile,—"my fists will take care of me."

One of the party that made up the game with 'Thanase was the fellow whom you may remember as having brought that first news of 'Thanase from camp to Carancro, and whom Zoséphine had discredited. The young husband had never liked him since.

But, as I say, 'Thanase was in high spirits. His jests came thick and fast, and some were hard and personal, and some were barbed with truth, and one, at length, ended in the word "deserter." The victim grew instantly fierce and red, leaped up crying "Liar," and was knocked backward to the ground by the long-reaching fist of 'Thanase. He rose again and dashed at his assailant. The rest of the company hastily made way to right and left, chairs were overturned, over went the table, the cards were underfoot. Men ran in from outside and from over the way. The two foes clash together, 'Thanase smites again with his fist, and the other grapples. They tug and strain—

"Separate them!" cry two or three of the packed crowd in suppressed earnestness. "Separate them! Bonaventure is coming! And here from the other side the curé too! Oh, get them apart!" But the half-hearted interference is shaken off. 'Thanase sees Bonaventure and the curé enter; mortification smites him; a smothered cry of rage bursts from his lips; he tries to hurl his antagonist from him; and just as the two friends reach out to lay hands upon the wrestling mass, it goes with a great thud to the ground. The crowd recoils and springs back again; then a cry of amazement and horror from all around, the arm of the under man lifted out over the back of the other, a downward flash of steel—another—and another! the long, subsiding wail of a strong man's sudden despair, the voice of one crying,—

"Zoséphine! Ah! Zoséphine! ma vieille! ma vieille!"—one long moan and sigh, and the finest horseman, the sweetest musician, the

41

bravest soldier, yes, and the best husband, in all Carancro, was dead.

Poor old Sosthène and his wife! How hard they tried, for days, for weeks, to comfort their widowed child! But in vain. Day and night she put them away in fierce grief and silence, or if she spoke wailed always the one implacable answer,—

"I want my husband!" And to the curé the same words,—

"Go tell God I want my husband!"

But when at last came one who, having come to speak, could only hold her hand in his and silently weep with her, she clung to his with both her own, and looking up into his young, thin face, cried,—not with grace of words, and yet with some grace in all her words' Acadian ruggedness,—

"Bonaventure! Ah! Bonaventure! thou who knowest the way—teach me, my brother, how to be patient."

And so—though the ex-governor had just offered him a mission in another part of the Acadians' land, a mission, as he thought, far beyond his deserving, though, in fact, so humble that to tell you what it was would force your smile—he staid.

A year went by, and then another. Zoséphine no longer lifted to heaven a mutinous and aggrieved countenance. Bonaventure was often nigh, and his words were a deep comfort. Yet often, too, her spirit flashed impatience through her eyes when in the childish philosophizing of which he was so fond he put forward—though ever so impersonally and counting himself least of all to have attained—the precepts of self-conquest and abnegation. And then as the flash passed away, with a moisture of the eye repudiated by the pride of the lip, she would slowly shake her head and say:

"It is of no use; I can't do it! I may be too young—I may be too bad, but—I can't learn it!"

At last, one September evening, Bonaventure stood at the edge of Sosthène's galérie, whither Zoséphine had followed out, leaving le vieux and la vieille in the house. On the morrow Bonaventure was to leave Carancro. And now he said,—

"Zoséphine, I must go."

"Ah, Bonaventure!" she replied, "my children—what will my children do? It is not only that you have taught them to spell and read, though God will be good to you for that! But these two years you have been every thing to them—every thing. They will be orphaned over again, Bonaventure." Tears shone in her eyes, and she turned away her face with her dropped hands clasped together.

The young man laid his hand upon her drooping brow. She turned again and lifted her eyes to his. His lips moved silently, but she read upon them the unheard utterance: it was a word of blessing and farewell. Slowly and tenderly she drew down his hand, laid a kiss upon it, and said,—

"Adjieu—adjieu," and they parted.

As Zoséphine, with erect form and firm, clear tread, went by her parents and into the inner room where her children lay in their trundle-bed, the old mother said to le vieux,—

"You can go ahead and repair the schoolhouse now. Our daughter will want to begin, even to-morrow, to teach the children of the village—les zonfants à la chapelle."

"You think so?" said Sosthène, but not as if he doubted.

"Yes; it is certain now that Zoséphine will always remain the Widow 'Thanase."

# GRANDE POINTE

## CHAPTER I

## A STRANGER

From College Point to Bell's Point, sixty miles above New Orleans, the Mississippi runs nearly from west to east. Both banks, or "coasts," are lined with large and famous sugar-plantations. Midway on the northern side, lie the beautiful estates of "Belmont" and "Belle Alliance." Early one morning in the middle of October, 1878, a young man, whose age you would have guessed fifteen years too much, stood in scrupulously clean, ill-fitting, flimsy garments, on the strong, high levee overlooking these two plantations. He was asking the way to a place called Grande Pointe. Grand Point, he called it, and so may we: many names in Louisiana that retain the French spelling are habitually given an English pronunciation.

A tattered negro mounted on a sunburnt, unshod, bare-backed mule, down in the dusty gray road on the land-side of the embankment, was his only hearer. Fifteen years earlier these two men, with French accents, strangers to each other, would hardly have conversed in English; but the date made the difference. We need not inexorably render the dialect of the white man; pretty enough to hear, it would often be hideous to print. The letter r, for instance, that plague of all nations—before consonants it disappeared; before vowels the tongue failed of that upward curve that makes the good strong r's of Italy and Great Britain.

The negro pointed over his mule's ears.

"You see Belle Alliance sugah-house yondeh? Well, behine dah you fine one road go stret thoo the plantation till de wood. Dass 'bout mile, you know. Den she keep stret on thoo de wood 'bout two mile' mo', an' dat fetch you at Gran' Point'. Hole on; I show you."

The two men started down the road, the negro on his mule, the stranger along the levee's crown.

"Dat Gran' Point'," resumed the black; "'tain't no point on de riveh, you know, like dat Bell' Point, w'at you see yondeh 'twixt dem ah batture willows whah de sun all spread out on the wateh; no, seh. 'Tis jis lil place back in de swamp, raise' 'bout five, six feet 'bove de

44

wateh. Yes, seh; 'bout t'ree mile' long, 'alf mile wide. Don't nobody but Cajun'[1] live back dah. Seem droll you goin' yondeh."

"'Tis the reason I go," said the other, without looking up.

"Yes, seh."—A short silence.—"Dass nigh fifty year', now, dat place done been settle'. Ole 'Mian Roussel he was gret hunter. He know dat place. He see 'tis rich groun'. One day he come dare, cut some tree', buil' house, plant lil tobahcah. Nex' year come ole man Le Blanc; den Poché, den St. Pierre, den Martin,—all Cajun'. Oh! dass mo'n fifty year' 'go. Dey all comes from dis yeh riveh coast; 'caze de rich Creole', dey buy 'em out. Yes, seh, dat use' be de Côte Acadien', right yeh whar yo' feet stan'in' on. C'est la côte Acadien', just ici, oui." The trudging stranger waived away the right of translation. He had some reason for preferring English. But his manner was very gentle, and in a moment the negro began again.

"Gret place, dat Gran' Point'. Yes, seh; fo' tobahcah. Dey make de bes' Périque tobahcah in de worl'. Yes, seh, right yond' at Gran' Point'; an' de bes' Périque w'at come from Gran' Point', dass de Périque of Octave Roussel, w'at dey use call 'im Chat-oué;[2] but he git tired dat name, and now he got lil boy 'bout twenny-five year' ole, an' dey call de ole man Catou, an' call his lil boy Chat-oué. Dey fine dat wuck mo' betteh. Yes, seh. An' he got bruddeh name' 'Mian Roussel. But dat not de ole, ole 'Mian—like dey say de ole he one. 'Caze, you know, he done peg out. Oh, yes, he peg out in de du'in' o' de waugh.[3] But he lef' heap-sight chillen; you know, he got a year' staht o' all de res', you know. Yes, seh. Dey got 'bout hund'ed fifty peop' yond' by Gran' Point', and sim like dey mos' all name Roussel. Sim dat way to me. An' ev'y las' one got a lil fahm so lil you can't plow her; got dig her up wid a spade. Yes, seh, same like you diggin' grave; yes, seh."

The gentle stranger interrupted, still without lifting his eyes from the path. "'Tis better narrowness of land than of virtue." The negro responded eagerly:

"Oh, dey good sawt o' peop', yes. Dey deals fair an' dey deals square. Dey keeps de peace. Dass 'caze dey mos'ly don't let whisky git on deir blin' side, you know. Dey does love to dance, and dey marries mawnstus young; but dey not like some niggehs: dey stays married. An' modess? Dey dess so modess dey shy! Yes, seh, dey de shyes', easy-goin'es', modesses', most p'esumin' peop' in de whole worl'! I don't see fo' why folks talk 'gin dem Cajun'; on'y dey a lil bit slow."

---

[1] Acadians.
[2] Raccoon.
[3] During the war.

45

The traveller on the levee's top suddenly stood still, a soft glow on his cheek, a distension in his blue eyes. "My friend, what was it, the first American industry? Was it not the Newfoundland fisheries? Who inaugu'ate them, if not the fishermen of Normandy and Bretagne? And since how long? Nearly fo' hundred years!"

"Dass so, boss," exclaimed the negro with the promptitude of an eye-witness; but the stranger continued:—

"The ancestors of the Acadian'—they are the fathers of the codfish!" He resumed his walk.

"Dass so, seh; dass true. Yes, seh, you' talkin' mighty true; dey a pow'ful ancestrified peop', dem Cajun'; dass w'at make dey so shy, you know. An' dey mighty good han' in de sugah-house. Dey des watchin', now, w'en dat sugah-cane git ready fo' biggin to grind; so soon dey see dat, dey des come a-lopin' in here to Mistoo Wallis' sugah-house here at Belle Alliance, an' likewise to Marse Louis Le Bourgeois yond' at Belmont. You see! de fust t'ing dey gwine ass you when you come at Gran' Point'—'Is Mistoo Wallis biggin to grind?' Well, seh, like I tell you, yeh de sugah-house, an' dah de road. Dat road fetch you at Gran' Point'."

# CHAPTER II

## IN A STRANGE LAND

An hour later the stranger, quite alone, had left behind him the broad smooth road, between rustling walls of sugar-cane, that had brought him through Belle Alliance plantation. The way before him was little more than a bridle-path along the earth thrown up beside a draining-ditch in a dense swamp. The eye could run but a little way ere it was confused by the tangle of vegetation. The trees of the all-surrounding forest—sweet-gums, water-oaks, magnolias— cast their shade obliquely along and across his way, and wherever it fell the undried dew still sparkled on the long grass.

A pervading whisper seemed to say good-by to the great human world. Scarce the note of an insect joined with his footsteps in the coarse herbage to break the stillness. He made no haste. Ferns were often about his feet, and vines were both there and everywhere. The soft blue tufts of the ageratum were on each side continually. Here and there in wet places clumps of Indian-shot spread their pale scroll leaves and sent up their green and scarlet spikes. Of stature greater than his own the golden-rod stood, crested with yellow plumes, unswayed by the still air. Often he had to push apart the brake-canes and press through with bowed head. Nothing met him in the path. Now and then there were faint signs underfoot as if wheels might have crushed the ragged turf long weeks before. Now and then the print of a hoof was seen in the black soil, but a spider had made it her home and spread across it her silken snares. If he halted and hearkened, he heard far away the hawk screaming to his mate, and maybe, looking up, caught a glimpse of him sailing in the upper air with the sunlight glowing in his pinions; or in some bush near by heard the soft rustle of the wren, or the ruffling whiff and nervous "chip" of the cardinal, or saw for an instant the flirt of his crimson robes as he rattled the stiff, jagged fans of the palmetto.

At length the path grew easier and lighter, the woods on the right gave place to a field half claimed for cotton and half given up to persimmon saplings, blackberry-bushes, and rampant weeds. A furry pony with mane and tail so loaded with cockleburs that he could not shake them, lifted his head and stared. A moment afterward the view opened to right and left, and the path struck a grassy road at right angles and ended. Just there stood an aged sow.

"Unclean one," said the grave wayfarer, "where dwells your master?—Ignore you the English tongue? But I shall speak not in another; 'tis that same that I am arriving to bring you."

The brute, with her small bestial eye fixed on him distrustfully and askance, moved enough to the right to let him pass on the other hand, and with his coat on his arm—so strong was the October sun—he turned into the road westward, followed one or two of its slight curves, and presently saw neat fields on either hand, walled in on each farther side by the moss-hung swamp; and now a small, gray, unpainted house, then two or three more, the roofs of others peering out over the dense verdure, and down at the end of the vista a small white spire and cross. Then, at another angle, two men seated on the roadside. Their diffident gaze bore that look of wild innocence that belongs to those who see more of dumb nature than of men. Their dress was homespun. The older was about fifty years old, the other much younger.

"Sirs, have I already reach Gran' Point'?"

The older replied in an affirmative that could but just be heard, laid back a long lock of his straight brown hair after the manner of a short-haired girl, and rose to his feet.

"I hunt," said the traveller slowly, "Mr. Maximian Roussel."

A silent bow.

47

"'Tis you?"

The same motion again.

The traveller produced a slip of paper folded once and containing a line or two of writing hastily pencilled that morning at Belle Alliance. Maximian received it timidly and held it helplessly before his downcast eyes with the lines turned perpendicularly, while the pause grew stifling, and until the traveller said:—

"'Tis Mr. Wallis make that introduction."

At the name of the owner of the beautiful plantation the man who had not yet spoken rose, covered with whittlings. It was like a steer getting up out of the straw. He spoke.

"M'sieu' Walleece, a commencé à mouliner? Is big-in to gryne?"

"He shall commence in the centre of the next week."

Maximian's eyes rose slowly from the undeciphered paper. The traveller's met them. He pointed to the missive.

"The schoolmaster therein alluded—'tis me."

"Oh!" cried the villager joyously, "maître d'école!—schooltitcher!"

"But," said the stranger, "not worthy the title." He accepted gratefully the hand of one and then of the other.

"Walk een!" said Maximian, "all hand', walk een house." They went, Indian file, across the road, down a sinuous footpath, over a stile, and up to his little single-story unpainted house, and tramped in upon the railed galérie.

"Et M'sieu' Le Bourgeois," said the host, as the schoolmaster accepted a split-bottomed chair, "he's big-in to gryne?"

Within this ground-floor veranda—chief appointment of all Acadian homes—the traveller accepted a drink of water in a blue tumbler, brought by the meek wife. The galérie just now was scattered with the husband's appliances for making Périque tobacco into "carats"—the carat-press. Its small, iron-ratcheted, wooden windlass extended along the top rail of the balustrade across one of the galérie's ends. Lines of half-inch grass rope, for wrapping the carats into diminished bulk and solid shape, lay along under foot. Beside one of the doors, in deep hickory baskets, were the parcels of cured tobacco swaddled in cotton cloths and ready for the torture of ropes and windlass. From the joists overhead hung the pods of tobacco-seed for next year's planting.

# CHAPTER III

## THE HANDSHAKING

There was news in Grande Pointe. The fair noon sky above, with its peaceful flocks of clouds; the solemn, wet forest round about; the harvested fields; the dishevelled, fragrant fallows; the reclining, ruminating cattle; the little chapel of St. Vincent de Paul in the midst, open for mass once a fortnight, for a sermon in French four times a year,—these were not more tranquil in the face of the fact that a schoolmaster had come to Grande Pointe to stay than outwardly appeared the peaceful-minded villagers. Yet as the tidings floated among the people, touching and drifting on like thistle-down, they were stirred within, and came by ones, by twos, slow-stepping, diffidently smiling, to shake hands with the young great man. They wiped their own before offering them—the men on their strong thighs, the women on their aprons. Children came, whose courage would carry them no nearer than the galérie's end or front edge, where they lurked and hovered, or gazed through the balustrade, or leaned against a galérie post and rubbed one brown bare foot upon another and crowded each other's shoulders without assignable cause, or lopped down upon the grass and gazed from a distance.

Little conversation was offered. The curiosity was as unobtrusive as the diffidence was without fear; and when a villager's soft, low speech was heard, it was generally in answer to inquiries necessary for one to make who was about to assume the high office of educator. Moreover, the schoolmaster revealed, with all gentleness, his preference for the English tongue, and to this many could only give ear. Only two or three times did the conversation rise to a pitch that kindled even the ready ardor of the young man of letters. Once, after a prolonged silence, the host, having gazed long upon his guest, said, without preface:—

"Tough jawb you got," and waved a hand toward the hovering children.

"Sir," replied the young scholar, "is it not the better to do whilse it is the mo' tough? The mo' toughness, the mo' honor." He rose suddenly, brushed back the dry, brown locks of his fine hair, and extending both hands, with his limp straw hat dangling in one, said: "Sir, I will ask you; is not the schoolmaster the true patriot? Shall his honor be less than that of the soldier? Yet I ask not honor;

for me, I am not fit; yet, after my poor capacities"—He resumed his seat.

An awesome quiet followed. Then some one spoke to him, too low to be heard. He bent forward to hear the words repeated, and 'Mian said for the timorous speaker:—

"Aw, dass nut'n; he jis only say, 'Is M'sieu' Walleece big-in to gryne?'"

Few tarried long, though one man—he whom the schoolmaster had found sitting on the roadside with Maximian—staid all day; and even among the villagers themselves there was almost no loquacity. Maximian, it is true, as the afternoon wore along, and it seemed plain that the reception was a great and spontaneous success, spoke with growing frequency and heartiness; and, when the guest sat down alone at a table within, where la vieille—the wife—was placing half-a-dozen still sputtering fried eggs, a great wheaten loaf, a yellow gallon bowl of boiled milk, a pewter ladle, a bowie-knife, the blue tumbler, and a towel; and out on the galérie the callers were still coming: his simple neighbors pardoned the elation that led him to take a chair himself a little way off, sit on it sidewise, cross his legs gayly, and with a smile and wave of his good brown hand say:—

"Servez-vous! He'p you'se'f! Eat much you like; till you swell up!"

Even he asked no questions. Only near the end of the day, when the barefoot children by gradual ventures had at length gathered close about and were softly pushing for place on his knees, and huddling under his arms, and he was talking French,—the only language most of them knew,—he answered the first personal inquiry put to him since arriving. "His name," he replied to the tiny, dark, big-eyed boy who spoke for his whispering fellows, "his name was Bonaventure—Bonaventure Deschamps."

As the great October sun began to dip his crimson wheel behind the low black line of swamp, and the chapel cross stood out against a band of yellow light that spanned the west, he walked out to see the village, a little girl on either hand and little boys round about. The children talked apace. Only the girl whose hand he held in his right was mute. She was taller than the rest; yet it was she to whom the little big-eyed boy pointed when he said, vain of his ability to tell it in English:—

"I don't got but eight year' old, me. I'm gran' for my age; but she, she not gran' for her age—Sidonie; no; she not gran' at all for her age."

They told the story of the chapel: how some years before, in the Convent of the Sacred Heart, at the parish seat a few miles away on the Mississippi, a nun had by the Pope's leave cast off the veil; how she had come to Grande Pointe and taken charge of her widowed brother's children; and how he had died, and she had found means, the children knew not how, to build this chapel. And now she was buried under it, they said. It seemed, from what they left unsaid as well as what they said, that the simple influence of her presence had kindled a desire for education in Grande Pointe not known before.

"Dass my tante—my hant. She was my hant befo' she die'," said the little man of eight years, hopping along the turf in front of the rest. He dropped into a walk that looked rapid, facing round and moving backward. "She learn me English, my tante. And she try to learn Sidonie; but Sidonie, Sidonie fine that too strong to learn, that English, Sidonie." He hopped again, talking as he hopped, and holding the lifted foot in his hand. He could do that and speak English at the same time, so talented was Toutou.

Thus the sun went down. And at Maximian's stile again Bonaventure Deschamps took the children's cheeks into his slender fingers and kissed them, one by one, beginning at the least, and so up, slowly, toward Sidonie Le Blanc. With very earnest tenderness it was done, some grave word of inspiration going before each caress; but when at last he said, "To-morrow, dear chil'run, the school-bell shall ring in Gran' Point'!" and turned to finish with Sidonie—she was gone.

# CHAPTER IV

## HOW THE CHILDREN RANG THE BELL

Where the fields go wild and grow into brakes, and the soil becomes fenny, on the north-western edge of Grande Pointe, a dark, slender thread of a bayou moves loiteringly north-eastward into a swamp of huge cypresses. In there it presently meets another like itself, the Bayou Tchackchou, slipping around from the little farm village's eastern end as silently as a little mother comes out of a bower where she has just put her babe to sleep. A little farther on they are joined as noiselessly by Blind River, and the united waters slip on northward through the dim, colonnaded, watery-floored, green-roofed, blue-vapored, moss-draped wilderness, till in the adjoining parish of Ascension they curve around to the east and issue into the sunny breadth of Lake Maurepas. Thus they make the Bayou des Acadiens. From Lake Maurepas one can go up Amite or Tickfaw River, or to Pass Manchac or Pontchatoula, anywhere in the world, in fact,—where a canoe can go.

On a bank of this bayou, no great way from Grande Pointe, but with the shadow of the swamp at its back and a small, bright prairie of rushes and giant reeds stretching away from the opposite shore, stood, more in the water than on the land, the palmetto-thatched fishing and hunting lodge and only home of a man who on the other side of the Atlantic you would have known for a peasant of Normandy, albeit he was born in this swamp,—the man who had tarried all day at the schoolmaster's handshaking.

What a day that had been! Once before he had witnessed a positive event. That was when, one day, he journeyed purposely to the levee of Belle Alliance, waited from morning till evening, and at last saw the steamer "Robert E. Lee" come by, and, as fortune would have it, land! loaded with cotton from the water to the hurricane deck. He had gone home resolved from that moment to save his money, and be something more than he was.

But that event had flashed before his eyes, and in a quarter-hour was gone, save in his memory. The coming of the schoolmaster, all unforeseen, had lasted a day, and he had seen it from beginning to end. All day long on 'Mian's galérie, standing now here, now there, he had got others to interpret for him, where he could not guess, the meanings of the wise and noble utterances that fell every now and then from the lips of the young soldier of learning, and stored them away in his now greedy mind.

One saying in particular, whose originality he did not dream of questioning, took profound hold of his conviction and admiration; and two or three times that evening, as his canoe glided homeward in the twilight, its one long, smooth ripple gleaming on this side and that as it widened away toward the bayou's dark banks, he rested for a moment on his tireless paddle, and softly broke the silence of the wilderness with its three simple words, so trite to our ears, so strange to his:—

"Knowledge is power."

In years he was but thirty-five; but he was a widower, and the one son who was his only child and companion would presently be fourteen.

"Claude," he said, as they rose that evening from their hard supper in the light and fumes of their small kerosene-lamp, "I' faut z-ahler coucher." (We must go to bed.)

"Quofoir?" asked the sturdy lad. (Pourquoi? Why?)

"Because," replied the father in the same strange French in which he had begun, "at daybreak to-morrow, and every day thereafter, you must be in your dug-out on your way to Grande Pointe, to school. My son, you are going to learn how to read!"

So came it that, until their alphabetical re-arrangement, the first of all the thirty-five names on the roll was Claude St. Pierre, and that every evening thenceforward when that small kerosene-lamp glimmered in the deep darkness of Bayou des Acadiens, the abecedarian Claude was a teacher.

But even before the first rough roll was made he was present, under the little chapel-tower, when for the first time its bell rang for school. The young master was there, and all the children; so that really there was nothing to ring the bell for. They could, all together, have walked quietly across the village green to the forlorn tobacco-shed that 'Mian had given them for a schoolhouse, and begun the session. Ah! say not so! It was good to ring the bell. A few of the stronger lads would even have sent the glad clang abroad before the time, but Bonaventure restrained them. For one thing, there must be room for every one to bear a hand. So he tied above their best reach three strands of "carat" cord to the main rope. Even then he was not ready.

"No, dear chil'run; but grasp hold, every one, the ropes, the cawds,—the shawt chil'run reaching up shawtly, the long chil'run the more longly."

Few understood his words, but they quietly caught the idea, and yielded themselves eagerly to his arranging hand. The highest grasp was Claude's. There was a little empty space under it, and then one only of Sidonie's hands, timid, smooth, and brown. And still the master held back the word.

"Not yet! not yet! The pear is not ripe!" He stood apart from them, near the chapel-door, where the light was strong, his silver watch open in his left hand, his form erect, his right hand lifted to the brim of his hat, his eyes upon the dial.

"Not yet, dear chil'run. Not yet. Two minute mo'.—Be ready.— Not yet!—One minute mo'!—Have the patience. Hold every one in his aw her place. Be ready! Have the patience." But at length when the little ones were frowning and softly sighing with the pain of upheld arms, their waiting eyes saw his dilate. "Be ready!" he said, with low intensity: "Be ready!" He soared to his tiptoes, the hat flounced from his head and smote his thigh, his eyes turned upon them blazing, and he cried, "Ring, chil'run, ring!"

The elfin crew leaped up the ropes and came crouching down. The bell pealed; the master's hat swung round his head. His wide

53

eyes were wet, and he cried again, "Ring! ring! for God, light, libbutty, education!" He sprang toward the leaping, sinking mass; but the right feeling kept his own hands off. And up and down the children went, the bell answering from above, peal upon peal; when just as they had caught the rhythm of Claude's sturdy pull, and the bell could sound no louder, the small cords gave way from their fastenings, the little ones rolled upon their backs, the bell gave one ecstatic double clang and turned clear over, the swift rope straightened upward from its coil, and Claude and Sidonie, her hands clasped upon each other about the rope and his hands upon hers, shot up three times as high as their finest leap could have carried them. For an instant they hung; then with another peal the bell turned back and they came blushing to the floor. A swarm of hands darted to the rope, but Bonaventure's was on it first.

"'Tis sufficient!" he said, his face all triumph. The bell gave a lingering clang or two and ceased, and presently the happy company walked across the green. "Sufficient," the master had said; but it was more than sufficient. In that moment of suspension, with Sidonie's great brown frightened eyes in his, and their four hands clasped together, Claude had learned, for his first lesson, that knowledge is not the only or the greatest power.

# CHAPTER V

## INVITED TO LEAVE

After that, every school-day morning Claude rang the bell. Always full early his pirogue came gliding out of the woods and up through the bushy fen to the head of canoe navigation and was hauled ashore. Bonaventure had fixed his home near the chapel and not far from Claude's landing-place. Thus the lad could easily come to his door each morning at the right moment—reading it by hunter's signs in nature's book—to get the word to ring. There were none of the usual reasons that the schoolmaster should live close to the schoolhouse. There was no demand for its key.

Not of that schoolhouse! A hundred feet length by twenty-five breadth, of earth-floored, clapboard-roofed, tumbling shed, rudely walled with cypress split boards,—pieux,—planted endwise in the earth, like palisades, a hand-breadth space between every two, and sunlight and fresh air and the gleams of green fields coming in; the scores of little tobacco-presses that had stood in ranks on the hard earth floor, the great sapling levers, and the festoons of curing tobacco that had hung from the joists overhead, all removed, only the odor left; bold gaps here and there in the pieux, made by that mild influence which the restless call decay, and serving for windows and doors; the eastern end swept clean and occupied by a few benches and five or six desks, strong, home-made, sixty-four pounders.

Life had broadened with Claude in two directions. On one side opened, fair and noble, the acquaintanceship of Bonaventure Deschamps, a man who had seen the outside world, a man of books, of learning, a man who could have taught even geography, had there been any one to learn it; and on the other side, like a garden of roses and spices, the schoolmateship of Sidonie Le Blanc. To you and me she would have seemed the merest little brown sprout of a thing, almost nothing but two big eyes—like a little owl. To Claude it seemed as though nothing older or larger could be so exactly in the prime of beauty; the path to learning was the widest, floweriest, fragrantest path he had ever trod.

Sidonie did not often speak with him. At recess she usually staid at her desk, studying, quite alone but for Bonaventure silently busy at his, and Claude himself, sitting farther away, whenever the teacher did not see him and drive him to the playground. If he would only drive Sidonie out! But he never did.

One day, after quite a contest of learning, and as the hour of dismission was scattering the various groups across the green, Toutou, the little brother who was grand for his age, said to Claude, hanging timidly near Sidonie:—

"Alle est plus smart' que vous." (She is smarter than you.)

Whereupon Sidonie made haste to say in their Acadian French, "Ah! Master Toutou, you forget we went to school to our dear aunt. And besides, I am small and look young, but I am nearly a year older than Claude." She had wanted to be kind, but that was the first thorn. Older than he!

And not only that; nearly fifteen! Why, at fifteen—at fifteen girls get married! The odds were heavy. He wished he had thought of that at first. He was sadly confused. Sometimes when Bonaventure spoke words of enthusiasm and regard to him after urging him fiercely up some hill of difficulty among the bristling heights of English pronunciation, he yearned to seek him alone and tell him this difficulty of the heart. There was no fear that Bonaventure would laugh; he seemed scarce to know how; and his smiles were all of tenderness and zeal. Claude did not believe the ten years between them would matter; had not Bonaventure said to him but yesterday that to him all loveliness was the lovelier for being very young? Yet when the confession seemed almost on Claude's lips it was driven back by an alien mood in the master's face. There were troubles in Bonaventure's heart that Claude wot not of.

One day who should drop in just as school was about to begin but the priest from College Point! Such order as he found! Bonaventure stood at his desk like a general on a high hill, his large hand-bell in his grasp, passed his eyes over the seventeen demure girls, with their large, brown-black, liquid eyes, their delicately pencilled brows, their dark, waveless hair, and sounded one tap! The sport outside ceased, the gaps at the shed's farther end were darkened by small forms that came darting like rabbits into their burrows, eighteen small hats came off, and the eighteen boys came softly forward and took their seats. Such discipline!

"Sir," said Bonaventure, "think you 'tis arising, f'om the strickness of the teacher? 'Tis f'om the goodness of the chil'run! How I long the State Sup'inten'ent Public Education to see them!"

The priest commended the sight and the wish with smiling affirmations that somehow seemed to lack sympathy. He asked the names of two or three pupils. That little fellow with soft, tanned, chubby cheeks and great black eyes, tiny mouth, smooth feet so shapely and small, still wet to their ankles with dew, and arms that he could but just get folded, was Toutou. That lad with the strong shoulders, good wide brows, steady eye, and general air of manliness,—that was Claude St. Pierre. And this girl over on the left here,—"You observe," said Bonaventure, "I situate the lambs on the left and the kids on the right,"—this little, slender crescent of human moonlight, with her hair in two heavy, black, down-falling plaits, meek, drooping eyes, long lashes, soft childish cheeks and full throat, was Sidonie Le Blanc. Bonaventure murmured:—

"Best scholah in the school, yet the only—that loves not her teacher. But I give always my interest, not according to the interestingness, but rather to the necessitude, of each."

The visit was not long. Standing, about to depart, the visitor seemed still, as at the first, a man of many reservations under his polite smiles. But just then he dropped a phrase that the teacher recognized as an indirect quotation, and Bonaventure cried, with greedy eyes:—

"You have read Victor Hugo?"

"Yes."

"Oh, sir, that grea-a-at man! That father of libbutty! Other patriots are the sons, but he the father! Is it not thus?"

The priest shrugged and made a mouth. The young schoolmaster's face dropped.

"Sir, I must ask you—is he not the frien' of the poor and downtrod?"

The visitor's smile quite disappeared. He said:—

"Oh!"—and waved a hand impatiently; "Victor Hugo"—another mouth—"Victor Hugo"—replying in French to the schoolmaster's English—"is not of my party." And then he laughed unpleasantly and said good-day.

The State Superintendent did not come, but every day—"It is perhaps he shall come to-mo'w, chil'run; have yo' lessons well!"

The whole tiny army of long, blue, ankle-hiding cottonade pantalettes and pantaloons tried to fulfil the injunction. Not one but had a warm place in the teacher's heart. But Toutou, Claude, Sidonie, anybody who glanced into that heart could see sitting there enthroned. And some did that kind of reconnoitring. Catou, 'Mian's older brother, was much concerned. He saw no harm in a little education, but took no satisfaction in the introduction of English speech; and speaking to 'Mian of that reminded him to say he believed the schoolmaster himself was aware of the three children's pre-eminence in his heart. But 'Mian only said:—

"Ah bien, c'est all right, alors!" (Well, then, it's all right.) Whether all right or not, Bonaventure was aware of it, and tried to hide it under special kindnesses to others, and particularly to the dullard of the school, grandson of Catou and nicknamed Crébiche[4]. The child loved him; and when Claude rang the chapel bell, and before its last tap had thrilled dreamily on the morning air, when the urchins playing about the schoolhouse espied another group coming slowly across the common with Bonaventure in the midst of them, his coat on his arm and the children's hands in his, there among them came Crébiche, now on one side, now running round to the other, hoping so to get a little nearer to the master.

"None shall have such kindness to-day as thou," Bonaventure would silently resolve as he went in through a gap in the pieux. And the children could not see but he treated them all alike. They saw no unjust inequality even when, Crébiche having three times spelt "earth" with an u, the master paced to and fro on the bare ground among the unmatched desks and break-back benches, running his hands through his hair and crying:—

---

[4] Écrevisse, crawfish.

"Well! well aht thou name' the crawfish; with such rapiditive celeritude dost thou progress backwardly!"

It must have been to this utterance that he alluded when at the close of that day he walked, as he supposed, with only birds and grasshoppers for companions, and they grew still, and the turtle-doves began to moan, and he smote his breast and cried:

"Ah! rules, rules! how easy to make, likewise break! Oh! the shame, the shame! If Victor Hugo had seen that! And if George Washington! But thou,"—some one else, not mentioned,—"thou sawedst it!"

The last word was still on the speaker's lips, when—there beside the path, with heavy eye and drunken frown, stood the father of Crébiche, the son of Catou, the little boy of twenty-five known as Chat-oué. He spoke:

"To who is dat you speak? Talk wid de dev'?"

Bonaventure murmured a salutation, touched his hat, and passed. Chat-oué moved a little, and delivered a broadside:

"Afteh dat, you betteh leave! Yes, you betteh leave Gran' Point'!"

"Sir," said Bonaventure, turning with flushed face, "I stay."

"Yes," said the other, "dass righ'; you betteh go way and stay. Magicien," he added as the schoolmaster moved on, "sorcier!—Voudou!—jackass!"

What did all this mean?

# CHAPTER VI

## WAR OF DARKNESS AND LIGHT

Catou, it seems, had gone one day to College Point with a pair of wild ducks that he had shot,—first of the season,—and offered them to the priest who preached for Grande Pointe once a quarter.

"Catou," said the recipient, in good French but with a cruel hardness of tone, "why does that man out there teach his school in English?" The questioner's intentions were not unkind. He felt a protector's care for his Acadian sheep, whose wants he fancied he, if not he only, understood. He believed a sudden overdose of enlightenment would be to them a real disaster, and he proposed to save them from it by the kind of management they had been accustomed to—they and their fathers—for a thousand years.

Catou answered the question only by a timid smile and shrug. The questioner spoke again:

"Why do you Grande Pointe folk allow it? Do you want your children stuffed full of American ideas? What is in those books they are studying? You don't know? Neither do I. I would not look into one of them. But you ought to know that to learn English is to learn free-thinking. Do you know who print those books that your children are rubbing their noses in? Yankees! Oh, I doubt not they have been sharp enough to sprinkle a little of the stuff they call religion here and there in them; 'tis but the bait on the hook! But you silly 'Cadians think your children are getting education, and that makes up for every thing else. Do you know what comes of it? Discontent. Vanity. Contempt of honest labor. Your children are going to be discontented with their lot. It will soon be good-by to sunbonnets; good-by to homespun; good-by to Grande Pointe,—yes, and good-by to the faith of your fathers. Catou, what do you know about that man, anyhow? You ask him no questions, you 'Cadians, and he—oh, he is too modest to tell you who or what he is. Who pays him?"

"He say pay is way behine. He say he don't get not'in' since he come yondeh," said Catou, the distress that had gathered on his face disappearing for a moment.

The questioner laughed contemptuously.

"Do you suppose he works that way for nothing? How do you know, at all, that his real errand is to teach school? A letter from Mr. Wallis! who simply told your simple-minded brother what the fellow told him! See here, Catou; you owe a tax as a raiser of tobacco, eh? And besides that, hasn't every one of you an absurd little sign stuck up on the side of his house, as required by the Government, to show that you owe another tax as a tobacco manufacturer? But still you have a little arrangement to neutralize that, eh? How do you know this man is not among you to look into that? Do you know that he can teach? No wonder he prefers to teach in English! I had a conversation with him the other day; I want no more; he preferred to talk to me in English. That is the good manners he is teaching; light-headed, hero-worshipping, free-thinker that he is."

Catou was sore dismayed. He had never heard of hero-worship or free-thinking before, but did not doubt their atrocity. It had never occurred to him that a man with a few spelling-books and elementary readers could be so dangerous to society.

"I wish he clear out from yondeh," said Catou. He really made his short responses in French, but in a French best indicated in bad English.

"Not for my sake," replied the priest, coldly smiling. "I shall just preach somewhere else on the thirteenth Sunday of each quarter, and let Grande Pointe go to the devil; for there is where your new friend is sure to land you. Good-day, I am very busy this morning."

These harsh words—harsh barking of the shepherd dog—spread an unseen consternation in Grande Pointe. Maximian was not greatly concerned. When he heard of the threat to cut off the spiritual table-crumbs with which the villagers had so scantily been fed, he only responded that in his opinion the dominie was no such a fool as that. But others could not so easily dismiss their fears. They began to say privately, leaning on fences and lingering at stiles, that they had felt from the very day of that first mad bell-ringing that the whole movement was too headlong; that this opening the sluices of English education would make trouble. Children shouldn't be taught what their parents do not understand. Not that there was special harm in a little spelling, adding, or subtracting, but—the notions they and the teacher produced! Here was the school's influence going through all the place like the waters of a rising tide. All Grande Pointe was lifting from the sands, and in danger of getting afloat and drifting toward the current of the great world's life. Personally, too, the schoolmaster seemed harmless enough. From the children and he loving each other, the hearts of the seniors had become entangled. The children had come home from the atmosphere of that old tobacco-shed, and persuaded the very grandmothers to understand vaguely—very vaguely and dimly—that the day of liberty which had come to the world at large a hundred years before had come at last to them; that in France their race had been peasants; in Acadia, forsaken colonists; in Massachusetts, Pennsylvania, Maryland, Virginia, exiles alien to the land, the language, and the times; in St. Domingo, penniless, sick, unwelcome refugees; and for just one century in Louisiana the jest of the proud Creole, held down by the triple fetter of illiteracy, poverty, and the competition of unpaid, half-clad, swarming slaves. But that now the slave was free, the school was free, and a new, wide, golden future waited only on their education in the greatest language of the world.

All this was pleasant enough to accept even in a dim way, though too good to be more than remotely grasped. But just when, as music in a sleeper's ear, it is taking hold of their impulses somewhat, comes the word of their hereditary dictator that this man is among them only for their destruction. What could they reply? They were a people around whom the entire world's thought had swirled and tumbled for four hundred years without once touching them. Their ancestors had left France before Descartes or Newton had begun to teach the modern world to think. They knew no method of reasoning save by precedent, and had never caught the faintest reflection from the mind of that great, sweet thinker who said, "A stubborn retention of customs is a turbulent thing, no less than the introduction of new." To such strangers in the world of to-day now came the contemptuous challenge of authority, defying them to prove that one who proposed to launch them forth upon a sea of changes out of sight of all precedent and tradition was not the hireling of some enemy's gold secretly paid to sap the foundations of all their spiritual and temporal interests and plunge them into chaos.

They blamed Bonaventure; he had got himself hated and them rebuked; it was enough. They said little to each other and nothing to him; but they felt the sleepy sense of injury we all know so well against one who was disturbing their slumber; and some began to suspect and distrust him, others to think hard of him for being suspected and distrusted. Yet all this reached not his ears, and the first betrayal of it was from the lips of Chat-oué, when, in his cups, he unexpectedly invited the schoolmaster to leave Grande Pointe.

After that, even the unconscious schoolmaster could feel the faint chill of estrangement. But he laid it not to his work, but to his personal unloveliness, and said to 'Mian he did not doubt if he were more engaging there would not be so many maidens kept at the wheel and loom in the priceless hours of school, or so many strapping youths sent, all unlettered, to the sugar-kettles of the coast plantations what time M'sieu' Walleece big-in to gryne.

"'Tain't dat," said 'Mian. He had intended to tell the true reason, but his heart failed him; and when Bonaventure asked what, then, it was, he replied:

"Aw, dey don't got no time. Time run so fas',—run like a scared dog. I dunno fo' w'at dey make dat time run so fas' dat way."

"O my friend," cried the young schoolmaster, leaping from his chair, "say not that! If God did not make time to p'oceed with rapidness, who would ever do his best?"

It was such lessons as this that made the children—Crébiche among them—still gather round the humble master and love to grasp his hand.

# CHAPTER VII

## LOVE AND DUTY

Time ran fast. The seasons were as inexorable at Grande Pointe as elsewhere. But there was no fierceness in them. The very frosts were gentle. Slowly and kindly they stripped the green robes from many a tree, from many a thicket ejected like defaulting tenants the blue linnet, the orchard oriole, the nonpareil, took down all its leafy hangings and left it open to the winds and rain of December. The wet ponies and kine turned away from the north and stood in the slanting storm with bowed heads. The great wall of cypress swamp grew spectral. But its depths, the marshes far beyond sight behind them, and the little, hidden, rushy lakes, were alive with game. No snake crossed the path. Under the roof, on the galérie, the wheel hummed, the loom pounded; inside, the logs crackled and blazed on the hearth; on the board were venison, mallard, teal, rice-birds, sirop de baterie, and quitte; round the fireside were pipes, pecans, old stories, and the Saturday-night contra-dance; and every now and then came sounding on the outer air the long, hoarse bellow of some Mississippi steamer, telling of the great world beyond the tree-tops, a little farther than the clouds and nearer than the stars.

Christmas passed, and New Year—time runs so fast! Presently yonder was 'Mian himself, spading a piece of ground to sow his tobacco-seed in; then Catou and his little boy of twenty-five doing likewise; and then others all about the scattered village. Then there was a general spreading of dry brush over the spaded ground, then the sweet, clean smell of its burning, and, hanging everywhere throughout the clearing, its thin blue smoke. The little frogs began to pipe to each other again in every wet place, the grass began to freshen, and almost in the calendar's midwinter the smiles of spring were wreathing everywhere.

What of the schoolmaster and the children? Much, much! The good work went on. Intense days for Bonaventure. The clouds of disfavor darkling in some places, but brightening in others, and, on the whole, he hoped and believed, breaking. A few days of vacation, and then a bright re-union and resumption, the children all his faithful adherents save one—Sidonie. She, a close student, too, but growingly distant and reticent. The State Superintendent still believed to be—

"Impending, impending, chil'run! he is impending! Any day he may precipitate upon us!"

Intense days, too, for Claude. Sidonie openly, and oh, so sweetly, his friend. Loving him? He could neither say nor know; enough, for the present, to be allowed to love her. His love knew no spirit of conquest yet; it was star-worship; it was angel adoration; seraphically pure; something so celestially refined that had it been a tangible object you could have held it up and seen the stars right through it. The thought of acquisition would have seemed like coveting the gold of a temple. And yet already the faintest hint of loss was intolerable. Oh! this happy, happy school-going,—this faring sumptuously on one smile a day! Ah, if it might but continue! But alas! how Sidonie was growing! Growing, growing daily! up, up, up! While he—there was a tree in the swamp where he measured his stature every day; but in vain, in vain! It never budged! And then— all at once—like the rose-vine on her galérie, Sidonie burst into bloom.

Her smiles were kinder and more frequent now than ever before; but the boy's heart was wrung. What chance now? In four long years to come he would not yet be quite nineteen, and she was fifteen now. Four years! He was in no hurry himself—could wait forever and be happy every day of it; but she? Such prize as she, somebody would certainly bear away before three years could run by, run they ever so fast.

Sitting and pondering one evening in the little bayou cabin, Claude caught the father's eye upon him, leaned his forehead upon the parent's knee, and silently wept. The rough woodman said a kind word, and the boy, without lifting his burning face, told his love. The father made no reply for a long time, and then he said in their quaint old French:

"Claude, tell the young schoolmaster. Of all men, he is the one to help you." And then in English, as you would quote Latin, "Knowledge is power!"

The next day he missed—failed miserably—in every lesson. At its close he sat at his desk, crushed. Bonaventure seemed scarce less tempest-tossed than he; and all about the school the distress spread as wintry gray overcasts a sky. Only Sidonie moved calmly her accustomed round, like some fair, silent, wide-winged bird circling about a wreck.

At length the lad and his teacher were left alone. Claude sat very still, looking at his toil-worn hands lying crossed on the desk. Presently there sank an arm across his shoulders. It was the master's. Drop—drop—two big tears fell upon the rude desk's sleeve-polished wood. The small, hard, right hand slowly left its fellow, and rubbed off the wet spots.

"Claude, you have something to disclose me?"

The drooping head nodded.

"And 'tis not something done wrongly?"

The lad shook his head.

"Then, my poor Claude,"—the teacher's own voice faltered for a moment,—"then—'tis—'tis she!" He stroked the weeping head that sank into its hands. "Ah! yes, Claude, yes; 'tis she; 'tis she! And you want me to help you. Alas! in vain you want me! I cannot even try-y-y to help you; you have mentioned it too lately! 'Tis right you come to me, despiting discrepancy of years; but alas! the difficulty lies in the contrary; for alas! Claude, our two heart' are of the one, same age!"

They went out; and walking side by side toward the failing sun, with the humble flowers of the field and path newly opened and craving leave to live about their feet and knees, Bonaventure Deschamps revealed his own childlike heart to the simple boy whose hand clasped his.

"Yes, yes; I conceal not from you, Claude, that 'tis not alone 'thou lovest,' but 'I love'! If with cause to hope, Claude, I know not. And I must not search to know whilst yet the schoolmaster. And the same to you, Claude, whilst yet a scholah. We mus' let the dissimulation like a worm in the bud to h-eat our cheek. 'Tis the voice of honor cry—'Silence.' And during the meanwhilst, you? Perchance at the last, the years passing and you enlarging in size daily and arriving to budding manhood, may be the successful; for suspect not I consider lightly the youngness of yo' passion. Attend what I shall reveal you. Claude, there once was a boy, yo' size, yo' age, but fierce, selfish, distemperate; still more selfish than yo' schoolmaster of to-day." And there that master went on to tell of an early—like Claude's, an all too early—rash, and boyish passion, whose ragged wound, that he had thought never could heal, was now only a tender scar.

"And you, too, Claude, though now it seem not possible—you shall recuperate from this. But why say I thus? Think you I would inoculate the idea that you must despair? Nay, perchance you shall achieve her." They stood near the lad's pirogue about to say adieu; the schoolmaster waved his hand backward toward the farther end of the village. "She is there; in a short time she will cease to continue scholah; then—try." And again, with still more courageous kindness, he repeated, "Try! 'Tis a lesson that thou shouldest heed—try, try again. If at the first thou doest not succeed, try, try again."

Claude gazed gratefully into the master's face. Boy that he

was, he did not read aright the anguish gathering there. From his own face the clouds melted into a glad sunshine of courage, resolve, and anticipation. Bonaventure saw the spark of hope that he had dropped into the boy's heart blaze up into his face. And what did Claude see? The hot blood mounting to the master's brow an instant ere he wheeled and hurried away.

"'Sieur Bonaventure!" exclaimed Claude; "'Sieur Bonaventure!"

But deaf to all tones alike, Bonaventure moved straight away along the bushy path, and was presently gone from sight. There is a repentance of good deeds. Bonaventure Deschamps felt it gnawing and tearing hard and harder within his bosom as he strode on through the wild vernal growth that closed in the view on every side. Soon he halted; then turned, and began to retrace his steps.

"Claude!" The tone was angry and imperative. No answer came. He quickened his gait. "Claude!" The voice was petulant and imperious. A turn of the path brought again to view the spot where the two had so lately parted. No one was there. He moaned and then cried aloud, "O thou fool, fool, fool!—Claude!" He ran; faster—faster—down the path, away from all paths, down the little bayou's margin, into the bushes, into the mud and water. "Claude! Claude! I told you wrongly! Stop! Arretez-la! I must add somewhat!—Claude!" The bushes snatched away his hat; tore his garments; bled him in hands and face; yet on he went into the edge of the forest. "Claude! Ah! Claude, thou hast ruin' me! Stop, you young rascal!—thief!—robber!—brigand!" A vine caught and held him fast. "Claude! Claude!"—The echoes multiplied the sound, and scared from their dead-tree roost a flock of vultures. The dense wood was wrapping the little bayou in its premature twilight. The retreating sun, that for a while had shot its flaming arrows through the black boles and branches, had sunk now and was gone. Only a parting ruby glow shone through the tangle where far and wide the echoes were calling for Claude.

"Claude! I mistook the facts in the case. There is no hope for you! 'Tis futile you try—the poem is not for you! I take every thing back!—all back! You shall not once try! You have grasp' the advantage! You got no business, you little rascal! You dare venture to attempt making love in my school! Claude St. Pierre, you are dismiss' the school! Mutiny! mutiny! Claude St. Pierre, for mutinizing, excluded the Gran' Point' school."

He tore himself from his fastenings and hastened back toward the village. The tempest within him was as fierce as ever; but already it, too, had turned and was coming out of the opposite quarter. The better Bonaventure—the Bonaventure purified by fires that Grande Pointe had no knowledge of—was coming back into his gentle self-mastery. And because that other, that old-time Bonaventure, bound in chains deep down within, felt already the triumph of a moment slipping from his grasp, he silently now to the outer air, but loudly within, railed and gnashed and tore himself the more.

He regained the path and hurried along it, hatless, dishevelled, bespattered, and oblivious to every thing save the war within. Presently there came upon him the knowledge, the certain knowledge, that Claude would come the next morning and ring the chapel bell, take his seat in school, stand in all his classes, know every lesson, and go home in the evening happy and all unchallenged of him. He groaned aloud.

"Ah! Claude! To dismiss or not to dismiss, it shall not be mine! But it shall be thine, Sidonie! And whether she is for thee, Claude—so juvenile!—or for me, so unfit, unfit, unfit!—Ah! Sidonie, choose not yet!"—He stood rooted to the spot; while within easy earshot of his lightest word tripped brightly and swiftly across the path from the direction of the chapel a fawn, Claude's gift, and its mistress, Sidonie—as though she neither saw nor heard.

# CHAPTER VIII

## AT CLAUDE'S MERCY

Time flagged not. The school shone on, within its walls making glad the teacher and the pupils with ever new achievements in knowledge and excellence. Some of the vanguard—Claude, Sidonie, Étienne, Madelaine, Henri, Marcelline—actually going into the Third Reader. Such perfection in lessons as they told about at home—such mastery of English, such satisfactory results in pronunciation and emphasis! Reading just as they talked? Oh, no, a thousand times no! The school's remoter light, its secondary influences, slowly spreading, but so slowly that only the eyes of enmity could see its increase. There were murmurs and head-shakings; but the thirteenth Sunday of the year's first quarter came, and the sermon whose withholding had been threatened was preached. And on the thirteenth Monday there was Bonaventure, still moving quietly across the green toward the schoolhouse with the children all about him. But a few days later the unexpected happened.

By this time Claude's father, whose teacher, you remember, was Claude, had learned to read. One day a surveyor, who had employed him as a guide, seeing the Acadian laboring over a fragment of rural newspaper, fell into conversation with him as they sat smoking by their camp-fire, and presently caught some hint of St. Pierre's aspirations for himself and his son.

"So there's a public school at Grande Pointe, is there?"

"Oh, yass; fine school; hondred feet long! and fine titcher; splendid titcher; titch English."

"Well, well!" laughed the surveyor. "Well, the next thing will be a railroad."

St. Pierre's eyes lighted up.

"You t'ink!"

"Why, yes; you can't keep railroads away from a place long, once you let in the public school and teach English."

"You t'ink dass good?"

"What, a railroad? Most certainly. It brings immigration."

"Whass dat—'migrash'n?"

The surveyor explained.

The next time St. Pierre came to Grande Pointe—to sell some fish—he came armed with two great words for the final overthrow of all opponents of enlightenment: "Rellroad!—'Migrash'n!"

They had a profound and immediate effect—exactly the opposite of what he had expected.

The school had just been dismissed; the children were still in sight, dispersing this way and that. Sidonie lingered a moment at her desk, putting it in order; Claude, taking all the time he could, was getting his canoe-paddle from a corner; Crébiche was waiting, by the master's command, to repair some default of the day; and Toutou, outside on his knees in the grass catching grasshoppers, was tarrying for his sister; when four or five of the village's best men came slowly and hesitatingly in. It required no power of divination for even the pre-occupied schoolmaster to guess the nature of their errand. 'Mian was not among them. Catou was at their head. They silently bowed. The schoolmaster as silently responded. The visitors huddled together. They came a step nearer.

"Well," said Catou, "we come to see you."

"Sirs, welcome to Gran' Point' school.—Sidonie, Crébiche, Claude, rest in yo' seats."

"Mo' betteh you tu'n 'em loose, I t'ink," said Catou amiably; "ain't it?"

67

"I rather they stay," replied Bonaventure. All sat down. There was a sustained silence, and then Catou said with quiet abruptness:

"We dawn't want no mo' school!"

"From what cause?"

"'Tain't no use."

"Sir—sirs, no use? 'Tis every use! The schoolhouse? 'tis mo' worth than the gole mine. Ah! sirs, tell me: what is gole without education?"

They confronted the riddle for a moment.

"Ed'cation want to change every thin'—rellroad—'migrash'n."

"Change every thing? Yes!—making every thing better! Sirs, where is that country that the people are sorry that the railroad and the schoolhouse have come?" Again the riddle went unanswered; but Catou sat as if in meditation, looking to one side, and presently said:

"I t'ink dass all humbug, dat titchin' English. What want titch English faw?"

"Sir," cried Bonaventure, "in America you mus' be American! Three Acadians have been governor of Louisiana! What made them thus to become?" He leaned forward and smote his hands together. "What was it? 'Twas English education!"

The men were silent again. Catou pushed his feet out, and looked at his shoes, put on for the occasion. Presently—

"Yass," he said, in an unconvinced tone; "yass, dass all right: but how we know you titch English? Nobody can't tell you titchin' him right or no."

"And yet—I do! And the time approach when you shall know! Sirs, I make to you a p'oposition. Time is passing. It must be soon the State Sup'inten'ent Public Education visit this school. The school is any time ready. Since long time are we waiting. He shall come—he shall examine! The chil'run shall be ignorant this arrangement! Only these shall know—Claude, Sidonie, Crébiche; they will not disclose! And the total chil'run shall exhibit all their previous learning! And welcome the day, when the adversaries of education shall see those dear chil'run stan' up befo' the assem'led Gran' Point' spelling co'ectly words of one to eight syllable' and reading from their readers! And if one miss—if one—one! miss, then let the school be shut and the schoolmaster banish-ed!"

It was so agreed. The debate did not cease at once, but it languished. Catou thought he had made one strong point when he objected to education as conducive to idle habits; but when the schoolmaster hurled back the fact that communities the world over are industrious just in proportion as they are educated, he was

68

done. He did not know, but when he confronted the assertion it looked so true that he could not doubt it. He only said:

"Well, anyhow, I t'ink 'tain't no use Crébiche go school no mo'." But when Bonaventure pleaded for the lad's continuance, that too was agreed upon. The men departed.

"Crébiche," said the master, holding the boy's hand at parting, "ah! Crébiche, if thou become not a good scholar"—and read a promise in the boy's swimming eyes.

"Claude, Claude, I am at yo' mercy now." But the honest gaze of Claude and the pressure of his small strong hand were a pledge. The grateful master turned to Sidonie, and again, as of old, no Sidonie was there.

# CHAPTER IX

## READY

Summer came. The song-birds were all back again, waking at dawn, and making the hoary cypress wood merry with their carollings to the wives and younglings in the nests. Busy times. Foraging on the helpless enemy—earth-worm, gnat, grub, grasshopper, weevil, sawyer, dragon-fly—from morning till night: watching for him; scratching for him; picking, pecking, boring for him; poising, swooping, darting for him; standing upside down and peering into chinks for him; and all for the luxury—not of knowledge, but of love and marriage. The mocking-bird had no rest whatever. Back and forth from dawn to dark, back and forth across and across Grande Pointe clearing, always one way empty and the other way with his beak full of marketing; and then sitting up on an average half the night—sometimes the whole of it—at his own concert. And with military duties too; patrolling the earth below, a large part of it, and all the upper air; driving off the weasel, the black snake, the hawk, the jay, the buzzard, the crow, and all that brigand crew—busy times! All nature in glad, gay earnest. Corn in blossom and rustling in the warm breeze; blackberries ripe; morning-glories under foot; the trumpet-flower flaring from its dense green vine high above on the naked, girdled tree; the cotton-plant blooming white, yellow, and red in the field beneath; honey a-

69

making in the hives and hollow trees; butterflies and bees lingering in the fields at sunset; the moth venturing forth at the first sign of dew; and Sidonie—a wild-rose tree.

Mark you, this was in Grande Pointe. I have seen the wild flower taken from its cool haunt in the forest, and planted in the glare of a city garden. Alas! the plight of it, poor outshone, wilting, odorless thing! And then I have seen it again in the forest; and pleasanter than to fill the lap with roses and tulips of the conservatory's blood-royal it was to find it there, once more the simple queen of that green solitude.

So Sidonie. Acadian maidens are shy as herons. They always see you first. They see you first, silently rise, and are gone—from the galérie. They are more shy than violets. You would think they lived whole days with those dark, black-fringed eyes cast down; but—they see you first. The work about the house is well done where they are; there are apt to be flowers outside round about; while they themselves are as Paul desired to see the women in bishop Timothy's church, "adorned in modest apparel, with shamefacedness and sobriety."

Flowers sprang plentifully where Sidonie dwelt. Her best homespun gown was her own weaving; the old dog lying on the galérie always thumped the floor with his tail and sank his obsequious head as that robe passed; the fawn—that Claude had brought—would come trotting and press its head against it; all the small living things of the dooryard would follow it about; and if she stood by the calf-pen the calves would push each other for the nearest place, lay their cheeks upon the fence's top, and roll their eyes—as many a youth of Grande Pointe would have done if he might. Chat-oué,—I fear I have omitted to mention that the father of Crébiche, like the father of Claude, had lost his wife before he was of age,—Chat-oué looked often over that fence.

When matters take that shape a girl must quit school. And yet Sidonie, when after a short vacation the school resumed its sessions, resumed with it. Toutou, who had to admit now that his sister was even more grand for her age than he, was always available for protection. There was no wonder that Sidonie wished to continue; Bonaventure explained why:

"So interesting is that McGuffey's Third Reader!"

Those at home hesitated, and presently it was the first of October. Now it was too late to withdraw; the examination was to take place. The school's opponents had expressed little impatience at the State Superintendent's weary delay, but at length Catou asked, "Why dat man don't nevva come!"

"The wherefore of his non-coming I ignore," said

Bonaventure, with a look of old pain in his young face; "but I am ready, let him come or let him come not."

"'Tain't no use wait no longer," said Catou; "jis well have yo' lil show widout him."

"Sir, it shall be had! Revolution never go backwood!"

Much was the toil, many the anxieties, of the preparation. For Bonaventure at once determined to make the affair more than an examination. He set its date on the anniversary of the day when he had come to Grande Pointe. From such a day Sidonie could not be spared. She was to say a piece, a poem, an apostrophe to a star. A child, beholding the little star in the heavens, and wondering what it can be, sparkling diamond-like so high up above the world, exhorts it not to stop twinkling on his account. But to its tender regret the school knew that no more thereafter was Sidonie to twinkle in its firmament.

"Learn yo' lessons hard, chil'run; if the State Sup'inten'ent, even at the last, you know"—Bonaventure could not believe that this important outpost had been forgotten.

# CHAPTER X

# CONSPIRACY

About this time a certain Mr. Tarbox—G. W. Tarbox—was travelling on horseback and touching from house to house of the great sugar-estates of the river "coast," seeing the country and people, and allowing the élite to subscribe to the "Album of Universal Information."

One Sunday, resting at College Point, he was led by curiosity to cultivate the acquaintance of three men who had come in from Grande Pointe. One of them was Chat-oué. He could understand them, and make them understand him, well enough to play vingt et un with them the whole forenoon. He won all their money, drank with them, and took their five subscriptions, Chat-oué taking three—one for himself, one for Catou, and one for Crébiche. There was no delivery of goods there and then; they could not write; but they made their marks, and it was agreed that when Mr. Tarbox should come along a few days later to deliver the volumes, they were not to be received or paid for until with his scholarly aid the impostor who pretended to teach English education at Grande Pointe had been put to confusion and to flight.

"All right," said Tarbox; "all right. I'm the kind of State Superintendent you want. I like an adventure; and if there's any thing I just love, it's exposing a fraud! What day shall I come? Yes, I understand—middle of the day. I'll be on hand."

The fateful day came. In every house and on every galérie the morning tasks were early done. Then the best of every wardrobe was put on, the sun soared high, and by noon every chair in Grande Pointe was in the tobacco-shed where knowledge poured forth her beams, and was occupied by one or two persons. And then, at last, the chapel bell above Claude's head pealed out the final signal, and the schoolmaster moved across the green. Bonaventure Deschamps was weary. Had aught gone wrong? Far from it. But the work had been great, and it was now done. Every thing was at stake: the cause of enlightenment and the fortunes of his heart hung on the issue of the next few hours. Three pupils, one the oftenest rebuked of all the school, one his rival in love, one the queen of his heart, held his fate in their hands and knew it. With these thoughts mingled the pangs of an unconfessed passion and the loneliness of a benevolent nature famishing for a word of thanks. Yea, and to-day he must be his own judge.

His coat was on his arm, and the children round about him in their usual way as they came across the common; but his words, always so kind, were, on this day of all days, so dejected and so few that the little ones stole glances into his face and grew silent. Then, all at once, he saw,—yea, verily, he saw,—standing near the school entrance, a man from the great outer world!

He knew it by a hundred signs—the free attitude, the brilliant silk hat, the shaven face, and every inch of the attire. As plainly as one knows a green tree from a dead one, the Crusoe of Grande Pointe recognized one who came from the haunts of men; from some great nerve-centre of human knowledge and power where the human mind, trained and equipped, had piled up the spoils of its innumerable conquests. His whole form lighted up with a new life. His voice trembled with pent feeling as he said in deep undertone:

"Be callm, chil'run; be callm. Refrain excitement. Who you behole befo' you, yondeh, I ignore. But who shall we expect to see if not the State Sup'inten'ent Public Education? And if yea, then welcome, thrice welcome, the surprise! We shall not inquire him; but as a stranger we shall show him with how small reso'ce how large result." He put on his coat.

Mr. Tarbox had just reached the school-ground. His horse was fastened by the bridle to a picket in a fence behind him. A few boys had been out before the schoolhouse, and it was the sudden cessation of their clamor that had drawn Bonaventure's attention. Some of them were still visible, silently slipping through the gaps in the pieux and disappearing within. Bonaventure across the distance marked him beckon persuasively to one of them. The lad stopped, came forward, and gave his hand; and thereupon a second, a third, fourth, fifth, tenth, without waiting for invitation, emerged again and advanced to the same grave and silent ceremony. Two or three men who stood near did the same. The handshaking was just ending when Bonaventure and the stranger raised their hats to each other.

"Trust I don't intrude?"

"Sir, we are honored, not intruded, as you shall witness. Will you give yourself the pain to enter the school-place? I say not schoolhouse; 'tis, as its humble teacher, not fitly so nominated. But you shall therein find a school which, the more taken by surprise, not the less prepared."

"The State ought to build you a good schoolhouse," said the stranger, with a slight frown that seemed official.

"Ah! sir," cried the young schoolmaster, beaming gratitude from his whole surface, "I—I"—he smote his breast,—"I would reimburst her in good citizen' and mother' of good citizen'! And both reading, writing, and also ciphering,—arithmeticulating, in the English tongue, and grammatically! But enter and investigate."

A hush fell upon the school and the audience beyond it as the two men came in. Every scholar was in place—the little ones with bare, dangling feet, their shapely sun-tanned ankles just peeping from pantaloons and pantalettes of equal length; the older lads beyond them; and off at the left the larger girls, and Sidonie. The visitor, as his eye fell last upon her, silently and all to himself drew a long whistle of admiration. The master stood and eyed him with unspoken but confessed pride. A little maiden of six slipped from the bench to the earth floor, came forward, gave her hand, and noiselessly returned. One by one, with eyes dropped, the remaining sixteen girls followed. It seemed for a moment as if the contagion might break out in the audience, but the symptom passed.

There was just room on the teacher's little platform for Bonaventure to seat his visitor a little at one side and stand behind his desk. The fateful moment had come. The master stood nervously drawn up, bell in hand. With a quick, short motion he gave it one tap, and set it down.

"That, sir, is to designate attention!" He waved a triumphant hand toward the spectacle before them.

"Perfect!" murmured the stranger. A look of earnest ecstasy

73

broke out upon the master's face. He turned at first upon the audience and then upon the school.

"Chil'run, chil'run, he p'onounce you perfect!" He turned again upon the visitor, threw high his right hand, flirted it violently, and cried:—

"At random! exclusively at random; state what class! at random!"

"I—I doubt if I under"—

"Name any class, exclusively at random, and you shall see with what promptness and quietude the chil'run shall take each one their exactly co'ect places."

"Oh, I understand. You want me to designate"—

"Any class! at yo' caprice."

"Well, if you have—third class in geography."

"Or spelling?" cried Bonaventure, a momentary look of dismay giving place to fresh enthusiasm.

"Yes—spell—I meant spelling."

"Third spelling!" The tongue of the bell fell with the emphasis, and as silently as sleep the tiniest seven in the school, four pairs of pantaloons, three of pantalettes, with seven of little bare feet at their borders and seven of hands pointed down stiffly at their sides, came out and stood a-row. The master turned to the visitor.

"Now, commencing wherever, even at the foot if desired! ask, sir, if you please, any English word of one syllable, of however difficult!"

"No matter how difficult?"

"Well, they are timid, as you see; advance by degrees."

"Very well, then," said the visitor with much kindness of tone; "I will ask the little boy at this end"—

"At the foot—but—still, 'tis well. Only—ah, Crébiche! every thing depend! Be prepared, Crébiche!"

"Yes," said the stranger; "I will ask him to spell hoss."

The child drew himself up rigidly, pointed his stiffened fingers down his thighs, rounded his pretty red mouth, and said slowly, in a low, melodious, distinct voice:—

"'O-double eth, awth."

Bonaventure leapt from the platform and ran to the child.

"Ah! mon p'tit garçon—ah! my lil boy! 'O-double eth, listten, my chile. O, sir, he did not hear the word precisely. Listten, my chile, to yo' teacher! remember that his honor and the school's honor is in yo' spelling!" He drew back a step, poised himself, and gave the word. It came like an anchor-chain crashing through a hawse-hole.

"Or-r-r-r-rus-seh!" And the child, winking at vacancy in the intensity of his attention, spelled:—

"Haich-o-r-eth-e, 'Orthe."

The breathless audience, leaning forward, read the visitor's commendation in his face. Bonaventure, beaming upon him, extended one arm, the other turned toward the child, and cried, shaking both hands tremulously:—

"Another! another word! another to the same!"

"Mouse," said the stranger, and Bonaventure turned and cried:—

"Mah-ooseh! my nob'e lil boy! Mah-ooseh!" and Crébiche, a speaking statue, spelled:—

"M-o-u-eth-e, mouthe."

"Co'ect, my chile! And yet, sir, and yet, 'tis he that they call Crébiche, because like the crawfish advancing backwardly. But to the next! another word! another word!"

The spelling, its excitements, its moments of agonizing suspense, and its triumphs, went on. The second class is up. It spells in two, even in three, syllables. Toutou is in it. He gets tremendously wrought up; cannot keep two feet on the ground at once; spells fast when the word is his; smiles in response to the visitor's smile, the only one who dares; leans out and looks down the line with a knuckle in his mouth as the spelling passes down; wrings one hand as his turn approaches again; catches his word in mid-air and tosses it off, and marks with ecstasy the triumph and pride written on the face of his master.

"But, sir," cries Bonaventure, "why consume the spelling-book? Give, yourself, if you please, to Toutou, a word not therein comprise'." He glanced around condescendingly upon the people of Grande Pointe. Chat-oué is in a front seat. Toutou gathers himself for the spring, and the stranger ponders a moment and then gives— "Florida!"

"F-l-o, flo, warr-de-warr-da,—Florida!"

A smile broke from the visitor's face unbidden, but—

"Right! my chile! co'ect, Toutou!" cried Bonaventure, running and patting the little hero on the back and head by turns. "Sir, let us"—He stopped short. The eyes of the house were on Chat-oué. He had risen to his feet and made a gesture for the visitor's attention. As the stranger looked at him he asked:—

"He spell dat las word r-i-i-ight?" But the visitor with quiet gravity said, "Yes, that was all right;" and a companion pulled the Raccoon down into his seat again. Bonaventure resumed.

"Sir, let us not exhoss the time with spelling! You shall now hear them read."

75

The bell taps, the class retires; again, and the reading class is up. They are the larger girls and boys. But before they begin the master has a word for their fathers and mothers.

"Friends and fellow-citizens of Gran' Point', think not at the suppi-zing goodness of yo' chil'run' reading. 'Tis to this branch has been given the largest attention and most assidu'ty, so thus to comprise puffection in the English tongue, whether speaking aw otherwise." He turned to the stranger beside him. "I am not satisfied whilst the slightest accent of French is remaining. But you shall judge if they read not as if in their own vernaculary. And you shall choose the piece!"

The visitor waived the privilege, but Bonaventure gently insisted, and he selected Jane Taylor's little poem, "The Violet," glancing across at Sidonie as he himself read out the first two lines:—

"Down in a green and shady bed
A modest violet grew."

Bonaventure proclaimed the title and page and said:—
"Claude, p'oceed!" And Claude read:—
"'Dthee vy—ee-lit. Dah-oon-a hin hay grin and-a shad-y bade—A mo-dest-a vy-ee-lit grŏo—Hits-a stallk whoz baint hit hawngg-a hits hade—Has hif-a too hah-ed-a frawm ve-ŏo. Hand h-yet it whoz a lo-vly flow'r—Hits-a co-lors-a brah-eet and fair-a—Heet maheet-a hāve grass-ed a rozzy bow'r—Heenstade-a hof hah-ee-dingg there"—

"Stop!" cried Bonaventure; "stop! You pronounciate' a word faultily!" He turned to the visitor. "I call not that a miss; but we must inoculate the idea of puffection. So soon the sly-y-test misp'onounciating I pass to the next." He turned again: "Next!" And a black-haired girl began in a higher key, and very slowly:—

"Yate there eet whoz cawntaint-a too bulloom—Heen mo-dest-a teent z-arrayed—And there-a heet sprade-a heets swit pre-fume-a—Whit-hin thee sy-y-lent-a shade"—

"Stop! Not that you mistook, but—'tis enough. Sir, will you give yourself the pain to tell—not for my sake or reputation, but to the encouragement of the chil'run, and devoid flattery—what is yo' opinion of that specimen of reading? Not t'oubling you, but, in two or three word' only—if you will give yo'self the pain"—

"Why, certainly; I think it is—I can hardly find words—it's remarkable." Bonaventure started with joy.

"Chil'run, do you hear? Remawkable! But do you not detect no slight—no small faultiness of p'onounciating?"

"No, not the slightest; I smile, but I was thinking of something

76

else." The visitor's eye, wandering a trifle, caught Chat-oué giving him one black look that removed his disposition to smile, yet he insisted, "No, sir; I can truthfully say I never heard such a pronunciation." The audience drank his words.

"Sir," cried the glad preceptor, "'tis toil have p'oduce it! Toil of the teacher, industry of the chil'run! But it has p'oduce' beside! Sir, look—that school! Since one year commencing the A B C—and now spelling word' of eight syllabl'!"

"Not this school?"

"Sir, you shall see—or, more p'operly, hear. First spelling!"

"Yes," said the stranger, seeing Sidonie rise, "I'd like to hear that class;" and felt Chat-oué looking at him again.

# CHAPTER XI

## LIGHT, LOVE, AND VICTORY

The bell tapped, and they came forth to battle. There was the line, there was the leader. The great juncture of the day was on him. Was not here the State's official eye? Did not victory hover overhead? His reserve, the darling regiment, the flower of his army, was dressing for the final charge. There was Claude. Next him, Sidonie!—and Étienne, and Madelaine, Henri and Marcelline,—all waiting for the word—the words—of eight syllables! Supreme moment! Would any betray? Banish the thought! Would any fail?

He waited an instant while two or three mothers bore out great armfuls of slumbering or fretting infancy and a number of young men sank down into the vacated chairs. Then he stepped down from the platform, drew back four or five yards from the class, opened the spelling-book, scanned the first word, closed the book with his finger at the place, lifted it high above his head, and cried:

"Claude! Claude, my brave scholar, always perfect, ah you ready?" He gave the little book a half whirl round, and dashed forward toward the chosen scholar, crying as he came:

"In-e-rad-i-ca-bility!"

Claude's face suddenly set in a stony vacancy, and with his eyes staring straight before him he responded:

"I-n, in-, e, inerad-, r-a-d, rad-, inerad-, ineraddy-, ineradica-, c-a, ca, ineradica-, ineradicabili-, b-i-elly-billy, ineradicabili-, ineradicabili-, t-y, ty, ineradicability."

"Right! Claude, my boy! my always good scholar, right!" The master drew back to his starting-place as he spoke, re-opened the book, shut it again, lifted it high in air, cried, "Madelaine, my dear chile, prepare!" whirled the book and rushed upon her with—

"In-de-fat-i-ga-bil-ly-ty!"

Madelaine turned to stone and began:

"I-n, een, d-e, de-, inde-, indefat-, indefat—fat—f-a-t, fat, indefat, indefatty, i, ty, indefati-, indefatiga-, g-a, ga, indefatiga-, indefatigabilly, b-i-elly, billy, indefatigabili-, t-y, ty, indefatigability."

"O, Madelaine, my chile, you make yo' teacher proud! prah-ood, my chile!" Bonaventure's hand rested a moment tenderly on her head as he looked first toward the audience and then toward the stranger. Then he drew off for the third word. He looked at it twice before he called it. Then—

"Sidonie! ah! Sidonie, be ready! be prepared! fail not yo' humble school-teacher! In-com"—He looked at the word a third time, and then swept down upon her:

"In-com-pre-hen-si-ca-bility!"

Sidonie flinched not nor looked upon him, as he hung over her with the spelling-book at arm's-reach above them; yet the pause that followed seemed to speak dismay, and throughout the class there was a silent recoil from something undiscovered by the master. But an instant later Sidonie had chosen between the two horns of her agonizing dilemma, and began:

"I-n, een, c-o-m, cawm, eencawm, eencawmpre, p-r-e, pre, eencawmpre, eencawmprehen, prehen, haich-e-n, hen, hen, eencawmprehensi, s-i, si, eencawmprehensi-, b-i-l"—

"Ah! Sidonie! Stop! Arretez! Si-do-nie-e-e-e! Oh! listen—écoutez—Sidonie, my dear!" The master threw his arms up and down in distraction, then suddenly faced his visitor, "Sir, it was my blame! I spoke the word without adequate distinction! Sidonie—maintenant—now!" But a voice in the audience interrupted with—

"Assoiez-vous la, Chat-oué! Seet down yondeh!" And at the potent voice of Maximian Roussel the offender was pushed silently into the seat he had risen from, and Bonaventure gave the word again.

"In-com-pre-hen-si-ca-bil-i-ty!" And Sidonie, blushing like fire, returned to the task:

"I-n, een"—She bit her lip and trembled.

"Right! Right! Tremble not, my Sidonie! fear naught! yo' loving school-teacher is at thy side!" But she trembled like a red leaf as she spelled on—"Haich-e-n, hen, eencawmprehen,

eencawmprehensi, s-i, si, eencawmprehensi-, eencawmprehensi-
billy-t-y, ty, incomprehensibility!"

The master dropped his hands and lifted his eyes in speechless despair. As they fell again upon Sidonie, her own met them. She moaned, covered her face in her hands, burst into tears, ran to her desk and threw her hands and face upon it, shaking with noiseless sobs and burning red to the nape of her perfect neck. All Grande Pointe rose to its feet.

"Lost!" cried Bonaventure in a heart-broken voice. "Every thing lost! Farewell, chil'run!" He opened his arms toward them and with one dash all the lesser ones filled them. They wept. Tears welled from Bonaventure's eyes; and the mothers of Grande Pointe dropped again into their seats and silently added theirs.

The next moment all eyes were on Maximian. His strong figure was mounted on a chair, and he was making a gentle, commanding gesture with one hand as he called:

"Seet down! Seet down, all han'!" And all sank down, Bonaventure in a mass of weeping and clinging children. 'Mian too resumed his seat, at the same time waving to the stranger to speak.

"My friends," said the visitor, rising with alacrity, "I say when a man makes a bargain, he ought to stick to it!" He paused for them—as many as could—to take in the meaning of his English speech, and, it may be, expecting some demonstration of approval; but dead silence reigned, all eyes on him save Bonaventure's and Sidonie's. He began again:

"A bargain's a bargain!" And Chat-oué nodded approvingly and began to say audibly, "Yass;" but 'Mian thundered out:

"Taise toi, Chat-oué! Shot op!" And the silence was again complete, while the stranger resumed.

"There was a plain bargain made." He moved a step forward and laid the matter off on the palm of his hand. "There was to be an examination; the school was not to know; but if one scholar should make one mistake the schoolhouse was to be closed and the schoolmaster sent away. Well, there's been a mistake made, and I say a bargain's a bargain." Dead silence still. The speaker looked at 'Mian. "Do you think they understand me?"

"Dey meck out," said 'Mian, and shut his firm jaws.

"My friends," said the stranger once more, "some people think education's a big thing, and some think it ain't. Well, sometimes it is and sometimes it ain't. Now, here's this man"—he pointed down to where Bonaventure's dishevelled crown was drooping to his knees—"claims to have taught over thirty of your children to read. Well, what of it? A man can know how to read, and be just as no account as he was before. He brags that he's taught them to talk English. Well, what does that prove? A man might speak English and starve

79

to death. He claims, I am told, to have taught some of them to write. But I know a man in the penitentiary that can write; he wrote too much."

Bonaventure had lifted his head and was sitting with his eyes upon the speaker in close attention. At this last word he said:

"Ah! sir! too true, too true ah yo' words; nevertheless, their cooelty! 'Tis not what is print' in the books, but what you learn through the books!"

"Yes; and so you hadn't never ought to have made the bargain you made; but, my friends, a bargain's a bargain, and the teacher's"—He paused invitingly, and an answer came from the audience. It was Catou who rose and said:

"Naw, sah. Naw; he don't got to go!" But again 'Mian thundered:

"Taise toi, Catou. Shot op!"

"I say," continued the stranger, "the mistake's been made. Three mistakes have been made!"

"Yass!" roared Chat-oué, leaping to his feet and turning upon the assemblage a face fierce with triumph. Suspense and suspicions were past now; he was to see his desire on his enemy. But instantly a dozen men were on their feet—St. Pierre, Catou, Bonaventure himself, with a countenance full of pleading deprecation, and even Claude, flushed with anger.

"Naw, sah! Naw, sah! Waun meesteck?"

"Seet down, all han'!" yelled 'Mian; "all han' seet dah-oon!" Only Chat-oué took his seat, glancing upon the rest with the exultant look of one who can afford to yield ground.

"The first mistake," resumed the stranger, addressing himself especially to the risen men still standing, and pointedly to Catou, "the first mistake was in the kind of bargain you made." He ceased, and passed his eyes around from one to another until they rested an instant on the bewildered countenance of Chat-oué. Then he turned again upon the people, who had sat down, and began to speak with the exultation of a man that feels his subject lifting him above himself.

"I came out here to show up that man as a fraud. But what do I find? A poor, unpaid, half-starved man that loves his thankless work better than his life, teaching what not one schoolmaster in a thousand can teach; teaching his whole school four better things than were ever printed in any school-book,—how to study, how to think, how to value knowledge, and to love one another and mankind. What you'd ought to have done was to agree that such a school should keep open, and such a teacher should stay, if jest one, one lone child should answer one single book-question right! But as I said before, a bargain's a bargain—Hold on there! Sit down! You

80

sha'n't interrupt me again!" Men were standing up on every side. There was confusion and a loud buzz of voices. "The second mistake," the stranger made haste to cry, "was thinking the teacher gave out that last word right. He gave it wrong! And the third mistake," he shouted against the rising commotion, "was thinking it was spelt wrong. She spelt it right! And a bargain's a bargain! The schoolmaster stays!"

He could say no more; the rumble of voices suddenly burst into a cheer. The women and children laughed and clapped their hands,—Toutou his feet also,—and Bonaventure, flirting the leaves of a spelling book till he found the place, looked, cried—"In-com-pre-hen-sibility!" wheeled and dashed upon Sidonie, seized her hands in his as she turned to fly, and gazed speechlessly upon her, with the tears running down his face. Feeling a large hand upon his shoulder, he glanced around and saw 'Mian pointing him to his platform and desk. Thither he went. The stranger had partly restored order. Every one was in his place. But what a change! What a gay flutter throughout the old shed! Bonaventure seemed to have bathed in the fountain of youth. Sidonie, once more the school's queen-flower, sat calm, with just a trace of tears adding a subtle something to her beauty.

"Chil'run, beloved chil'run," said Bonaventure, standing once more by his desk, "yo' school-teacher has the blame of the sole mistake; and, sir, gladly, oh, gladly, sir, would he always have the blame rather than any of his beloved school-chil'run! Sir, I will boldly ask you—ah you not the State Sup'inten'ent Public Education?"

"No, I"—

"But surely, sir, than a greater?—Yes, I discover it, though you smile. Chil'run—friends—not the State Sup'inten'ent, but greater!—Pardon; have yo' chair, sir."

"Why, the examination's over, isn't it? Guess you'd better call it finished, hadn't you?" He made the suggestion softly, but Bonaventure answered aloud:

"Figu'atively speaking, 'tis conclude'; but—pardon—you mention' writing. Shall you paht f'om us not known—not leaving yo' name—in a copy-book, for examp'?"

"With pleasure. You do teach writing?"

"If I teach writing? To such with desks, yes. 'Twould be to all but for the privation of desks. You perceive how we have here nothing less than a desk famine. Madelaine! Claude! Sidonie!— present copy-book'! Sir, do you not think every chile should be provided a desk?—Ah! I knew 'twould be yo' verdic'. But how great trouble I have with that subjec'! Me, I think yes; but the parents,"— he looked tenderly over among them,—"they contend no. Now, sir,

81

here are three copy-books. Inspect; criticise. No, commence rather, if you please, with the copy-book of Madelaine; then p'oceed to the copy-book of Claude, and finally conclude at the copy-book of Sidonie; thus rising by degrees: good, more good, most good."

"How about," asked the stranger, with a smile, as he turned the leaves, "about Toutou and Crébiche; don't they write?"

"Ah! sir," said Bonaventure, half to the stranger and half to the assemblage, "they write, yes; but—they ah yet in the pot-hook and chicken-track stage. And now, chil'run, in honor of our eminent friend's visitation, and of the excellence with which you have been examine', I p'onounce the exhibition finish'—dispensing with 'Twink', twink' lil stah.' And now, in the book of the best writing scholar in the school—you, sir, deciding that intricacy—shall now be written the name of the eminent frien' of learning hereinbefo' confronting.—Claude! a new pen!"

The stranger made his choice among the books.

"Chil'run, he has select' the book of Sidonie!" Bonaventure reached and swung a chair into place at his desk. The visitor sat down. Bonaventure stood over him, gazing down at the hand that poised the pen. The silence was profound.

"Chil'run—sh-sh-sh!" said the master, lifting his left arm but not his eyes. The stranger wrote a single initial.

"G! chil'run; G!—Sir, does it not signify George?"

"Yes," murmured the writer; "it stands for George." He wrote another.

"W! my chil'run; George W!—Sir, does it not sig—My chil'run! George Washington! George Washington, my chil'run! George Washington, the father of his country! My chil'run and fellow-citizen' of Gran' Point', he is nominated for George Washington, the father of his country! Sir, ah you not a relation?"

"I really can't tell you," said the writer, with a calm smile. "I've always been too busy to look it up." He finished his signature as he talked. Bonaventure bent over it.

"Tar-box. Chil'run and friends and fellow-citizen', I have the p'oudness to int'oduce you the hono'able George Washington Tarbox! And now the exhibition is dismiss'; but stop! Sir, if some—aw all—desire gratefully to shake hand'?"

"I should feel honored."

"Attention, everybody! Make rank! Everybody by two by two, the school-chil'run coming last,—Claude and Sidonie resting till the end,—pass 'round—shake hand'—walk out—similah a fu-nial."

So came, shook hands, and passed out and to their simple homes, the manhood, motherhood, maidenhood, childhood of

82

Grande Pointe, not knowing that before many days every household in the village was to be a subscriber to the "Album of Universal Information."

One of the last of the householders was Chat-oué. But when he grasped the honored hand, he also held it, fixing upon its owner a generous and somewhat bacchanalian smile.

"I'm a fool, but I know. You been put op a jawb on me. Dass four, five days now I been try to meck out what dat niggah at Belle Alliance holla to me when I gallop down de road." (Chat-oué's English had been acquired from negroes in the sugar-house, and was like theirs.) "He been braggin' dat day befo'"—turning to Bonaventure—"how 'twas him show you de road to Gran' Point' las' year; and so I git mad and tell him, me," addressing the stranger again, "how we goin' git school shot op. Well, dat night I mit him comin' fum Gran' Point' and he hol' at me. I been try evva since meck out what he say. Yass. An' I jis meck it out! He say, 'Watch out, watch out, 'Mian Roussel and dat book-fellah dawn't put op jawb on you.' Well, I'm a fool, but I know. You put op jawb on me; I know. But dass all right—I don't take no book." He laughed with the rest, scratched his tipsy head, and backed out through the pieux.

Only a fairy number remained, grouped around the honorable Tarbox. They were St. Pierre, Bonaventure,—Maximian detaining a middle-aged pair, Sidonie's timorous guardians,—and two others, who held back, still waiting to shake hands.

"Claude," cried Bonaventure; "Sidonie."

They came. Claude shook hands and stepped inside. Sidonie, with eyes on the ground, put forth her hand. The honored guest held it lingeringly, and the ceremonies were at an end.

"Come," said 'Mian, beckoning away the great G. W.'s probable relative. They passed out together. "Come!" he repeated, looking back and beckoning again; "walk een! all han'! walk een house!"

The guardian pair followed, hand in hand.

"Claude," said Bonaventure tenderly; but—

"Claude," more firmly said St. Pierre.

The boy looked for one instant from the master's face to Sidonie's; then turned, grasped his father's hand, and followed the others.

A blaze of light filled Bonaventure's heart. He turned to Sidonie to give his hand—both her hands were clasped upon each other, and they only tightened. But their eyes met—ah! those Acadian maidens, they do it all with their eyes!—and lover and maiden passed out and walked forth side by side. They are going that way still, only—with hands joined.

83

# AU LARGE

## CHAPTER I

## THE POT-HUNTER

The sun was just rising, as a man stepped from his slender dug-out and drew half its length out upon the oozy bank of a pretty bayou. Before him, as he turned away from the water, a small gray railway-platform and frame station-house, drowsing on long legs in the mud and water, were still veiled in the translucent shade of the deep cypress swamp, whose long moss drapings almost overhung them on the side next the brightening dawn. The solemn gray festoons did overhang the farthest two or three of a few flimsy wooden houses and a saw-mill with its lumber, logs, and sawdust, its cold furnace and idle engine.

As with gun and game this man mounted by a short, rude ladder to firmer footing on the platform, a negro, who sat fishing for his breakfast on the bank a few yards up the stream, where it bent from the north and west, slowly lifted his eyes, noted that the other was a white man, an Acadian, and brought his gaze back again to hook and line.

He had made out these facts by the man's shape and dress, for the face was in shade. The day, I say, was still in its genesis. The waters that slid so languidly between the two silent men as not to crook one line of the station-house's image inverted in their clear dark depths, had not yet caught a beam upon their whitest water-lily, nor yet upon their tallest bulrush; but the tops of the giant cypresses were green and luminous, and as the Acadian glanced abroad westward, in the open sky far out over the vast marshy breadths of the "shaking prairie,"[5] two still clouds, whose under surfaces were yet dusky and pink, sparkled on their sunward edges like a frosted fleece. You could not have told whether the Acadian saw the black man or not. His dog, soiled and wet, stood beside his

---

[5] The "shaking prairie," "trembling prairie," or prairie tremblante, is low, level, treeless delta land, having a top soil of vegetable mould overlying immense beds of quicksand.

knee, pricked his ears for a moment at sight of the negro, and then dropped them.

It was September. The comfortable air could only near by be seen to stir the tops of the high reeds whose crowding myriads stretched away south, west, and north, an open sea of green, its immense distances relieved here and there by strips of swamp forest tinged with their peculiar purple haze. Eastward the railroad's long causeway and telegraph-poles narrowed on the view through its wide axe-hewn lane in the overtowering swamp. New Orleans, sixty miles or more away, was in that direction. Westward, rails, causeway, and telegraph, tapered away again across the illimitable hidden quicksands of the "trembling prairie" till the green disguise of reeds and rushes closed in upon the attenuated line, and only a small notch in a far strip of woods showed where it still led on toward Texas. Behind the Acadian the smoke of woman's early industry began to curl from two or three low chimneys.

But his eye lingered in the north. He stood with his dog curled at his feet beside a bunch of egrets,—killed for their plumage,—the butt of his long fowling-piece resting on the platform, and the arm half outstretched whose hand grasped the barrels near the muzzle. The hand, toil-hardened and weather-browned, showed, withal, antiquity of race. His feet were in rough muddy brogans, but even so they were smallish and shapely. His garments were coarse, but there were no tatters anywhere. He wore a wide Campeachy hat. His brown hair was too long, but it was fine. His eyes, too, were brown, and, between brief moments of alertness, sedate. Sun and wind had darkened his face, and his pale brown beard curled meagre and untrimmed on a cheek and chin that in forty years had never felt a razor.

Some miles away in the direction in which he was looking, the broadening sunlight had struck and brightened the single red lug-sail of a boat whose unseen hull, for all the eye could see, was coming across the green land on a dry keel. But the bayou, hidden in the tall rushes, was its highway; for suddenly the canvas was black as it turned its shady side, and soon was red again as another change of direction caught the sunbeams upon its tense width and showed that, with much more wind out there than it would find by and by in here under the lee of the swamp, it was following the unseen meanderings of the stream. Presently it reached a more open space where a stretch of the water lay shining in the distant view. Here the boat itself came into sight, showed its bunch of some half-dozen passengers for a minute or two, and vanished again, leaving only its slanting red sail skimming nautilus-like over the vast breezy expanse.

85

Yet more than two hours later the boat's one blue-shirted, barefoot Sicilian sailor in red worsted cap had with one oar at the stern just turned her drifting form into the glassy calm by the railway-station, tossed her anchor ashore, and was still busy with small matters of boat-keeping, while his five passengers clambered to the platform.

The place showed somewhat more movement now. The negro had long ago wound his line upon its crooked pole, gathered up his stiffened fishes from the bank, thrust them into the pockets of his shamelessly ragged trousers, and was gone to his hut in the underbrush. But the few amphibious households round about were passing out and in at the half-idle tasks of their slow daily life, and a young white man was bustling around, now into the station and now out again upon the platform, with authority in his frown and a pencil and two matches behind his ear. It was Monday. Two or three shabby negroes with broad, collapsed, glazed leather travelling-bags of the old carpet-sack pattern dragged their formless feet about, waiting to take the train for the next station to hire out there as rice harvesters, and one, with his back turned, leaned motionless against an open window gazing in upon the ticking telegraph instruments. A black woman in blue cotton gown, red-and-yellow Madras turban, and some sportsman's cast-off hunting-shoes minus the shoe-strings, crouched against the wall. Beside her stood her shapely mulatto daughter, with head-covering of white cotton cloth, in which female instinct had discovered the lines of grace and disposed them after the folds of the Egyptian fellah head—dress. A portly white man, with decided polish in his commanding air, evidently a sugar-planter from the Mississippi "coast" ten miles northward, moved about in spurred boots, and put personal questions to the negroes, calling them "boys," and the mulattress, "girl."

The pot-hunter was still among them; or rather, he had drawn apart from the rest, and stood at the platform's far end, leaning on his gun, an innocent, wild-animal look in his restless eyes, and a slumberous agility revealed in his strong, supple loins. The station-agent went to him, and with abrupt questions and assertions, to which the man replied in low, grave monosyllables, bought his game,—as he might have done two hours before, but—an Acadian can wait. There was some trouble to make exact change, and the agent, saying "Hold on, I'll fix it," went into the station just as the group from the Sicilian's boat reached the platform. The agent came bustling out again with his eyes on his palm, counting small silver.

"Here!" But he spoke to the empty air. He glanced about with an offended frown.

"Achille!" There was no reply. He turned to one of the

negroes: "Where's that 'Cajun?" Nobody knew. Down where his canoe had lain, tiny rillets of muddy water were still running into its imprint left in the mire; but canoe, dog, and man had vanished into the rank undergrowth of the swamp.

# CHAPTER II

## CLAUDE

Of the party that had come in the Sicilian's boat four were men and one a young woman. She was pretty; so pretty, and of such restful sweetness of countenance, that the homespun garb, the brand-new creaking gaiters, and a hat that I dare not describe were nothing against her. Her large, soft, dark eyes, more sweetly but not less plainly than the attire, confessed her a denizen of the woods.

Not so the man who seemed to be her husband. His dress was rustic enough; and yet you would have seen at once that it was not the outward circumstance, but an inward singularity, that had made him and must always keep him a stranger to the ordinary ways of men. There was an emotional exaltation in his face as he hastily led his companions with military directness to the ticket window. Two others of the men were evidently father and son, the son barely twenty years of age, the parent certainly not twice as old; and the last of the group was a strong, sluggish man of years somewhat near, but under, fifty.

They bought but one ticket; but, as one may say, they all bought it, the youngest extricating its price with difficulty from the knotted corner of his red handkerchief, and the long, thin hand of the leader making the purchase, while the eyes of the others followed every movement with unconscious absorption.

The same unemotional attentiveness was in their forms as their slow feet drifted here and there always after the one leader, their eyes on his demonstrative hands, and their ears drinking in his discourse. He showed them the rails of the track, how smooth they were, how they rested on their cross-ties, and how they were spiked in place always the same width apart. They crowded close about him at the telegraph-window while he interpreted with unconscious originality the wonders of electricity. Their eyes rose slowly from the window up and out along the ascending wires to where they mounted the poles and eastward and westward leaped away sinking and rising from insulator to insulator. One of the party pointed at these green dots of glass and murmured a question, and the leader's wife laid her small hand softly upon his arm to check the energy of his utterance as he said, audibly to all on the platform, and with a strong French accent:

"They?—are there lest the heat of the telegraph fluid inflame the post-es!" He laid his own hand tenderly upon his wife's in response to its warning pressure, yet turned to the sugar-planter and asked:

"Sir, pardon; do I not explain truly?"

The planter, with restrained smile, was about to reply, when some one called, "There she comes!" and every eye was turned to the east.

"Truly!" exclaimed the inquirer, in a voice made rich with emotion. "Truly, she comes! She comes! The iron horse, though they call him 'she'!" He turned to the planter—"Ah! sir, why say they thus many or thus many horse-power, when truly"—his finger-tip pattered upon his temple—"truly it is mind-power!"

The planter, smiling decorously, turned away, and the speaker looked again down the long vacant track to where the small dark focus of every one's attention was growing on the sight. He spoke again, in lower voice but with larger emotion.

"Mind-power! thought-power! knowledge-power! learning and thinking power!" He caught his wife's arm. "See! see, Sidonie, my dear! See her enhancing in magnitude so fastly approaching!" As he spoke a puff of white vapor lifted from the object and spread out against the blue, the sunbeams turned it to silver and pearl, and a moment later came the far-away, long, wild scream of the locomotive.

"Retire!" exclaimed the husband, drawing back all his gazing companions at once. "Retire! retire! the whisttel is to signify warning to retire from too close the edge of the galérie! There! rest at this point. 'Tis far enough. Now, each and all resolve to stand and shrink not whilst that iron mare, eating coal, drinking hot water, and spitting fire, shall seem, but falsely, threatening to come on the platform. Ah! Claude!" he cried to the youngest of the group, "now shall you behold what I have told you—that vast am-azement of civilize-ation anni-high-lating space and also time at the tune of twenty miles the hour!" He wheeled upon the planter—"Sir, do I exaggerate?"

"Forty miles," replied the planter; "sometimes fifty."

"Friends,—confirmated! more than twicefold confirmated.

88

Forty, sometimes fifty! Thou heardest it, Maximian Roussel! Not from me, but from the gentleman himself! Forty, sometimes fifty! Such the march, the forward march of civilize-ation!"

His words were cut short by the unearthly neigh of the engine. Sidonie smote herself backward against her husband.

"Nay, Sidonie, fear thou nothing! Remember, dear Sidonie, thy promise of self-control! Stand boldly still, St. Pierre; both father and son, stand." The speaker was unheard. Hissing, clanging, thundering, and shaking the earth, the engine and train loomed up to the platform and stopped.

"Come!" cried Bonaventure Deschamps; "lose no moment, dear friends. Tide and time—even less the railroad—wait for nobody. Claude, remember; give your ticket of passage to none save the conductor only. 'Tis print' in letter' of gold on front his cap—'Conductor'—Stop! he is here.—Sir, this young man, inexperienced, is taking passage for"—

"Shoot him aboard," replied a uniformed man, and walked on without a pause. Claude moved toward the train. Bonaventure seized him by both arms and gazed on him.

"Claude St. Pierre! Claude, my boy, pride of Grande Pointe, second only with Sidonie, farewell!"

Tears leaped into the eyes of both. Bonaventure snatched Claude to his arms and kissed him. It was less than nothing to him that every eye on and off the train was on them. He relaxed his grasp. "Sidonie! tell him farewell!—ah! nay! shake not hands only! Kiss her, Claude! Kiss him, my own Sidonie, kiss him farewell!"

It was done. Claude blushed red, and Sidonie stepped back, wiping her eyes. Maximian moved into the void, and smiling gave his hand to the young adventurer.

"Adjieu, Claude." He waved a hand awkwardly. "Teck care you'seff," and dropped the hand audibly against his thigh.

Claude's eye sought his father. St. Pierre pressed forward, laid his right hand upon his son's shoulder, and gazed into his face. His voice was low and husky. He smiled.

"Claude,"—tears rose in his eyes, but he swallowed them down,—"Claude,—my baby,"—and the flood came. The engine-bell rang. The conductor gave the warning word, the youth leaped upon his father's neck. St. Pierre thrust him off, caught his two cheeks between fluttering palms and kissed him violently; the train moved, the young man leaped aboard, the blue uniforms disappeared, save one on the rear platform, the bell ceased, the gliding mass shrunk and dwindled away, the rails clicked more and more softly, the tearful group drew closer together as they gazed after the now-unheard train. It melted to a point and disappeared, the stillness of

89

forest and prairie fell again upon the place, the soaring sun shone down, and Claude St. Pierre was gone to seek his fortune.

# CHAPTER III

## THE TAVERN FIRESIDE

I call to mind a certain wild, dark night in November. St. Pierre lay under his palmetto thatch in the forest behind Grande Pointe, and could not sleep for listening to the wind, and wondering where his son was, in that wild Texas norther. On the Mississippi a steamer, upward bound, that had whistled to land at Belmont or Belle Alliance plantation, seemed to be staying there afraid to venture away. Miles southward beyond the river and the lands on that side, Lake des Allemands was combing with the tempest and hissing with the rain. Still farther away, on the little bayou and at the railway-station in the edge of the swamp that we already know, and westward over the prairie where Claude had vanished into the world, all life was hidden and mute. And farther still, leagues and leagues away, the mad tempest was riding the white-caps in Berwick's Bay and Grande Lake; and yet beyond, beyond New Iberia, and up by Carancro, and around again by St. Martinville, Breaux Bridge, Grand Coteau, and Opelousas, and down once more across the prairies of Vermilion, the marshes about Côte Blanche Bay, and the islands in the Gulf, it came bounding, screaming, and buffeting. And all the way across that open sweep from Mermentau to Côte Gelée it was tearing the rain to mist and freezing it wherever it fell, only lulling and warming a little about Joseph Jefferson's Island, as if that prank were too mean a trick to play upon his orange-groves.

In Vermilionville the wind came around every corner piercing and pinching to the bone. The walking was slippery; and though it was still early bedtime and the ruddy lamp-light filled the wet panes of some window every here and there, scarce a soul was stirring without, on horse or afoot, to be guided by its kindly glow.

At the corner of two streets quite away from the court-house square, a white frame tavern, with a wooden Greek porch filling its whole two-story front and a balcony built within the porch at the second-story windows in oddest fashion, was glowing with hospitable firelight. It was not nearly the largest inn of the place, nor the oldest, nor the newest, nor the most accessible. There was no clink of glass there. Yet in this, only third year of its present management, it was the place where those who knew best always put up.

Around the waiting-room fire this evening sat a goodly semicircle of men,—commercial travellers. Some of them were quite dry and comfortable, and  wore an air of superior fortune over others whose shoes and lower garments sent out more or less steam and odor toward the open fireplace. Several were smoking. One who neither smoked nor steamed stood with his back to the fire and the skirts of his coat lifted forward on his wrists. He was a rather short, slight, nervy man, about thirty years of age, with a wide pink baldness running so far back from his prominent temples and forehead that when he tipped his face toward the blue joists overhead, enjoying the fatigue of a well-filled day, his polished skull sent back the firelight brilliantly. There was a light skirmish of conversation going on, in which he took no part. No one seemed really acquainted with another. Presently a man sitting next on the left of him put away a quill toothpick in his watch-pocket, looked up into the face of the standing man, and said, with a faint smile:

"That job's done!"

With friendly gravity the other looked down and replied, "I never use a quill toothpick."

"Yes," said the one who sat, "it's bad. Still I do it."

"Nothing," continued the other,—"nothing harder than a sharpened white-pine match should ever go between the teeth. Brush thoroughly but not violently once or twice daily with a moderately stiff brush dipped in soft water into which has been dropped a few drops of the tincture of myrrh. A brush of badger's hair is best. If tartar accumulates, have it removed by a dentist. Do not bite thread or crack nuts with the teeth, or use the teeth for other purposes than those  for which nature designed them." He bent toward his hearer with a smile of irresistible sweetness, drew his lips away from his gums, snapped his teeth together loudly twice or thrice, and smiled again, modestly. The other man sought defence in buoyancy of manner.

"Right you are!" he chirruped. He reached up to his adviser's blue and crimson neck-scarf, and laid his finger and thumb upon a large, solitary pear-shaped pearl. "You're like me; you believe in the real thing."

"I do," said the pearl's owner; "and I like people that like the real thing. A pearl of the first water is real. There's no sham there;

no deception—except the iridescence, which is, as you doubtless know, an optical illusion attributable to the intervention of rays of light reflected from microscopic corrugations of the nacreous surface. But for that our eye is to blame, not the pearl. See?"

The seated man did not reply; but another man on the speaker's right, a large man, widest at the waist, leaned across the arm of his chair to scrutinize the jewel. Its owner turned his throat for the inspection, despite a certain grumness and crocodilian aggressiveness in the man's interest.

"I like a diamond, myself," said the new on-looker, dropped back in his chair, and met the eyes of the pearl's owner with a heavy glance.

"Tastes differ," kindly responded the wearer of the pearl. "Are you acquainted with the language of gems?"

The big-waisted man gave a negative grunt, and spat bravely into the fire. "Didn't know gems could talk," he said.

"They do not talk, they speak," responded their serene interpreter. The company in general noticed that, with all his amiability of tone and manner, his mild eyes held the big-waisted man with an uncomfortable steadiness. "They speak not to the ear, but to the eye and to the thought:

*Thought is deeper than all speech;*
*Feeling deeper than all thought;*
*Souls to souls can never teach*
*What unto themselves was taught.'"*

The speaker's victim writhed, but the riveted gaze and an uplifted finger pinioned him. "You should know—every one should know—the language of gems. There is a language of flowers:

*'To me the meanest flower that blows can give*
*Thoughts that do often lie too deep for tears.'*

But the language of gems is as much more important than that of flowers as the imperishable gem is itself more enduring than the withering, the evanescent blossom. A gentleman may not with safety present to a lady a gem of whose accompanying sentiment he is ignorant. But with the language of gems understood between them, how could a sentiment be more exquisitely or more acceptably expressed than by the gift of a costly gem uttering that sentiment with an unspoken eloquence! Did you but know the language of gems, your choice would not be the diamond. 'Diamond me no diamonds,' emblems of pride—

*'Pride in their port, defiance in their eye,*
*I see the lords of humankind pass by.'*

92

"Your choice would have been the pearl, symbol of modest loveliness.

*'Full many a gem of purest ray serene
The dark, unfathomed caves of ocean bear;'*

*'Orient pearls at random strung;'*

*'Fold, little trembler, thy fluttering wing,
Freely partake of love's fathomless spring;
So hallowed thy presence, the spirit within
Hath whispered, "The angels protect thee from sin."'"*

The speaker ceased, with his glance hovering caressingly over the little trembler with fluttering wing, that is, the big-waisted man. The company sat in listening expectancy; and the big-waisted man, whose eyes had long ago sought refuge in the fire, lifted them and said, satirically, "Go on," at the same time trying to buy his way out with a smile.

"It's your turn," quickly responded the jewel's owner, with something droll in his manner that made the company laugh at the other's expense. The big-waisted man kindled, then smiled again, and said:

"Was that emblem of modest loveliness give' to you symbolically, or did you present it to yourself?"

"I took it for a debt," replied the wearer, bowing joyously.

"Ah!" said the other. "Well, I s'pose it was either that or her furniture?"

"Thanks, yes." There was a pause, and then the pearl's owner spoke on. "Strange fact. That was years ago. And yet"—he fondled his gem with thumb and finger and tender glance—"you're the first man I've met to whom I could sincerely and symbolically present it, and you don't want it. I'm sorry."

"I see," said the big-waisted man, glaring at him.

"So do I," responded the pearl's owner. A smile went round, and the company sat looking into the fire. Outside the wind growled and scolded, shook and slapped the house, and thrashed it with the rain. A man sitting against the chimney said:

"If this storm keeps on six hours longer I reduce my estimate of the cotton-crop sixty-five thousand bales." But no one responded; and as the importance died out of his face he dropped his gaze into the fire with a pretence of deep meditation. Presently another, a good-looking young fellow, said:

"Well, gents, I never cared much for jewelry. But I like a nice scarf-pin; it's nobby. And I like a handsome seal-ring." He drew one from a rather chubby finger, and passed it to his next neighbor, following it with his eyes, and adding: "That's said to be a real intaglio. But—now, one thing I don't like, that's to see a lady wear a quantity of diamond rings outside of her glove, and heavy gold chains, and"—He was interrupted. A long man, with legs stiffened out to the fire, lifted a cigar between two fingers, sent a soft jet of smoke into the air, and began monotonously:

"*'Chains on a Southern woman? Chains?'*

I know the lady that wrote that piece." He suddenly gathered himself up for some large effort. "I can't recite it as she used to, but"—And to the joy of all he was interrupted.

"Gentlemen," said one, throwing a cigarette stump into the fire, "that brings up the subject of the war. By the by, do you know what that war cost the Government of the United States?" He glanced from one to another until his eye reached the wearer of the pearl, who had faced about, and stood now, with the jewel glistening in the firelight, and who promptly said:

"Yes; how much?"

"Well," said the first questioner with sudden caution, "I may be mistaken, but I've heard that it cost six—I think they say six—billion dollars. Didn't it?"

"It did," replied the other, with a smile of friendly commendation; "it cost six billion, one hundred and eighty-nine million, nine hundred and twenty-nine thousand, nine hundred and eight dollars. The largest item is interest; one billion, seven hundred and one million, two hundred and fifty-six thousand, one hundred and ninety-eight dollars, forty-two cents. The next largest, the pay of troops; the next, clothing the army. If there's any item of the war's expenses you would like to know, ask me. Capturing president Confederate States—ninety-seven thousand and thirty-one dollars, three cents." The speaker's manner grew almost gay. The other smiled defensively, and responded:

"You've got a good memory for sta-stistics. I haven't; and yet I always did like sta-stistics. I'm no sta-stitian, and yet if I had the time sta-stistics would be my favorite study; I s'pose it's yours."

The wearer of the pearl shook his head. "No. But I like it. I like the style of mind that likes it." The two bowed with playful graciousness to each other. "Yes, I do. And I've studied it, some little. I can tell you the best time of every celebrated trotter in this country; the quickest trip a steamer ever made between Queenstown and New York, New York and Queenstown, New Orleans and New York; the greatest speed ever made on a railroad or by a yacht, pedestrian, carrier-pigeon, or defaulting cashier; the rate of postage to every foreign country; the excess of women over men in every State of the Union so afflicted—or blessed, according to how you look at it; the number of volumes in each of the world's ten largest libraries; the salary of every officer of the United-States Government; the average duration of life in a man, elephant, lion, horse, anaconda, tortoise, camel, rabbit, ass, etcetera-etcetera; the age of every crowned head in Europe; each State's legal and commercial rate of interest; and how long it takes a healthy boy to digest apples, baked beans, cabbage, dates, eggs, fish, green corn, h, i, j, k, l-m-n-o-p, quinces, rice, shrimps, tripe, veal, yams, and any thing you can cook commencing with z. It's a fascinating study. But it's not my favorite.

*'The proper study of mankind is man.*
*\*\*\*\*\**

*Sole judge of truth, in endless error hurled,*
*The glory, jest, and riddle of the world!'*

"I love to study human nature. That's my favorite study! The art of reading the inner human nature by the outer aspect is of immeasurable interest and boundless practical value, and the man who can practise it skilfully and apply it sagaciously is on the high road to fortune, and why? Because to know it thoroughly is to know whom to trust and how far; to select wisely a friend, a confidant, a partner in any enterprise; to shun the untrustworthy, to anticipate and turn to our personal advantage the merits, faults, and deficiencies of all, and to evolve from their character such practical results as we may choose for our own ends; but a thorough knowledge is attained only by incessant observation and long practice; like music, it demands a special talent possessed by different individuals in variable quantity or not at all. You, gentlemen, all are, what I am not, commercial tourists. Before you I must be modest. You, each of you, have been chosen from surrounding hundreds or thousands for your superior ability, natural or acquired, to scan the human face and form and know whereof you see. I look you in the eye—you look me in the eye—for the eye, though it does not tell all, tells much—it is the key of character—it has been called the mirror of the soul—

*'And looks commercing with the skies,*
*Thy rapt soul sitting in thine eyes.'*

And so looking you read me. You say to yourself, 'There's a man with no concealments, yet who speaks not till he's spoken to; knows when to stop, and stops.' You note my pale eyebrows, my slightly prominent and pointed chin, somewhat over-sized mouth; small, well-spread ears, faintly aquiline nose; fine, thin, blonde hair, a depression in the skull where the bump of self-conceit ought to be, and you say, 'A man that knows his talents without being vain of them; who not only minds his own business, but loves it, and who in that business, be it buggy-whips or be it washine, or be it something far nobler,'—which, let me say modestly, it is,—'simply goes to the head of the class and stays there.' Yes, sirs, if I say that reading the human countenance is one of my accomplishments, I am diffidently mindful that in this company, I, myself, am read, perused; no other probably so well read—I mean so exhaustively perused. For there is one thing about me, gentlemen, if you'll allow me to say it, I'm short metre, large print, and open to the public seven days in the week. And yet you probably all make one mistake about me: you take me for the alumni of some university. Not so. I'm a self-made man. I made myself; and considering that I'm the first man I ever made, I think—pardon the seeming egotism—I think I've done well. A few years ago there dwelt in humble obscurity among the granite hills of New England, earning his bread by the sweat of his brow upon his father's farm, a youth to fortune and to fame unknown. But one day a voice within him said, 'Tarbox'—George W.,—namesake of the man who never told a lie,—'do you want to succeed in life? Then leave the production of tobacco and cider to unambitious age, and find that business wherein you can always give a man ten times as much for his dollar as his dollar is worth.' The meaning was plain, and from that time forth young Tarbox aspired to become a book-agent. 'Twas not long ere he, like

*'Young Harry Bluff, left his friends and his home,*
*And his dear native land, o'er the wide world to roam.'*

Books became his line, and full soon he was the head of the line. And why? Was it because in the first short twelve months of his career he sold, delivered, and got the money for, 5107 copies of 'Mend-me-at-Home'? No. Was it, then, because three years later he sold in one year, with no other assistance than a man to drive the horse and wagon, hold the blackboard, and hand out the books, 10,003 copies of 'Rapid 'Rithmetic'? It was not. Was it, then, because in 1878, reading aright the public mind, he said to his publishers, whose confidence in him was unbounded, 'It ain't "Mend-me-at-Home" the people want most, nor "Rapid 'Rithmetic," nor "Heal Thyself," nor "I meet the Emergency," nor the "Bouquet of Poetry and Song." What they want is all these in one.'— 'Abridged?' said the publishers. 'Enlarged!' said young Tarbox,— 'enlarged and copiously illustrated, complete in one volume, price, cloth, three dollars, sheep four, half morocco, gilt edges, five; real value to the subscriber, two hundred and fifty; title, "The Album of

Universal Information; author, G. W. Tarbox; editor, G. W. T.; agent for the United States, the Canadas, and Mexico, G. W. Tarbox," that is to say, myself.' That, gentlemen, is the reason I stand at the head of my line; not merely because on every copy sold I make an author's as well as a solicitor's margin; but because, being the author, I know whereof I sell. A man that's got my book has got a college education; and when a man taps me,—for, gentlemen, I never spout until I'm tapped,—and information bursts from me like water from a street hydrant, and he comes to find out that every thing I tell is in that wonderful book, and that every thing that is in that wonderful book I can tell, he wants to own a copy; and when I tell him I can't spare my sample copy, but I'll take his subscription, he smiles gratefully"—

A cold, wet blast, rushing into the room from the hall, betrayed the opening of the front door. The door was shut again, and a well-formed, muscular young man who had entered stood in the parlor doorway lifting his hat from his head, shaking the rain from it, and looking at it with amused diffidence. Mr. Tarbox turned about once more with his back to the fire, gave the figure a quick glance of scrutiny, then a second and longer one, and then dropped his eyes to the floor. The big-waisted man shifted his chair, tipped it back, and said:

"He smiles gratefully, you say?"

"Yes."

"And subscribes?"

"If he's got any sense," Mr. Tarbox replied in a pre-occupied tone. His eyes were on the young man who still stood in the door. This person must have reached the house in some covered conveyance. Even his boot-tops were dry or nearly so. He was rather pleasing to see; of good stature, his clothing cheap. A dark-blue flannel sack of the ready-made sort hung on him not too well. Light as the garment was, he showed no sign that he felt the penetrating cold out of which he had just come. His throat and beardless face had the good brown of outdoor life, his broad chest strained the two buttons of his sack, his head was well-poised, his feet were shapely, and but for somewhat too much roundness about the shoulder-blades, noticeable in the side view as he carefully stood a long, queer package that was not buggy-whips against the hat-rack, it would have been fair to pronounce him an athlete.

The eyes of the fireside group were turned toward him; but not upon him. They rested on a girl of sixteen who had come down the hall, and was standing before the new-comer just beyond the door. The registry-book was just there on a desk in the hall. She stood with a freshly dipped pen in her hand, ignoring the gaze from

97

the fireside with a faintly overdone calmness of face. The new guest came forward, and, in a manner that showed slender acquaintance with the operation, slowly registered his name and address.

He did it with such pains-taking, that, upside down as the writing was, she read it as he wrote. As the Christian name appeared, her perfunctory glance became attention. As the surname followed, the attention became interest and recognition. And as the address was added, Mr. Tarbox detected pleasure dancing behind the long fringe of her discreet eyes, and marked their stolen glance of quick inspection upon the short, dark locks and strong young form still bent over the last strokes of the writing. But when he straightened up, carefully shut the book, and fixed his brown eyes upon hers in guileless expectation of instructions, he saw nothing to indicate that he was not the entire stranger that she was to him.

"You done had sopper?" she asked. The uncommon kindness of such a question at such an hour of a tavern's evening was lost on the young man's obvious inexperience, and as one schooled to the hap-hazard of forest and field he merely replied:

"Naw, I didn' had any."

The girl turned—what a wealth of black hair she had!—and disappeared as she moved away along the hall. Her voice was heard: "Mamma?" Then there was the silence of an unheard consultation. The young man moved a step or two into the parlor and returned toward the door as a light double foot-fall approached again down the hall and the girl appeared once more, somewhat preceded by a small, tired-looking, pretty woman some thirty-five years of age, of slow, self-contained movement and clear, meditative eyes.

But the guest, too, had been re-enforced. A man had come silently from the fireside, taken his hand, and now, near the doorway, was softly shaking it and smiling. Surprise, pleasure, and reverential regard were mingled in the young man's face, and his open mouth was gasping—

"Mister Tarbox!"

"Claude St. Pierre, after six years, I'm glad to see you.—Madame, take good care of Claude.—No fear but she will, my boy; if anybody in Louisiana knows how to take care of a traveller, it's Madame Beausoleil." He smiled for all. The daughter's large black eyes danced, but the mother asked Claude, with unmoved countenance and soft tone:

"You are Claude St. Pierre?—from Gran' Point'?"

"Yass."

"Dass lately since you left yondah?"

"About two month'."

"Bonaventure Deschamps—he was well?"

98

"Yass." Claude's eyes were full of a glad surprise, and asked a question that his lips did not dare to venture upon. Madame Beausoleil read it, and she said:

"We was raise' together, Bonaventure and me." She waved her hand toward her daughter. "He teach her to read. Seet down to the fire; we make you some sopper."

# CHAPTER IV

## MARGUERITE

Out in the kitchen, while the coffee was dripping and the ham and eggs frying, the mother was very silent, and the daughter said little, but followed her now and then with furtive liftings of her young black eyes. Marguerite remembered Bonaventure Deschamps well and lovingly. For years she had seen the letters that at long intervals came from him at Grande Pointe to her mother here. In almost every one of them she had read high praises of Claude. He had grown, thus, to be the hero of her imagination. She had wondered if it could ever happen that he would come within her sight, and if so, when, where, how. And now, here at a time of all times when it would have seemed least possible, he had, as it were, rained down.

She wondered to-night, with more definiteness of thought than ever before, what were the deep feelings which her reticent little mother—Marguerite was an inch the taller—kept hid in that dear breast. Rarely had emotion moved it. She remembered its terrible heavings at the time of her father's death, and the later silent downpour of tears when her only sister and brother were taken in one day. Since then, those eyes had rarely been wet; yet more than once or twice she had seen tears in them when they were reading a letter from Grande Pointe. Had her mother ever had something more than a sister's love for Bonaventure? Had Bonaventure loved her? And when? Before her marriage, or after her widowhood?

The only answer that came to her as she now stood, knife in hand, by the griddle, was a roar of laughter that found its way through the hall, the dining-room, and two closed doors, from the

99

men about the waiting-room fireside. That was the third time she had heard it. What could have put them so soon into such gay mood? Could it be Claude? Somehow she hoped it was not. Her mother reminded her that the batter-cakes would burn. She quickly turned them. The laugh came again.

When by and by she went to bid Claude to his repast, the laughter, as she reached the door of the waiting-room, burst upon her as the storm would have done had she opened the front door. It came from all but Claude and Mr. Tarbox. Claude sat with a knee in his hands, smiling. The semicircle had widened out from the fire, and in the midst Mr. Tarbox stood telling a story, of which Grande Pointe was the scene, Bonaventure Deschamps the hero, a school-examination the circumstance, and he, G. W., the accidental arbiter of destinies that hung upon its results. The big-waisted man had retired for the night, and half an eye could see that the story-teller had captivated the whole remaining audience. He was just at the end as Marguerite re-appeared at the door. The laugh suddenly ceased, and then all rose; it was high bedtime.

"And did they get married?" asked one. Three or four gathered close to hear the answer.

"Who? Sidonie and Bonnyventure? Yes. I didn't stay to see. I went away into Mississippi, Tennessee, and Alabama, and just only a few weeks ago took a notion to try this Attakapas and Opelousas region. But that's what Claude tells me to-night—married more than five years ago.—Claude, your supper wants you. Want me to go out and sit with you? Oh, no trouble! not the slightest! It will make me feel as if I was nearer to Bonnyventure."

And so the group about Claude's late supper numbered four. And because each had known Bonaventure, though each in a very different way from any other, they were four friends when Claude had demolished the ham and eggs, the strong black coffee, and the griddle-cakes and sirop-de-batterie.

At the top of the hall stairway, as Mr. Tarbox was on his way to bed, one of the dispersed fireside circle stopped him, saying:

"That's an awful good story!"

"I wouldn't try a poor one on you."

"Oh!—but really, now, in good earnest, it is good. It's good in more ways than one. Now, you know, that man, hid away there in the swamp at Grande Pointe, he little thinks that six or eight men away off here in Vermilionville are going to bed to-night better men—that's it, sir—yes, sir, that's it—yes, sir!—better men—just for having heard of him!"

Mr. Tarbox smiled with affectionate approval, and began to move away; but the other put out a hand—

"Say, look here; I'm going away on that two o'clock train to-night. I want that book of yours. And I don't want to subscribe and wait. I want the book now. That's my way. I'm just that kind of a man; I'm the nowest man you ever met up with. That book's just the kind of thing for a man like me who ain't got no time to go exhaustively delving and investigating and researching into things, and yet has got to keep as sharp as a brier."

Mr. Tarbox, on looking into his baggage, found he could oblige this person. Before night fell again he had done virtually the same thing, one by one, for all the rest. By that time they were all gone; but Mr. Tarbox made Vermilionville his base of operations for several days.

Claude also tarried. For reasons presently to appear, the "ladies parlor," a small room behind the waiting-room, with just one door, which let into the hall at the hall's inner end, was given up to his use; and of evenings not only Mr. Tarbox, but Marguerite and her mother as well, met with him, gathering familiarly about a lamp that other male lodgers were not invited to hover around.

The group was not idle. Mr. Tarbox held big hanks of blue and yellow yarn, which Zoséphine wound off into balls. A square table quite filled the centre of the room. There was a confusion of objects on it, and now on one side and now on another Claude leaned over it and slowly toiled, from morning until evening alone, and in the evening with these three about him; Marguerite, with her sewing dropped upon the floor, watching his work with an interest almost wholly silent, only making now and then a murmured comment, her eyes passing at intervals from his pre-occupied eyes to his hands, and her hand now and then guessing and supplying his want as he looked for one thing or another that had got out of sight. What was he doing?

As to Marguerite, more than he was aware of, Zoséphine Beausoleil saw, and was already casting about somewhat anxiously in her mind to think what, if any thing, ought to be done about it. She saw her child's sewing lie forgotten on the floor, and the eyes that should have been following the needle, fixed often on the absorbed, unconscious, boyish-manly face so near by. She saw them scanning the bent brows, the smooth bronzed cheek, the purposeful mouth, and the unusual length of dark eyelashes that gave its charm to the whole face; and she saw them quickly withdrawn whenever the face with those lashes was lifted and an unsuspecting smile of young companionship broke slowly about the relaxing lips and the soft, deep-curtained eyes. No; Claude little knew what he was doing. Neither did Marguerite. But, aside from her, what was his occupation? I will explain.

101

About five weeks earlier than this, a passenger on an eastward-bound train of Morgan's Louisiana and Texas Railway stood at the rear door of the last coach, eying critically the track as it glided swiftly from under the train and shrank perpetually into the west. The coach was nearly empty. No one was near him save the brakeman, and by and by he took his attention from the track and let it rest on this person. There he found a singular attraction. Had he seen that face before, or why did it provoke vague reminiscences of great cypresses overhead, and deep-shaded leafy distances with bayous winding out of sight through them, and cane-brakes impenetrable to the eye, and axe-strokes—heard but unseen—slashing through them only a few feet away? Suddenly he knew.

"Wasn't it your father," he said, "who was my guide up Bayou des Acadiens and Blind River the time I made the survey in that big swamp north of Grande Pointe? Isn't your name Claude St. Pierre?" And presently they were acquainted.

"You know I took a great fancy to your father. And you've been clear through the arithmetic twice? Why, see here; you're just the sort of man I—Look here; don't you want to learn to be a surveyor?" The questioner saw that same ambition which had pleased him so in the father, leap for joy in the son's eyes.

An agreement was quickly reached. Then the surveyor wandered into another coach, and nothing more passed between them that day save one matter, which, though trivial, has its place. When the surveyor returned to the rear train, Claude was in a corner seat gazing pensively through the window and out across the wide, backward-flying, purpling green cane-fields of St. Mary, to where on the far left the live-oaks of Bayou Teche seemed hoveringly to follow on the flank of their whooping and swaggering railway-train. Claude turned and met the stranger's regard with a faint smile. His new friend spoke first.

"Matters may turn out so that we can have your father"—

Claude's eyes answered with a glad flash. "Dass what I was t'inkin'!" he said, with a soft glow that staid even when he fell again into revery.

But when the engineer—for it seems that he was an engineer, chief of a party engaged in redeeming some extensive waste swamp and marsh lands—when the chief engineer, on the third day afterward, drew near the place where he suddenly recollected Claude would be waiting to enter his service, and recalled this part of their previous interview, he said to himself, "No, it would be good for the father, but not best for the son," and fell to thinking how often parents are called upon to wrench their affections down into cruel bounds to make the foundations of their children's prosperity.

102

Claude widened to his new experience with the rapidity of something hatched out of a shell. Moreover, accident was in his favor; the party was short-handed in its upper ranks, and Claude found himself by this stress taken into larger and larger tasks as fast as he could, though ever so crudely, qualify for them.

"'Tisn't at all the best thing for you," said one of the surveyors, "but I'll lend you some books that will teach you the why as well as the how."

In the use of these books by lantern-light certain skill with the pen showed itself; and when at length one day a despatch reached camp from the absent "chief" stating that in two or three days certain matters would take him to Vermilionville, and ordering that some one be sent at once with all necessary field notes and appliances, and give his undivided time to the making of certain urgently needed maps, and the only real draughtsman of the party was ill with swamp-fever, Claude was sent.

On his last half-day's journey toward the place, he had fallen in with an old gentleman whom others called "Governor," a tall, trim figure, bent but little under fourscore years, with cheerful voice and ready speech, and eyes hidden behind dark glasses and flickering in their deep sockets.

"Go to Madame Beausoleil's," he advised Claude. "That is the place for you. Excellent person; I've known her from childhood; a woman worthy a higher station." And so, all by accident, chance upon chance, here was Claude making maps; and this delightful work, he thought, was really all he was doing, in Zoséphine's little inner parlor.

By and by it was done. The engineer had not yet arrived. The storm had delayed work in one place and undone work in another, and he was detained beyond expectation. But a letter said he would come in a day or two more, and some maps of earlier surveys, drawn by skilled workmen in great New Orleans, arrived; seeing which, Claude blushed for his own and fell to work to make them over.

"If at first you not succeed," said Claude,—

"Try—try aga-a-ain," responded Marguerite; "Bonaventure learn me that poetry; and you?"

"Yass," said Claude. He stood looking down at his work and not seeing it. What he saw was Grande Pointe in the sunset hour of a spring day six years gone, the wet, spongy margin of a tiny bayou under his feet, the great swamp at his back, the leafy undergrowth all around; his canoe and paddle waiting for him, and Bonaventure repeating to him—swamp urchin of fourteen—the costliest words of kindness—to both of them the costliest—that he had ever heard, ending with these two that Marguerite had spoken. As he resumed his work, he said, without lifting his eyes:

"Seem' to me 'f I could make myself like any man in dat whole worl', I radder make myself like Bonaventure. And you?"

She was so slow to answer that he looked at her. Even then she merely kept on sweeping her fingers slowly and idly back and forth on the table, and, glancing down upon them, said without enthusiasm: "Yass."

Yet they both loved Bonaventure, each according to knowledge of him. Nor did their common likings stop with him. The things he had taught Claude to love and seek suddenly became the admiration of Marguerite. Aspirations—aspirations!—began to stir and hum in her young heart, and to pour forth like waking bees in the warm presence of spring. Claude was a new interpretation of life to her; as one caught abed by the first sunrise at sea, her whole spirit leaped, with unmeasured self-reproach, into fresh garments and to a new and beautiful stature, and looked out upon a wider heaven and earth than ever it had seen or desired to see before. All at once the life was more than meat and the body than raiment. Presently she sprang to action. In the convent school, whose white belfry you could see from the end of Madame Beausoleil's balcony, whither Zoséphine had sent her after teaching her all she herself knew, it had been "the mind for knowledge;" now it was "knowledge for the mind." Mental training and enrichment had a value now, never before dreamed of. The old school-books were got down, recalled from banishment. Nothing ever had been hard to learn, and now she found that all she seemed to have forgotten merely required, like the books, a little beating clear of dust.

And Claude was there to help. "If C"——C!—--"having a start of one hundred miles, travels"—so  and so, and so and so,—"how fast must I travel in order to"—etc. She cannot work the problem for thinking of what it symbolizes. As C himself takes the slate, her dark eyes, lifted an instant to his, are large with painful meaning, for she sees at a glance she must travel—if the arithmetical is the true answer—more than the whole distance now between them. But Claude says there is an easy way. She draws her chair nearer and nearer to his; he bows over the problem, and she cannot follow his pencil without bending her head very close to his—closer—closer—until fluffy bits of her black hair touch the thick locks on his temples. Look to your child, Zoséphine Beausoleil, look to her! Ah! she can look; but what can she do?

She saw the whole matter; saw more than merely an unripe girl smitten with the bright smile, goodly frame, and bewitching eyes of a promising young rustic; saw her heart ennobled, her

104

nature enlarged, and all the best motives of life suddenly illuminated by the presence of one to be mated with whom promised the key-note of all harmonies; promised heart-fellowship in the ever-hoping effort to lift poor daily existence higher and higher out of the dust and into the light. What could she say? If great spirits in men or maidens went always or only with high fortune, a mere Acadian lass, a tavern maiden, were safe enough, come one fate or another. If Marguerite were like many a girl in high ranks and low, to whom any husband were a husband, any snug roof a home, and any living life—But what may a maiden do, or a mother bid her do, when she looks upon the youth so shaped without and within to her young soul's belief in its wants, that all other men are but beasts of the field and creeping things, and he alone Adam? To whom could the widow turn? Father, mother?— Gone to their rest. The curé who had stood over her in baptism, marriage, and bereavement?—Called long ago to higher dignities and wider usefulness in distant fields. Oh for the presence and counsel of Bonaventure! It is true, here was Mr. Tarbox, so kind, and so replete with information; so shrewd and so ready to advise. She spurned the thought of leaning on him; and yet the oft-spurned thought as often returned. Already his generous interest had explored her pecuniary affairs, and his suggestions, too good to be ignored, had moulded them into better shape, and enlarged their net results. And he could tell how many eight-ounce tacks make a pound, and what electricity is, and could cure a wart in ten minutes, and recite "Oh! why should the spirit of mortal be proud?" And this evening, the seventh since the storm, when for one weak moment she had allowed the conversation to drift toward wedlock, he had stated a woman's chances of marrying between the ages of fifteen and twenty, to wit, 14½ per cent; and between thirty and thirty-five, 15½.

"Hah!" exclaimed Zoséphine, her eyes flashing as they had not done in many a day, "'tis not dat way!—not in Opelousas!"

"Arithmetically speaking!" the statistician quickly explained. He ventured to lay a forefinger on the back of her hand, but one glance of her eye removed it. "You see, that's merely arithmetically considered. Now, of course, looking at it geographically—why, of course! And—why, as to that, there are ladies"—

Madame Beausoleil rose, left Mr. Tarbox holding the yarn, and went down the hall, whose outer door had opened and shut. A moment later she entered the room again.

"Claude!"

Marguerite's heart sank. Her guess was right: the chief engineer had come. And early in the morning Claude was gone.

105

# CHAPTER V

## FATHER AND SON

Such strange things storms do,—here purifying the air, yonder treading down rich harvests, now replenishing the streams, and now strewing shores with wrecks; here a blessing, there a calamity. See what this one had done for Marguerite! Well, what? She could not lament; she dared not rejoice. Oh! if she were Claude and Claude were she, how quickly—

She wondered how many miles a day she could learn to walk if she should start out into the world on foot to find somebody, as she had heard that Bonaventure had once done to find her mother's lover. There are no Bonaventures now, she thinks, in these decayed times.

"Mamma,"—her speech was French,—"why do we never see Bonaventure? How far is it to Grande Pointe?"

"Ah! my child, a hundred miles; even more."

"And to my uncle Rosamond's,—Rosamond Robichaux, on Bayou Terrebonne?"

"Fully as far, and almost the same journey."

There was but one thing to be done,—crush Claude out of her heart.

The storm had left no wounds on Grande Pointe. Every roof was safe, even the old tobacco-shed where Bonaventure had kept school before the schoolhouse was built. The sheltering curtains of deep forest had broken the onset of the wind, and the little cotton, corn, and tobacco fields, already harvested, were merely made a little more tattered and brown. The November air was pure, sunny, and mild, and thrilled every now and then with the note of some lingering bird. A green and bosky confusion still hid house from house and masked from itself the all but motionless human life of the sleepy woods village. Only an adventitious China-tree here and there had been stripped of its golden foliage, and kept but its ripened berries with the red birds darting and fluttering around them like so many hiccoughing Comanches about a dramseller's tent. And here, if one must tell a thing so painful, our old friend the mocking-bird, neglecting his faithful wife and letting his home go to decay, kept dropping in, all hours of the day, tasting the berries' rank pulp, stimulating, stimulating, drowning care, you know,— "Lost so many children, and the rest gone off in ungrateful forgetfulness of their old hard-working father; yes;" and ready to sing or fight, just as any other creature happened not to wish; and going home in the evening scolding and swaggering, and getting to bed barely able to hang on to the roost. It would have been bad enough, even for a man; but for a bird—and a mocking-bird!

But the storm wrought a great change in one small house not in Grande Pointe, yet of it. Until the storm, ever since the day St. Pierre had returned from the little railway-station where Claude had taken the cars, he had seemed as patiently resigned to the new loneliness of Bayou des Acadiens as his thatched hut, which day by day sat so silent between the edges of the dark forest and the darker stream, looking out beyond the farther bank, and far over the green waste of rushes with its swarms of blackbirds sweeping capriciously now this way and now that, and the phantom cloud-shadows passing slowly across from one far line of cypress wood to another. But since that night when the hut's solitary occupant could not sleep for the winds and for thought of Claude, there was a great difference inside. And this did not diminish; it grew. It is hard for a man to be both father and mother, and at the same time be childless. The bonds of this condition began slowly to tighten around St. Pierre's heart and then to cut into it. And so, the same day on which Claude in Vermilionville left the Beausoleils' tavern, the cabin on Bayou des Acadiens, ever in his mind's eye, was empty, and in Grande Pointe his father stood on the one low step at the closed door of Bonaventure's little frame schoolhouse.

He had been there a full minute and had not knocked. Every movement, to-day, came only after an inward struggle. Many associations crowded his mind on this doorstep. Six years before, almost on this spot, a mere brier-patch then, he and Maximian Roussel had risen from the grassy earth and given the first two welcoming hand-grasps to the schoolmaster. And now, as one result, Claude, who did not know his letters then, was rising—nay, had risen—to greatness! Claude, whom once he would have been glad to make a good fisherman and swamper, or at the utmost a sugar-boiler, was now a greater, in rank at least, than the very schoolmaster. Truly "knowledge is power"—alas! yes; for it had stolen away that same Claude. The College Point priest's warning had come true: it was "good-by to Grande Pointe!"—Nay, nay, it must not be! Is that the kind of power education is? Power to tear children from their parents? Power to expose their young heads to midnight storms? Power to make them eager to go, and willing to stay away, from their paternal homes? Then indeed the priest had said only too truly, that these public schools teach every thing except morals and religion! From the depth of St. Pierre's heart there quickly came a denial of the charge; and on the moment, like a

107

chanted response, there fell upon his listening ear a monotonous intonation from within the door. A reading-class had begun its exercise. He knew the words by heart, so often had Claude and he read them together. He followed the last stanza silently with his own lips.

> *"Remember, child, remember*
> *That you love, with all your might,*
> *The God who watches o'er us*
> *And gives us each delight,*
> *Who guards us ever in the day,*
> *And saves as in the night."*

Tears filled the swamper's eyes. He moved as if to leave the place. But again he paused, with one foot half lowered to the ground. His jaws set, a frown came between his eyes; he drew back the foot, turned again to the door, and gave a loud, peremptory knock.

Bonaventure came to the door. Anxiety quickly overspread his face as he saw the gloom on St. Pierre's. He stood on the outer edge of the sill, and drew the door after him.

"I got good news," said St. Pierre, with no softening of countenance.

"Good news?"

"Yass.—I goin' make Claude come home."

Bonaventure could only look at him in amazement. St. Pierre looked away and continued:

"'S no use. Can't stand it no longer." He turned suddenly upon the schoolmaster. "Why you di'n' tell me ed'cation goin' teck my boy 'way from me?" In Bonaventure a look of distressful self-justification quickly changed to one of anxious compassion.

"Wait!" he said. He went back into the schoolroom, leaving St. Pierre in the open door, and said:

"Dear chil'run, I perceive generally the aspects of fatigue. You have been good scholars. I pronounce a half-hollyday till to-morrow morning. Come, each and every one, with lessons complete."

The children dispersed peaceably, jostling one another to shake the schoolmaster's hand as they passed him. When they were gone he put on his coarse straw hat, and the two men walked slowly, conversing as they went, down the green road that years before had first brought the educator to Grande Pointe.

"Dear friend," said the schoolmaster, "shall education be to blame for this separation? Is not also non-education responsible? Is it not by the non-education of Grande Pointe that there is nothing fit here for Claude's staying?"

"You stay!"

"I? I stay? Ah! sir, I stay, yes! Because like Claude, leaving my home and seeking by wandering to find the true place of my utility, a voice spake that I come at Grande Pointe. Behole me! as far from my childhood home as Claude from his. Friend,—ah! friend, what shall I,—shall Claude,—shall any man do with education! Keep it? Like a miser his gol'? What shall the ship do when she is load'? Dear friend,"—they halted where another road started away through the underbrush at an abrupt angle on their right,—"where leads this narrow road? To Belle Alliance plantation only, or not also to the whole worl'? So is education! That road here once fetch me at Grande Pointe; the same road fetch Claude away. Education came whispering, 'Claude St. Pierre, come! I have constitute' you citizen of the worl'. Come, come, forgetting self!' Oh, dear friend, education is not for self alone! Nay, even self is not for self!"

"Well, den,"—the deep-voiced woodman stood with one boot on a low stump, fiercely trimming a branch that he had struck from the parent stem with one blow of his big, keen clasp-knife,—"self not for self,—for what he gone off and lef' me in de swamp?"

"Ah, sir!" replied Bonaventure, "what do I unceasingly tell those dear school-chil'run? 'May we not make the most of self, yet not for self?'" He laid his hand upon St. Pierre's shoulder. "And who sent Claude hence if not his unselfish father?"

"I was big fool," said St. Pierre, whittling on.

"Nay, wise! Discovering the great rule of civilize-ation. Every man not for self, but for every other!"

The swamper disclaimed the generous imputation with a shake of the head.

"Naw, I dunno nut'n' 'bout dat. I look out for me and my boy, me.—And beside,"—he abruptly threw away the staff he had trimmed, shut his knife with a snap, and thrust it into his pocket,— "I dawn't see ed'cation make no diff'ence. You say ed'cation—priest say religion—me, I dawn't see neider one make no diff'ence. I see every man look out for hisself and his li'l' crowd. Not you, but"—He waved his hand bitterly toward the world at large.

"Ah, sir!" cried Bonaventure, "'tis not something what you can see all the time, like the horns on a cow! And yet, sir,—and yet!"—he lifted himself upon tiptoe and ran his fingers through his thin hair— "the education that make' no difference is but a dead body! and the religion that make' no difference is a ghost! Behole! behole two thing' in the worl', where all is giving and getting, two thing', contrary, yet resem'ling! 'Tis the left han'—alas, alas!—giving only to get; and the right, blessed of God, getting only to give! How much resem'ling, yet how contrary! The one—han' of all strife; the other—

109

of all peace. And oh! dear friend, there are those who call the one civilize-ation, and the other religion. Civilize-ation? Religion? They are one! They are body and soul! I care not what religion the priest teach you; in God's religion is comprise' the total mécanique of civilize-ation. We are all in it; you, me, Claude, Sidonie; all in it! Each and every at his task, however high, however low, working not to get, but to give, and not to give only to his own li'l' crowd, but to all, to all!" The speaker ceased, for his hearer was nodding his head with sceptical impatience.

"Yass," said the woodman, "yass; but look, Bonaventure. Di'n' you said one time, 'Knowledge is power'?"

"Yes, truly; and it is."

"But what use knowledge be power if goin' give ev't'in' away?"

Bonaventure drew back a step or two, suddenly jerked his hat from his head, and came forward again with arms stretched wide and the hat dangling from his hand. "Because—because God will not let it sta-a-ay given away! 'Give—it shall be give' to you.' Every thing given out into God's worl' come back to us roun' God's worl'! Resem'ling the stirring of water in a bucket."

But St. Pierre frowned. "Yass,—wat' in bucket,—yass. Den no man dawn't keep nut'n'. Dawn't own nut'n' he got."

"Ah! sir, there is a better owning than to own. 'Tis giving, dear friend; 'tis giving. To get? To have? That is not to own. The giver, not the getter; the giver! he is the true owner. Live thou not to get, but to give." Bonaventure's voice trembled; his eyes were full of tears.

The swamper stood up with his own eyes full, but his voice was firm. "Bonaventure, I don't got much. I got dat li'l' shanty on Bayou des Acadiens, and li'l' plunder inside—few kittle', and pan',—cast-net, fish-line', two, t'ree gun', and—my wife' grave, yond' in graveyard. But I got Claude,—my boy, my son. You t'ink God want me give my son to whole worl'?"

The schoolmaster took the woodsman's brown wrist tenderly into both his hands, and said, scarce above a whisper, "He gave His, first. He started it. Who can refuse, He starting it? And thou wilt not refuse." The voice rose—"I see, I see the victory! Well art thou nominated 'St. Pierre!' for on that rock of giving"—

"Naw, sir! Stop!" The swamper dashed the moisture from his eyes and summoned a look of stubborn resolve. "Mo' better you call me St. Pierre because I'm a fisherman what cuss when I git mad. Look! You dawn't want me git Claude back in Gran' Point'. You want me to give, give. Well, all right! I goin' quit Gran' Point' and give myself, me, to Claude. I kin read, I kin write, I t'ink kin do better 'long wid Claude dan livin' all 'lone wid snake' and alligator. I t'ink

110

dass mo' better for everybody; and anyhow, I dawn't care; I dawn't give my son to nobody; I give myself to Claude."

Bonaventure and his friend gazed into each other's wet eyes for a moment. Then the schoolmaster turned, lifted his eyes and one arm toward the west, and exclaimed:

"Ah, Claude! thou receivest the noblest gift in Gran' Point'!"

# CHAPTER VI

## CONVERGING LINES

On the prairies of Vermilion and Lafayette, winter is virtually over by the first week in February. From sky to sky, each tree and field, each plain and plantation grove, are putting on the greenery of a Northern May. Even on Côte Gelée the housewife has persuaded le vieux to lay aside his gun, and the early potatoes are already planted. If the moon be at the full, much ground is ready for the sower; and those ploughmen and pony teams and men working along behind them with big, clumsy hoes, over in yonder field, are planting corn. Those silent, tremulous strands of black that in the morning sky come gliding, high overhead, from the direction of the great sea-marshes and fade into the northern blue, are flocks that have escaped the murderous gun of the pot-hunter. Spring and Summer are driving these before them as the younger and older sister, almost abreast, come laughing, and striving to outrun each other across the Mexican Gulf.

Those two travellers on horseback, so dwarfed by distance, whom you see approaching out of the north-west, you shall presently find have made, in their dress, no provision against cold. At Carancro, some miles away to the north-east, there is a thermometer; and somewhere in Vermilionville, a like distance to the south-east, there might possibly be found a barometer; but there is no need of either to tell that the air to-day is threescore and ten and will be more before it is less. Before the riders draw near you have noticed that only one is a man and the other a woman. And now you may see that he is sleek and alert, blonde and bland, and the savage within us wants to knock off his silk hat. All the more so for that she is singularly pretty to be met in his sole care. The years

111

count on her brows, it is true, but the way in which they tell of matronhood—and somehow of widowhood too—is a very fair and gentle way. Her dress is plain, but its lines have a grace that is also dignity; and the lines of her face—lines is too hard a word for them—are not those of time, but of will and of care, that have chastened and refined one another. She speaks only now and then. Her companion's speech fills the wide intervals.

"Yesterday morning," he says, "as I came along here a little after sunrise, there was a thin fog lying only two or three feet deep, close to the level ground as far as you could see, hiding the whole prairie, and making it look for all the world like a beautiful lake, with every here and there a green grove standing out of it like a real little island."

She replies that she used to see it so in her younger days. The Acadian accent is in her words. She lifts her black eyes, looks toward Carancro, and is silent.

"You're thinking of the changes," says her escort.

"Yass; 'tis so. Dey got twenty time' many field' like had befo'. Peop' don't raise cattl' no more; raise crop'. Dey say even dat land changin'."

"How changing?"

"I dunno. I dunno if 'tis so. Dey say prairie risin' mo' higher every year. I dunno if 'tis so. I t'ink dat land don't change much; but de peop', yass."

"Still, the changes are mostly good changes," responds the male rider. "'Tisn't the prairie, but the people that are rising. They've got the schoolhouse, and the English language, and a free paid labor system, and the railroads, and painted wagons, and Cincinnati furniture, and sewing-machines, and melodeons, and Horsford's Acid Phosphate; and they've caught the spirit of progress!"

"Yass, 'tis so. Dawn't see nobody seem satisfied—since de army—since de railroad."

"Well, that's right enough; they oughtn't to be satisfied. You're not satisfied, are you? And yet you've never done so well before as you have this season. I wish I could say the same for the 'Album of Universal Information;' but I can't. I tell you that, Madame Beausoleil; I wouldn't tell anybody else."

Zoséphine responds with a dignified bow. She has years ago noticed in herself, that, though she has strength of will, she lacks clearness and promptness of decision. She is at a loss, now, to know what to do with Mr. Tarbox. Here he is for the seventh time. But there is always a plausible explanation of his presence, and a person

112

of more tactful propriety, it seems to her, never put his name upon her tavern register or himself into her company. She sees nothing shallow or specious in his dazzling attainments; they rekindle the old ambitions in her that Bonaventure lighted; and although Mr. Tarbox's modest loveliness is not visible, yet a certain fundamental rectitude, discernible behind all his nebulous gaudiness, confirms her liking. Then, too, he has earned her gratitude. She has inherited not only her father's small fortune, but his thrift as well. She can see the sagacity of Mr. Tarbox's advice in pecuniary matters, and once and once again, when he has told her quietly of some little operation into which he and the ex-governor—who "thinks the world of me," he says—were going to dip, and she has accepted his invitation to venture in also, to the extent of a single thousand dollars, the money has come back handsomely increased. Even now, the sale of all her prairie lands to her former kinsmen-in-law, which brought her out here yesterday and lets her return this morning, is made upon his suggestion, and is so advantageous that somehow, she doesn't know why, she almost fears it isn't fair to the other side. The fact is, the country is passing from the pastoral to the agricultural life, the prairies are being turned into countless farms, and the people are getting wealth. So explains Mr. Tarbox, whose happening to come along this morning bound in her direction is pure accident—pure accident.

"No, the 'A. of U. I.' hasn't done its best," he says again. "For one thing, I've had other fish to fry. You know that." He ventures a glance at her eyes, but they ignore it, and he adds, "I mean other financial matters."

"'Tis so," says Zoséphine; and Mr. Tarbox hopes the reason for this faint repulse is only the nearness of this farmhouse peeping at them through its pink veil of blossoming peach-trees, as they leisurely trot by.

"Yes," he says; "and, besides, 'Universal Information' isn't what this people want. The book's too catholic for them."

"Too Cat'oleek!" Zoséphine raises her pretty eyebrows in grave astonishment—"'Cadian' is all Cat'oleek."

"Yes, yes, ecclesiastically speaking, I know. That wasn't my meaning. Your smaller meaning puts my larger one out of sight; yes, just as this Cherokee hedge puts out of sight the miles of prairie fields, and even that house we just passed. No, the 'A. of U. I.,'—I love to call it that; can you guess why?" There is a venturesome twinkle in his smile, and even a playful permission in her own as she shakes her head.

"Well, I'll tell you; it's because it brings U and I so near together."

113

"Hah!" exclaims Madame Beausoleil, warningly, yet with sunshine and cloud on her brow at once. She likes her companion's wit, always so deep, and yet always so delicately pointed! His hearty laugh just now disturbs her somewhat, but they are out on the wide plain again, without a spot in all the sweep of her glance where an eye or an ear may ambush them or their walking horses.

"No," insists her fellow-traveller; "I say again, as I said before, the 'A. of U. I.'"—he pauses at the initials, and Zoséphine's faint smile gives him ecstasy—"hasn't done its best. And yet it has done beautifully! Why, when did you ever see such a list as this?" He dexterously draws from an extensive inner breast-pocket, such as no coat but a book-agent's or a shoplifter's would be guilty of, a wide, limp, morocco-bound subscription-book. "Here!" He throws it open upon the broad Texas pommel. "Now, just for curiosity, look at it—oh! you can't see it from away off there, looking at it sideways!" He gives her a half-reproachful, half-beseeching smile and glance, and gathers up his dropped bridle. They come closer. Their two near shoulders approach each other, the two elbows touch, and two dissimilar hands hold down the leaves. The two horses playfully bite at each other; it is their way of winking one eye.

"Now, first, here's the governor's name; and then his son's, and his nephew's, and his other son's, and his cousin's. And here's Pierre Cormeaux, and Baptiste Clément, you know, at Carancro; and here's Basilide Sexnailder, and Joseph Cantrelle, and Jacques Hébert; see? And Gaudin, and Laprade, Blouin, and Roussel,—old Christofle Roussel of Beau Bassin,—Duhon, Roman and Simonette Le Blanc, and Judge Landry, and Thériot,—Colonel Thériot,—Martin, Hébert again, Robichaux, Mouton, Mouton again, Robichaux again, Mouton—oh, I've got 'em all!—Castille, Beausoleil—cousin of yours? Yes, he said so; good fellow, thinks you're the greatest woman alive." The two dissimilar hands, in turning a leaf, touch, and the smaller one leaves the book. "And here's Guilbeau, and Latiolais, and Thibodeaux, and Soudrie, and Arcenaux—flowers of the community—'I gather them in,'—and here's a page of Côte Gelée people, and—Joe Jefferson hadn't got back to the Island yet, but I've got his son; see? And here's—can you make out this signature? It's written so small"—

Both heads,—with only the heavens and the dear old earth-mother to see them,—both heads bend over the book; the hand that had retreated returns, but bethinks itself and withdraws again; the eyes of Mr. Tarbox look across their corners at the sedate brow so much nearer his than ever it has been before, until that brow feels the look, and slowly draws away. Look to your mother, Marguerite; look to her! But Marguerite is not there, not even in Vermilionville;

nor yet in Lafayette parish; nor anywhere throughout the wide prairies of Opelousas or Attakapas. Triumph fills Mr. Tarbox's breast.

"Well," he says, restoring the book to its hiding-place, "seems like I ought to be satisfied with that; doesn't it to you?"

It does; Zoséphine says so. She sees the double meaning, and Mr. Tarbox sees that she sees it, but must still move cautiously. So he says:

"Well, I'm not satisfied. It's perfect as far as it goes, but don't expect me to be satisfied with it. If I've seemed satisfied, shall I tell you why it was, my dear—friend?"

Zoséphine makes no reply; but her dark eyes meeting his for a moment, and then falling to her horse's feet, seem to beg for mercy.

"It's because," says Mr. Tarbox, while her heart stands still, "it's because I've made"—there is an awful pause—"more money without the 'A. of U. I.' this season than I've made with it."

Madame Beausoleil catches her breath, shows relief in every feature, lifts her eyes with sudden brightness, and exclaims:

"Dass good! Dass mighty good, yass! 'Tis so."

"Yes, it is; and I tell you, and you only, because I'm proud to believe you're my sincere friend. Am I right?"

Zoséphine busies herself with her riding-skirt, shifts her seat a little, and with studied carelessness assents.

"Yes," her companion repeats; "and so I tell you. The true business man is candid to all, communicative to none. And yet I open my heart to you. I can't help it; it won't stay shut. And you must see, I'm sure you must, that there's something more in there besides money; don't you?" His tone grows tender.

Madame Beausoleil steals a glance toward him,—a grave, timid glance. She knows there is safety in the present moment. Three horsemen, strangers, far across the field in their front, are coming toward them, and she feels an almost proprietary complacence in a suitor whom she can safely trust to be saying just the right nothings when those shall meet them and ride by. She does not speak; but he says:

"You know there is, dear Jos——friend!" He smiles with modest sweetness. "G. W. Tarbox doesn't run after money, and consequently he never runs past much without picking it up." They both laugh in decorous moderation. The horsemen are drawing near; they are Acadians. "I admit I love to make money. But that's not my chief pleasure. My chief pleasure is the study of human nature.

*The proper study of mankind is man.*

115

*Sole judge of truth, in endless error hurled,*
*The glory, jest, and riddle of the world.'*

"This season I've been studying these Acadian people. And I like them! They don't like to be reminded that they're Acadians. Well, that's natural; the Creoles used to lord it over them so when the Creoles were slave-holding planters and they were small farmers. That's about past now. The Acadians are descended from peasants, that's true, while some Creoles are from the French nobility. But, hooh! wouldn't any fair-minded person"—the horsemen are within earshot; they are staring at the silk hat—"Adjieu."

"Adjieu." They pass.

"—Wouldn't any fair-minded person that knows what France was two or three hundred years ago—show you some day in the 'Album'—about as lief be descended from a good deal of that peasantry as from a good deal of that nobility? I should smile! Why, my dear—friend, the day's coming when the Acadians will be counted as good French blood as there is in Louisiana! They're the only white people that ever trod this continent—island or mainland—who never on their own account oppressed anybody. Some little depredation on their British neighbors, out of dogged faithfulness to their king and church,—that's the worst charge you can make. Look at their history! all poetry and pathos! Look at their character! brave, peaceable, loyal, industrious, home-loving"—

But Zoséphine was looking at the speaker. Her face is kindled with the inspiration of his praise. His own eyes grow ardent.

"Look at their women! Ah, Josephine, I'm looking at one! Don't turn away.

—*'One made up*
*Of loveliness alone;*
*A woman, of her gentle sex*
*The seeming paragon.'*

*'The reason firm, the temperate will,*
*Endurance, foresight, strength, and skill;*
*A perfect woman nobly planned,*
*To warn, to comfort, and command.'*

"You can't stop me, Josephine; it's got to come, and come right now. I'm a homeless man, Josephine, tired of wandering, with a heart bigger and weaker than I ever thought I had. I want you! I love you! I've never loved anybody before in my life except myself, and I don't find myself as lovely as I used. Oh, take me, Josephine! I

116

don't ask you to love as if you'd never loved another. I'll take what's left, and be perfectly satisfied! I know you're ambitious, and I love you for that! But I do think I can give you a larger life. With you for a wife, I believe I could be a man you needn't be ashamed of. I'm already at the head of my line. Best record in the United States, Josephine, whether by the day, week, month, year, or locality. But if you don't like the line, I'll throw up the 'A. of U. I.' and go into any thing you say; for I want to lift you higher, Josephine. You're above me already, by nature and by rights, but I can lift you, I know I can. You've got no business keeping tavern; you're one of Nature's aristocrats. Yes, you are! and you're too young and lovely to stay a widow—in a State where there's more men than there's women. There's a good deal of the hill yet to climb before you start down. Oh, let's climb it together, Josephine! I'll make you happier than you are, Josephine; I haven't got a bad habit left; such as I had, I've quit; it don't pay. I don't drink, chew, smoke, tell lies, swear, quarrel, play cards, make debts, nor belong to a club—be my wife! Your daughter 'll soon be leaving you. You can't be happy alone. Take me! take me!" He urges his horse close—her face is averted—and lays his hand softly but firmly on her two, resting folded on the saddle-horn. They struggle faintly and are still; but she slowly shakes her hanging head.

"O Josephine! you don't mean no, do you? Look this way! you don't mean no?" He presses his hand passionately down upon hers. Her eyes do not turn to his; but they are lifted tearfully to the vast, unanswering sky, and as she mournfully shakes her head again, she cries,—

"I dunno! I dunno! I can't tell! I got to see Marguerite."

"Well, you'll see her in an hour, and if she"—

"Naw, naw! 'tis not so; Marguerite is in New Orleans since Christmas."

Very late in the evening of that day Mr. Tarbox entered the principal inn of St. Martinville, on the Teche. He wore an air of blitheness which, though silent, was overdone. As he pushed his silk hat back on his head, and registered his name with a more than usual largeness of hand, he remarked:

> "'Man wants but little here below,
> Nor wants that little long.'

"Give me a short piece of candle and a stumpy candlestick—and

> 'Take me up, and bear me hence
> Into some other chamber'"—

117

"Glad to see you back, Mr. Tarbox," responded the host; and as his guest received the candle and heard the number of his room,—"books must 'a' went well this fine day."

Mr. Tarbox fixed him with his eye, drew a soft step closer, said in a low tone:

> *"'My only books*
> *Were woman's looks,*
> *And folly's all they've taught me.'"*

The landlord raised his eyebrows, rounded his mouth, and darted out his tongue. The guest shifted the candle to his left hand, laid his right softly upon the host's arm, and murmured:

"List! Are we alone? If I tell thee something, wilt thou tell it never?"

The landlord smiled eagerly, shook his head, and bent toward his speaker.

"Friend Perkins," said Mr. Tarbox, in muffled voice—

> *"'So live, that when thy summons comes to join*
> *The innumerable caravan which moves*
> *To that mysterious realm where each shall take*
> *His chamber in the silent halls of death,*
> *Thou go not, like the quarry-slave, at night,*
> *Scourged to his dungeon, but, sustained and soothed*
> *By an unfaltering trust, approach thy grave*
> *Like one that wraps the drapery of his couch*
> *About him, and lies down to pleasant dreams.'*

"Don't let the newspapers get hold of it—good-night."

But it was only at daybreak that Mr. Tarbox disordered the drapery of his couch to make believe he had slept there, and at sunrise he was gone to find Claude.

# CHAPTER VII

## 'THANASE'S VIOLIN

Had Marguerite gone to New Orleans the better to crush Claude out of her heart? No, no! Her mother gave an explanation interesting and reasonable enough, and at the same time less uncomfortably romantic. Marguerite had gone to the city to pursue studies taught better there than in Opelousas; especially music.

Back of this was a reason which she had her mother's promise not to mention,—the physician's recommendation—a change of scene. He spoke of slight malarial influences, and how many odd forms they took; of dyspepsia and its queer freaks; of the confining nature of house cares, and of how often they "ran down the whole system." His phrases were French, but they had all the weary triteness of these; while Marguerite rejoiced that he did not suspect the real ailment, and Zoséphine saw that he divined it perfectly.

A change of scene. Marguerite had treated the suggestion lightly, as something amusingly out of proportion to her trivial disorder, but took pains not to reject it. Zoséphine had received it with troubled assent, and mentioned the small sugar-farm and orangery of the kinsman Robichaux, down on Bayou Terrebonne. But the physician said, "If that would not be too dull;" mentioned, casually, the city, and saw Marguerite lighten up eagerly. The city was chosen; the physician's sister, living there, would see Marguerite comfortably established. All was presently arranged.

"And you can take your violin with you, and study music," he said. Marguerite had one, and played it with a taste and skill that knew no competitor in all the surrounding region.

It had belonged to her father. Before she was born, all Lafayette parish had known it tenderly. Before she could talk she had danced—courtesied and turned, tiptoed and fallen and risen again, latter end first, to the gay strains he had loved to wring from it. Before it seemed safe, for the instrument, to trust it in her hands, she had learned to draw its bow; and for years, now, there had been no resident within the parish who could not have been her scholar better than to be her teacher.

When Claude came, she had shut the violin in its case, and left the poor thing hidden away, despising its powers to charm, lost in self-contempt, and helpless under the spell of a chaste passion's first enchantment. When he went, she still forgot the instrument for many days. She returned with more than dutiful energy to her full

119

part in the household cares, and gave every waking hour not so filled to fierce study. If she could not follow him—if a true maiden must wait upon faith—at least she would be ready if fate should ever bring him back.

But one night, when she had conned her simple books until the words ran all together on the page, some good angel whispered, "The violin!" She took it and played. The music was but a song, but from some master of song. She played it, it may be, not after the best rules, yet as one may play who, after life's first great billow has gone over him, smites again his forgotten instrument. With tears, of all emotions mingled, starting from her eyes, and the bow trembling on the strings, she told the violin her love. And it answered her:

"Be strong! be strong! you shall not love for naught. He shall—he shall come back—he shall come back and lead us into joy." From that time the violin had more employment than ever before in all its days.

So it and Marguerite were gone away to the great strange city together. The loneliness they left behind was a sad burden to Zoséphine. No other one thing had had so much influence to make so nearly vulnerable the defences of her heart when Mr. Tarbox essayed to storm them. On the night following that event, the same that he had spent so sleeplessly in St. Martinville, she wrote a letter to Marguerite, which, though intended to have just the opposite effect, made the daughter feel that this being in New Orleans, and all the matter connected with it, were one unmixed mass of utter selfishness. The very written words that charged her to stay on seemed to say, "Come home!" Her strong little mother! always quiet and grave, it is true, and sometimes sad; yet so well poised, so concentrated, so equal to every passing day and hour!—she to seem—in this letter—far out of her course, adrift, and mutely and dimly signalling for aid! The daughter read the pages again and again. What could they mean? Here, for instance, this line about the mother's coming herself to the city, if, and if, and if!

The letter found Marguerite in the bosom of a family that dwelt in the old Rue Bourbon, only a short way below Canal Street, the city's centre. The house stands on the street, its drawing-room windows opening upon the sidewalk, and a narrow balcony on the story above shading them scantily at noon. A garden on the side is visible from the street through a lofty, black, wrought-iron fence. Of the details within the enclosure, I remember best the vines climbing the walls of the tall buildings that shut it in, and the urns and vases, and the evergreen foliage of the Japan plum-trees. A little way off, and across the street, was the pleasant restaurant and salesroom of the Christian Women's Exchange.

The family spoke English. Indeed, they spoke it a great deal; and French—also a great deal. The younger generation, two daughters and a son, went much into society. Their name was that of an ancient French noble house, with which, in fact, they had no connection. They took great pains to call themselves Creoles, though they knew well enough they were Acadians. The Acadian caterpillar often turns into a Creole butterfly. Their great-grandfather, one of the children of the Nova-Scotian deportation, had been a tobacco-farmer on the old Côte Acadien in St. John the Baptist parish. Lake des Allemands lay there, just behind him. In 1815, his son, their grandfather, in an excursion through the lake and bayou beyond, discovered, far south-eastward in the midst of the Grande Prairie des Allemands, a "pointe" of several hundred acres extent. Here, with one or two others, he founded the Acadian settlement of "La Vacherie," and began to build a modest fortune. The blood was good, even though it was not the blood of ancient robbers; and the son in the next generation found his way, by natural and easy stages, through Barataria and into the city, and became the "merchant" of his many sugar and rice planting kinsmen and neighbors.

It was a great favor to Marguerite to be taken into such a household as this. She felt it so. The household felt it so. Yet almost from the start they began to play her, in their social world, as their best card—when they could. She had her hours of school and of home study; also her music, both lessons and practice; was in earnest both as to books and violin, and had teachers who also were in earnest; and so she found little time for social revels. Almost all sociality is revel in New-Orleans society, and especially in the society she met.

But when she did appear, somehow she shone. A native instinct in dress,—even more of it than her mother had at the same age,—and in manners and speech, left only so little rusticity as became itself a charm rather than a blemish, suggested the sugar-cane fields; the orange-grove; the plantation-house, with pillared porch, half-hidden in tall magnolias and laurestines and bushes of red and white camellias higher and wider than arms can reach, and covered with their regal flowers from the ground to their tops; and the bayou front lined with moss-draped live-oaks, their noonday shadows a hundred feet across. About her there was not the faintest hint of the country tavern. She was but in her seventeenth year; but on her native prairies, where girls are women at fourteen, seventeen was almost an advanced stage of decay. She seemed full nineteen, and a very well-equipped nineteen as social equipments went in the circle she had entered. Being a schoolgirl was no drawback; there

121

are few New-Orleans circles where it is; and especially not in her case, for she needed neither to titter nor chatter,—she could talk. And then, her violin made victory always easy and certain.

Sometimes the company was largely of down-town Creoles; sometimes of up-town people,—"Americans;" and often equally of the two sorts, talking French and English in most amusing and pleasing confusion. For the father of the family had lately been made president of a small bank, and was fairly boxing the social compass in search of depositors. Marguerite had not yet discovered that—if we may drag the metaphor ashore—to enter society is not to emerge upon an unbroken table-land, or that she was not on its highest plateau. She noticed the frequency with which she encountered unaccomplished fathers, stupid mothers, rude sons and daughters, and ill-distributed personal regard; but she had the common-sense not to expect more of society than its nature warrants, guessed rightly that she would find the same thing anywhere else, and could not know that these elements were less mixed with better here than in many other of the city's circles, of whose existence she had not even heard. However:

Society, at its very best, always needs, and at its best or worst always contains, a few superior members, who make themselves a blessing by working a constant, tactful redistribution of individuals by their true values, across the unworthy lines upon which society ever tends to stratify. Such a person, a matron, sat with Marguerite one April evening under a Chinese lantern in the wide, curtained veranda of an Esplanade-street house whose drawing-room and Spanish garden were filled with company.

Marguerite was secretly cast down. This lady had brought her here, having met her but a fortnight before and chosen her at once, in her own private counsels, for social promotion. And Marguerite had played the violin. In her four months' advanced training she had accomplished wonders. Her German professor made the statement, while he warned her against enthusiastic drawing-room flattery. This evening she had gotten much praise and thanks. Yet these had a certain discriminative moderation that was new to her ear, and confirmed to her, not in the pleasantest way, the realization that this company was of higher average intelligence and refinement than any she had met before. She little guessed that the best impression she had ever made she made here to-night.

Of course it was not merely on account of the violin. She had beauty, not only of face and head, but of form and carriage. So that when she stood with her instrument, turning, as it were, every breath of air into music, and the growing volume of the strains called forth all her good Acadian strength of arms and hand, she charmed not merely the listening ear, but the eye, the reason, and the imagination in its freest range.

But, indeed, it was not the limitations of her social triumphs themselves that troubled her. Every experience of the evening had helped to show her how much wider the world was than she had dreamed, and had opened new distances on the right, on the left, and far ahead; and nowhere in them all could eye see, or ear hear, aught of that one without whom to go back to old things was misery, and to go on to new was mere weariness. And the dear little mother at home!—worth nine out of any ten of all this crowd—still at home in that old tavern-keeping life, now intolerable to think of, and still writing those yearning letters that bade the daughter not return! No wonder Marguerite's friend had divined her feelings, and drawn her out to the cool retreat under the shadow of the veranda lanterns.

A gentleman joined them, who had "just come," he said. Marguerite's companion and he were old friends. Neither he nor Marguerite heard each other's name, nor could see each other's face more than dimly. He was old enough to be twitted for bachelorhood, and to lay the blame upon an outdoor and out-of-town profession. Such words drew Marguerite's silent but close attention.

The talk turned easily from this to the ease with which the fair sex, as compared with the other, takes on the graces of the drawing-room. "Especially," the two older ones agreed, "if the previous lack is due merely to outward circumstances." But Marguerite was still. Here was a new thought. One who attained all those graces and love's prize also might at last, for love's sake, have to count them but dross, or carry them into retirement, the only trophies of abandoned triumphs. While she thought, the conversation went on.

"Yes," said her friend, replying to the bachelor, "we acquire drawing-room graces more easily; but why? Because most of us think we must. A man may find success in one direction or another; but a woman has got to be a social success, or she's a complete failure. She can't snap her fingers at the drawing-room."

"Ah!" exclaimed Marguerite, "she can if she want!" She felt the strength to rise that moment and go back to Opelousas, if only—and did not see, until her companions laughed straight at her, that the lady had spoken in jest.

"Still," said the bachelor, "the drawing-room is woman's element—realm—rather than man's, whatever the reasons may be. I had a young man with me last winter"—

"I knew it!" thought Marguerite.

"—until lately, in fact; he's here in town now,—whom I have tried once or twice to decoy into company in a small experimental

123

way. It's harder than putting a horse into a ship. He seems not to know what social interchange is for."

"Thinks it's for intellectual profit and pleasure," interrupted the ironical lady.

"No, he just doesn't see the use or fun of it. And yet, really, that's his only deficiency. True, he listens better than he talks—overdoes it; but when a chap has youth, intelligence, native refinement, integrity, and good looks, as far above the mean level as many of our society fellows are below it, it seems to me he ought to be"—

"Utilized," suggested the lady, casting her eyes toward Marguerite and withdrawing them as quickly, amused at the earnestness of her attention.

"Yes," said the bachelor, and mused a moment. "He's a talented fellow. It's only a few months ago that he really began life. Now he's outgrown my service."

"Left the nest," said the lady.

"Yes, indeed. He has invented"—

"Oh, dear!"

The bachelor was teased. "Ah! come, now; show your usual kindness; he has, really, made a simple, modest agricultural machine that—meets a want long felt. Oh! you may laugh; but he laughs last. He has not only a patent for it, but a good sale also, and is looking around for other worlds to conquer."

"And yet spurns society? Ours!"

"No, simply develops no affinity for it; would like to, if only to please me; but can't. Doesn't even make intimate companions among men; simply clings to his fond, lone father, and the lone father to him, closer than any pair of twin orphan girls that ever you saw. I don't believe any thing in life could divide them."

"Ah, don't you trust him! Man proposes, Cupid disposes. A girl will stick to her mother; but a man? Why, the least thing—a pair of blue eyes, a yellow curl"—

The bachelor gayly shook his head, and, leaning over with an air of secrecy, said: "A pair of blue eyes have shot him through and through, and a yellow curl is wound all round him from head to heel, and yet he sticks to his father."

"He can't live," said the lady. Marguerite's hand pressed her arm, and they rose. As the bachelor drew the light curtain of a long window aside, that they might pass in, the light fell upon Marguerite's face. It was entirely new to him. It seemed calm. Yet instantly the question smote him, "What have I done? what have I said?" She passed, and turned to give a parting bow. The light fell upon him. She was right; it was Claude's friend, the engineer.

When he came looking for them a few minutes later, he only caught, by chance, a glimpse of them, clouded in light wraps and passing to their carriage. It was not yet twelve.

Between Marguerite's chamber and that of one of the daughters of the family there was a door that neither one ever fastened. Somewhere down-stairs a clock was striking three in the morning, when this door softly opened and the daughter stole into Marguerite's room in her night-robe. With her hair falling about her, her hands unconsciously clasped, her eyes starting, and an outcry of amazement checked just within her open, rounded mouth, she stopped and stood an instant in the brightly lighted chamber.

Marguerite sat on the bedside exactly as she had come from the carriage, save that a white gossamer web had dropped from her head and shoulders, and lay coiled about her waist. Her tearless eyes were wide and filled with painful meditation, even when she turned to the alarmed and astonished girl before her. With suppressed exclamations of wonder and pity the girl glided forward, cast her arms about the sitting figure, and pleaded for explanation.

"It is a headache," said Marguerite, kindly but firmly lifting away the intwining arms.—"No, no, you can do nothing.—It is a headache.—Yes, I will go to bed presently; you go to yours.—No, no"—

The night-robed girl looked for a moment more into Marguerite's eyes, then sank to her knees, buried her face in her hands, and wept. Marguerite laid her hands upon the bowed head and looked down with dry eyes. "No," she presently said again, "it is a headache. Go back to your bed.—No, there is nothing to tell; only I have been very, very foolish and very, very selfish, and I am going home to-morrow. Good-night."

The door closed softly between the two. Then Marguerite sank slowly back upon the bed, closed her eyes, and rocking her head from side to side, said again and again, in moans that scarcely left the lips:

"My mother! my mother! Take me back! Oh! take me back, my mother! my mother!"

At length she arose, put off her attire, lay down to rest, and, even while she was charging sleep with being a thousand leagues away—slept.

When she awoke, the wide, bright morning filled all the room. Had some sound wakened her? Yes, a soft tapping came again upon her door. She lay still. It sounded once more. For all its softness, it seemed nervous and eager. A low voice came with it:

"Marguerite!"

She sprang from her pillow.—"Yes!"

125

While she answered, it came again,—

"Marguerite!"

With a low cry, she cast away the bed-coverings, threw back the white mosquito-curtain and the dark masses of her hair, and started up, lifted and opened her arms, cried again, but with joy, "My mother! my mother!" and clasped Zoséphine to her bosom.

## CHAPTER VIII

## THE SHAKING PRAIRIE

Manifestly it was a generous overstatement for Claude's professional friend to say that Claude had outgrown his service. It was true only that by and by there had come a juncture in his affairs where he could not, without injustice to others, make a place for Claude which he could advise Claude to accept, and they had parted with the mutual hope that the separation would be transient. But the surveyor could not but say to himself that such incidents, happening while we are still young, are apt to be turning-points in our lives, if our lives are going to have direction and movement of their own at all.

St. Pierre had belted his earnings about him under the woollen sash that always bound his waist, shouldered his rifle, taken one last, silent look at the cabin on Bayou des Acadiens, stood for a few moments with his hand in Bonaventure's above one green mound in the churchyard at Grande Pointe, given it into the schoolmaster's care, and had gone to join his son. Of course, not as an idler; such a perfect woodsman easily made himself necessary to the engineer's party. The company were sorry enough to lose him when Claude went away; but no temptation that they could invent could stay him from following Claude. Father and son went in one direction, and the camp in another.

I must confess to being somewhat vague as to just where they were. I should have to speak from memory, and I must not make another slip in topography. The changes men have made in Southern Louisiana these last few years are great. I say nothing, again, of the vast widths of prairie stripped of the herds and turned into corn and cane fields: when I came, a few months ago, to that

126

station on Morgan's Louisiana and Texas Railroad where Claude first went aboard a railway-train, somebody had actually moved the bayou, the swamp, and the prairie apart!

However, the exact whereabouts of the St. Pierres is not important to us. Mr. Tarbox, when in search of the camp he crossed the Teche at St. Martinville, expected to find it somewhere north-eastward, between that stream and the Atchafalaya. But at the Atchafalaya he found that the work in that region had been finished three days before, and that the party had been that long gone to take part in a new work down in the prairies tremblantes of Terrebonne Parish. The Louisiana Land Reclamation Company,—I think that was the name of the concern projecting the scheme. This was back in early February, you note.

Thither Mr. Tarbox followed. The "Album of Universal Information" went along, and "did well." It made his progress rather slow, of course; but one of Mr. Tarbox's many maxims was, never to make one day pay for another when it could be made to pay for itself, and during this season—this Louisiana campaign, as he called it—he had developed a new art,—making each day pay for itself several times over.

"Many of these people," he said,—but said it solely and silently to himself,—"are ignorant, shiftless, and set in their ways; and even when they're not they're out of the current, as it were; they haven't headway; and so they never—or seldom ever—see any way to make money except somehow in connection with the plantations. There's no end of chances here to a man that's got money-sense, and nerve to use it." He wrote that to Zoséphine, but she wrote no answer. A day rarely passed that he did not find  some man making needless loss through ignorance or inactivity; whereupon he would simply put in the sickle of his sharper wit, and garner the neglected harvest. Or, seeing some unesteemed commodity that had got out of, or had never been brought into, its best form, time, or place, he knew at sight just how, and at what expense, to bring it there, and brought it.

"Give me the gains other men pass by," he said, "and I'll be satisfied. The saying is, 'Buy wisdom;' but I sell mine. I like to sell. I enjoy making money. It suits my spirit of adventure. I like an adventure. And if there's any thing I love, it's an adventure with money in it! But even that isn't my chief pleasure: my chief pleasure's the study of human nature.

*'The proper study of mankind is man.*
*****

*Sole judge of truth, in endless error hurled,*
*The glory, jest, and riddle of the world.'"*

127

This spoiling of Assyrian camps, so to speak, often detained Mr. Tarbox within limited precincts for days at a time; but "Isn't that what time is for?" he would say to those he had been dealing with, as he finally snapped the band around his pocket-book; and they would respond, "Yes, that's so."

And then he would wish them a hearty farewell, while they were thinking that at least he might know it was his treat.

Thus it was the middle of February when at Houma, the parish seat of Terrebonne, he passed the last rootlet of railway, and, standing finally under the blossoming orange-trees of Terrebonne Bayou far down toward the Gulf, heard from the chief of the engineering party that Claude was not with him.

"He didn't leave us; we left him; and up to the time when we left he hadn't decided where he would go or what he would do. His father and he are together, you know, and of course that makes it harder for them to know just how to move."

The speaker was puzzled. What could this silk-hatted, cut-away-coated, empearled, free lance of a fellow want with Claude? He would like to find out. So he added, "I may get a letter from him to-morrow; suppose you stay with me until then." And, to his astonishment, Mr. Tarbox quickly jumped at the proposition.

No letter came. But when the twenty-four hours had passed, the surveyor had taken that same generous—not to say credulous—liking for Mr. Tarbox that we have seen him show for St. Pierre and for Claude. He was about to start on a tour of observation eastward through a series of short canals that span the shaking prairies from bayou to bayou, from Terrebonne to Lafourche, Lafourche to Des Allemands, so through Lake Ouacha into and up Barataria, again across prairie, and at length, leaving Lake Cataouaché on the left, through cypress-swamp to the Mississippi River, opposite New Orleans. He would have pressed Mr. Tarbox to bear him company; but before he could ask twice, Mr. Tarbox had consented. They went in a cat-rigged skiff, with a stalwart negro rowing or towing whenever the sail was not the best.

"It's all of sixty miles," said the engineer; "but if the wind doesn't change or drop we can sleep to-night in Achille's hut, send this man and skiff back, and make Achille, with his skiff, put us on board the Louisiana-avenue ferry-launch to-morrow afternoon."

"Who is Achille?"

"Achille? Oh! he's merely a 'Cajun pot-hunter living on a shell bank at the edge of Lake Cataouaché, with an Indian wife. Used to live somewhere on Bayou des Allemands, but last year something or other scared him away from there. He's odd—seems to be a sort of self-made outcast. I don't suppose he's ever done anybody any harm; but he just seems to be one of that kind that can't bear to even try to keep up with the rest of humanity; the sort of man swamps and shaking prairies were specially made for, you know. He's living right on top of a bank of fossil shells now,—thousands of barrels of them,—that he knows would bring him a little fortune if only he could command the intelligence and the courage to market them in New Orleans. There's a chance for some bright man who isn't already too busy. Why didn't I think to mention it to Claude? But then neither he nor his father have got the commercial knowledge they would need. Now"—The speaker suddenly paused, and, as the two men sat close beside each other under an umbrella in the stern of the skiff, looked into Mr. Tarbox's pale-blue eyes, and smiled, and smiled.

"I'm here," said Mr. Tarbox.

"Yes," responded the other, "and I've just made out why! And you're right, Tarbox; you and Claude, with or without his father, will make a strong team. You've got no business to be canvassing books, you"—

"It's my line," said the canvasser, smiling fondly and pushing his hat back,—it was wonderful how he kept that hat smooth,—"and I'm the head of the line:

'A voice replied far up the height,
Excelsior!'

I was acquainted with Mr. Longfellow."

"Tarbox," persisted the engineer, driving away his own smile, "you know what you are; you are a born contractor! You've found it out, and"—smiling again—"that's why you're looking for Claude."

"Where is he?" asked Mr. Tarbox.

"Well, I told you the truth when I said I didn't know; but I haven't a doubt he's in Vermilionville."

"Neither have I," said the book-agent; "and if I had, I wouldn't give it room. If I knew he was in New Jersey, still I'd think he was in Vermilionville, and go there looking for him. And wherefore? For occult reasons." The two men looked at each other smilingly in the eye, and the boat glided on.

The wind favored them. With only now and then the cordelle, and still more rarely the oars, they moved all day across the lands and waters that were once the fastnesses of the Baratarian pirates. The engineer made his desired observations without appreciable delays, and at night they slept under Achille's thatch of rushes.

As the two travellers stood alone for a moment next morning, the engineer said:

"You seem to be making a study of my pot-hunter."

129

"It's my natural instinct," replied Mr. Tarbox. "The study of human nature comes just as natural to me as it does to a new-born duck to scratch the back of its head with its hind foot; just as natural—and easier. The pot-hunter is a study; you're right."

"But he reciprocates," said the engineer; "he studies you."

The student of man held his smiling companion's gaze with his own, thrust one hand into his bosom, and lifted the digit of the other: "The eyes are called the windows of the soul,—

> *'And looks commercing with the skies,*
> *Thy rapt soul sitting in thine eyes.'*

"Have you tried to look into his eyes? You can't do it. He won't let you. He's got something in there that he doesn't want you to see."

In the middle of the afternoon, when Achille's skiff was already re-entering the shades of the swamp on his way homeward, and his two landed passengers stood on the levee at the head of Harvey's Canal with the Mississippi rolling by their feet and on its farther side the masts and spires of the city, lighted by the western sun, swinging round the long bend of her yellow harbor, Mr. Tarbox offered his hand to say good-by. The surveyor playfully held it.

"I mean no disparagement to your present calling," he said, "but the next time we meet I hope you'll be a contractor."

"Ah!" responded Tarbox, "it's not my nature. I cannot contract; I must always expand. And yet—I thank you.

> *'"Pure thoughts are angel visitors.*
> *Be such The frequent inmates of thy guileless breast.'*

"Good luck! Good-by!"

One took the ferry; the other, the west bound train at Gretna.

# CHAPTER IX

## NOT BLUE EYES, NOR YELLOW HAIR

When the St. Pierres found themselves really left with only each other's faces to look into, and the unbounded world around them, it was the father who first spoke:

"Well, Claude, where you t'ink 'better go?"

There had been a long, silent struggle in both men's minds. And now Claude heard with joy this question asked in English. To ask it in their old Acadian tongue would have meant retreat; this meant advance. And yet he knew his father yearned for Bayou des Acadiens. Nay, not his father; only one large part of his father's nature; the old, French, home-loving part.

What should Claude answer? Grande Pointe? Even for St. Pierre alone that was impossible. "Can a man enter a second time into his mother's womb?" No; the thatched cabin stood there,—stands there now; but, be he happy or unhappy, no power can ever make St. Pierre small enough again to go back into that shell. Let it stand, the lair of one of whom you may have heard, who has retreated straight backward from Grande Pointe and from advancing enlightenment and order,—the village drunkard, Chatoué.

Claude's trouble, then, was not that his father's happiness beckoned in one direction and his in another; but that his father's was linked on behind his. Could the father endure the atmosphere demanded by the son's widening power? Could the second nature of lifetime habits bear the change? Of his higher spirit there was no doubt. Neither father nor son had any conception of happiness separate from noble aggrandizement. Nay, that is scant justice; far more than they knew, or than St. Pierre, at least, would have acknowledged, they had caught the spirit of Bonaventure, to call it by no higher name, and saw that the best life for self is to live the best possible for others. "For all others," Bonaventure would have insisted; but "for Claude," St. Pierre would have amended. They could not return to Grande Pointe.

Where, then, should they go? Claude stood with his arms akimbo, looked into his father's face, tried to hide his perplexity under a smile, and then glanced at their little pile of effects. There lay their fire-arms, the same as ever; but the bundles in Madras handkerchiefs had given place to travelling-bags, and instead of pots and pans here were books and instruments. What reply did

131

these things make? New Orleans? The great city? Even Claude shrank from that thought.

No, it was the name of quite a different place they spoke; a name that Claude's lips dared not speak, because, for lo! these months and months his heart had spoken it,—spoken it at first in so soft a whisper that for a long time he had not known it was his heart he heard. When something within uttered and re-uttered the place's name, he would silently explain to himself: "It is because I am from home. It is this unfixed camp-life, this life without my father, without Bonaventure, that does it. This is not love, of course; I know that: for, in the first place, I was in love once, when I was fourteen, and it was not at all like this; and in the second place, it would be hopeless presumption in me, muddy-booted vagabond that I am; and in the third place, a burnt child dreads fire. And so it cannot be love. When papa and I are once more together, this unaccountable longing will cease."

But, instead of ceasing, it had grown. The name of the place was still the only word the heart would venture; but it meant always one pair of eyes, one young face, one form, one voice. Still it was not love—oh, no! Now and then the hospitality of some plantation-house near the camp was offered to the engineers; and sometimes, just to prove that this thing was not love, he would accept such an invitation, and even meet a pretty maiden or two, and ask them for music and song—for which he had well-nigh a passion—and talk enough to answer their questions and conjectures about a surveyor's life, etc.; but when he got back to camp, matters within his breast were rather worse than better.

He had then tried staying in camp, but without benefit,—nothing cured, every thing aggravated. And yet he knew so perfectly well that he was not in love, that just to realize the knowledge, one evening, when his father was a day's march ahead, and he was having a pleasant chat with the "chief," no one else nigh, and they were dawdling away its closing hour with pipes, metaphysics, psychology, and like trifles, which Claude, of course, knew all about,—Claude told him of this singular and amusing case of haunting fantasy in his own experience. His hearer had shown even more amusement than he, and had gone on smiling every now and then afterward, with a significance that at length drove Claude to bed disgusted with him and still more with himself. There had been one offsetting comfort; an unintentional implication had somehow slipped in between his words, that the haunting fantasy had blue eyes and yellow hair.

"All right," the angry youth had muttered, tossing on his iron couch, "let him think so!" And then he had tossed again, and said below his breath, "It is not love: it is not. But I must never answer its call; if I do, love is what it will be. My father, my father! would that I could give my whole heart to thee as thou givest all to me!"

God has written on every side of our nature,—on the mind, on the soul, yes, and in our very flesh,—the interdict forbidding love to have any one direction only, under penalty of being forever dwarfed. This Claude vaguely felt; but lacking the clear thought, he could only cry, "Oh, is it, is it, selfishness for one's heart just to be hungry and thirsty?"

And now here sat his father, on all their worldly goods, his rifle between his knees, waiting for his son's choice, and ready to make it his own. And here stood the son, free of foot to follow that voice which was calling to-day louder than ever before, but feeling assured that to follow it meant love without hope for him, and for this dear father the pain of yielding up the larger share of his son's heart,—as if love were subject to arithmetic!—yielding it to one who, thought Claude, cared less for both of them than for one tress of her black hair, one lash of her dark eyes. While he still pondered, the father spoke.

"Claude, I tell you!" his face lighted up with courage and ambition. "We better go—Mervilionville!"

Claude's heart leaped, but he kept his countenance. "Vermilionville? No, papa; you will not like Vermilionville."

"Yaas! I will like him. 'Tis good place! Bonaventure come from yondah. When I was leav' Gran' Point', Bonaventure, he cry, you know, like I tole you. He tell Sidonie he bringin' ed'cation at Gran' Point' to make Gran' Point' more better, but now ed'cation drive bes' men 'way from Gran' Point'. And den he say, 'St. Pierre, may bee you go Mervilionville; dat make me glad,' he say: 'dat way,' he say, 'what I rob Peter I pay John.' Where we go if dawn't go Mervilionville? St. Martinville, Opelousas, New Iberia? Too many Creole yondah for me. Can't go to city; city too big to live in. Why you dawn't like Mervilionville? You write me letter, when you was yondah, you like him fus' class!"

Claude let silence speak consent. He stooped, and began to load himself with their joint property. He had had, in his life, several sorts of trouble of mind; but only just now at twenty was he making the acquaintance of his conscience. Vermilionville was the call that had been sounding within him all these months, and Marguerite was the haunting fantasy.

# CHAPTER X

## A STRONG TEAM

I would not wish to offend the self-regard of Vermilionville. But—what a place in which to seek enlargement of life! I know worth and greatness have sometimes, not to say ofttimes, emerged from much worse spots; from little lazy villages, noisy only on Sunday, with grimier court-houses, deeper dust and mud, their trade more entirely in the hands of rat-faced Isaacs and Jacobs, with more frequent huge and solitary swine slowly scavenging about in abysmal self-occupation, fewer vine-clad cottages, raggeder negroes, and more decay. Vermilionville is not the worst, at all. I have seen large, and enlarging, lives there.

Hither came the two St. Pierres. "No," Claude said; "they would not go to the Beausoleil house." Privately he would make himself believe he had not returned to any thing named Beausoleil, but only and simply to Vermilionville. On a corner opposite the public square there was another "hotel;" and it was no great matter to them if it was mostly pine-boards, pale wall-paper, and transferable whitewash. But, not to be outdone by its rival round the corner, it had, besides, a piano, of a quality you may guess, and a landlady's daughter who seven times a day played and sang "I want to be somebody's darling," and had no want beyond. The travellers turned thence, found a third house full, conjectured the same of the only remaining one, and took their way, after all, towards Zoséphine's. It was quite right, now, to go there, thought Claude, since destiny led; and so he let it lead both his own steps and the thrumping boots of this dear figure in Campeachy hat and soft untrimmed beard, that followed ever at his side.

And then, after all!—looking into those quiet black eyes of Zoséphine's,—to hear that Marguerite was not there! Gone! Gone to the great city, the place "too big to live in." Gone there for knowledge, training, cultivation, larger life, and finer uses! Gone to study an art,—an art! Risen beyond him "like a diamond in the sky." And he fool enough to come rambling back, blue-shirted and brown-handed, expecting to find her still a tavern maid! So, farewell fantasy! 'Twas better so; much better. Now life was simplified. Oh, yes; and St. Pierre made matters better still by saying to Zoséphine:

"I dinn' know you got one lill gal. Claude never tell me 'bout dat. I spec' dat why he dawn't want 'come yeh. He dawn't like gal; he run f'om 'em like dog from yalla-jacket. He dawn't like none of 'm.

What he like, dass his daddy. He jus' married to his daddy." The father dropped his hand, smilingly, upon his son's shoulder with a weight that would have crushed it in had it been ordinary cast-iron.

Claude took the hand and held it, while Zoséphine smiled and secretly thanked God her child was away. In her letters to Marguerite she made no haste to mention the young man's re-appearance, and presently a small thing occurred that made it well that she had left it untold.

With Claude and his father some days passed unemployed. Yet both felt them to be heavy with significance. The weight and pressure of new and, to them, large conditions, were putting their inmost quality to proof. Claude saw, now, what he could not see before; why his friend the engineer had cast him loose without a word of advice as to where he should go or what he should do. It was because by asking no advice he had really proposed to be his own master. And now, could he do it? Dare he try it?

The first step he took was taken, I suppose, instinctively rather than intelligently; certainly it was perilous: he retreated into himself. St. Pierre found work afield, for of this sort there was plenty; the husbandmen's year, and the herders' too, were just gathering good momentum. But Claude now stood looking on empty-handed where other men were busy with agricultural utensils or machines; or now kept his room, whittling out a toy miniature of some apparatus, which when made was not like the one he had seen, at last. A great distress began to fill the father's mind. There had been a time when he could be idle and whittle, but that time was gone by; that was at Grande Pointe; and now for his son—for Claude—to become a lounger in tavern quarters—Claude had not announced himself to Vermilionville as a surveyor, or as any thing—Claude to be a hater of honest labor—was this what Bonaventure called civilize-ation? Better, surely better, go back to the old pastoral life. How yearningly it was calling them to its fragrant bosom! And almost every thing was answering the call. The town was tricking out its neglected decay with great trailing robes of roses. The spade and hoe were busy in front flower-beds and rear kitchen-gardens. Lanes were green, skies blue, roads good. In the bas fonds the oaks of many kinds and the tupelo-gums were hiding all their gray in shimmering green; in these coverts and in the reedy marshes, all the feathered flocks not gone away north were broken into nesting pairs; in the fields, crops were springing almost at the sower's heels; on the prairie pastures, once so vast, now being narrowed so rapidly by the people's thrift, the flocks and herds ate eagerly of the bright new grass, and foals, calves, and lambs stood and staggered on their first legs, while in the door-yards housewives, hens, and mother-geese warned away the puppies and children from downy broods under the shade of the China-trees. But Claude? Even his books lay unstudied, and his instruments gathered dust, while he pottered over two or three little wooden things that a boy could not play with without breaking. At last St. Pierre could bear it no longer.

"Well, Claude, dass ten days han'-runnin' now, we ain't do not'in' but whittlin'."

Claude slowly pushed his model from him, looked, as one in a dream, into his father's face, and suddenly and for the first time saw what that father had suffered for a fortnight. But into his own face there came no distress; only, for a moment, a look of tender protestation, and then strong hope and confidence.

"Yass," he said, rising, "dass true. But we dawn't got whittle no mo'." He pointed to the model, then threw his strong arms akimbo and asked, "You know what is dat?"

"Naw," replied the father, "I dunno. I t'ink 'taint no real mash-in' machine 'cause I dawn't never see nuttin' like dat at Belle Alliance plant-ation, neider at Belmont; and I know, me, if anybody got one mash-in', any place, for do any t'in' mo' betteh or mo' quicker, Mistoo Walleece an' M'sieu Le Bourgeois dey boun' to 'ave 'im. Can't hitch nuttin' to dat t'ing you got dare; she too small for a rat. What she is, Claude?"

A yet stronger hope and courage lighted Claude's face. He laid one hand upon the table before him and the other upon the shoulder of his sitting companion:

"Papa, if you want to go wid me to de city, we make one big enough for two mule'. Dass a mash-in'—a new mash-in'—my mash-in'—my invention!"

"Invench? What dat is—invench?"

Some one knocked on the door. Claude lifted the model, moved on tiptoe, and placed it softly under the bed. As he rose and turned again with reddened face, a card was slipped under the door. He took it and read, in a pencil scrawl,—

"State Superintendent of Public Education,"—

looked at his father with a broad grin, and opened the door.

Mr. Tarbox had come at the right moment. There was a good hour and a half of the afternoon still left, and he and Claude took a walk together. Beyond a stile and a frail bridge that spanned a gully at one end of the town, a noble avenue of oaks leads toward Vermilion River. On one side of this avenue the town has since begun to spread, but at that time there were only wide fields on the right hand and on the left. At the farther end a turn almost at right angles to the left takes you through a great gate and across the

136

railway, then along a ruined hedge of roses, and presently into the oak-grove of the old ex-governor's homestead. This was their walk.

By the time they reached the stile, Claude had learned that his friend was at the head of his line, and yet had determined to abandon that line for another

> *"Far up the height—*
> *Excelsior!"*

Also that his friend had liked him, had watched him, would need him, and was willing then and there to assure him a modest salary, whose amount he specified, simply to do whatever he might call upon him to do in his (Claude's) "line."

They were walking slowly, and now and then slower still. As they entered the avenue of oaks, Claude declined the offer. Then they went very slowly indeed. Claude learned that Mr. Tarbox, by some chance not explained, had been in company with his friend the engineer; that the engineer had said, "Tarbox, you're a born contractor," and that Claude and he would make a "strong team;" that Mr. Tarbox's favorite study was human nature; that he knew talent when he saw it; had studied Claude; had fully expected him to decline to be his employee, and liked him the better for so doing.

"That was just a kind of test vote; see?"

Then Mr. Tarbox offered Claude a partnership; not an equal one, but withal a fair interest.

"We've got to commence small and branch out gradually; see?" And Claude saw.

"Now, you wonder why I don't go in alone. Well, I'll tell you; and when I tell you, I'll astonish you. I lack education! Now, Claude, I'm taking you into my confidence. You've done nothing but go to school and study for about six years. I had a different kind of father from yours; I never got one solid year's schooling, all told, in my life. I've picked up cords of information, but an ounce of education's worth a ton of information. Don't you believe that? eh? it is so! I say it, and I'm the author of the A. of U. I. I like to call it that, because it brings you and I so near together; see?" The speaker smiled, was still, and resumed:

"That's why I need you. And I'm just as sure you need me. I need not only the education you have now, but what you're getting every day. When you see me you see a man who is always looking awa-a-ay ahead. I see what you're going to be, and I'm making this offer to the Claude St. Pierre of the future."

Mr. Tarbox waited for a reply. The avenue had been passed, the railway crossed, and the hedge skirted. They loitered slowly into the governor's grove, under whose canopy the beams of the late

137

afternoon sun were striking and glancing. But all their light seemed hardly as much as that which danced in the blue eyes of Mr. Tarbox while Claude slowly said:

"I dunno if we can fix dat. I was glad to see you comin'. I reckon you jus' right kind of man I want. I jus' make a new invention. I t'ink 'f you find dat's good, dat be cawntrac' enough for right smart while. And beside', I t'ink I invent some mo' b'fo' long."

But Mr. Tarbox was not rash. He only asked quiet and careful questions for some time. The long sunset was sending its last rays across the grove-dotted land, and the birds in every tree were filling the air with their sunset song-burst, when the two friends re-entered the avenue of oaks. They had agreed to join their fortunes. Now their talk drifted upon other subjects.

"I came back to Vermilionville purposely to see you," said Mr. Tarbox. "But I'll tell you privately, you wasn't the only cause of my coming."

Claude looked at him suddenly. Was this another haunted man? Were there two men haunted, and only one fantasy? He felt ill at ease. Mr. Tarbox saw, but seemed not to understand. He thought it best to speak plainly.

"I'm courting her, Claude; and I think I'm going to get her."

Claude stopped short, with jaws set and a bad look in his eye.

"Git who?"

But Mr. Tarbox was calm—even complacent. He pushed his silk hat from his forehead, and said:

> ... "'One made up
> Of loveliness alone;
> A woman, of her gentle sex
> The seeming paragon.'

I refer to the Rose of Vermilionville, the Pearl of the Parish, the loveliest love and fairest fair that ever wore the shining name of Beausoleil. She's got to change it to Tarbox, Claude. Before yon sun has run its course again, I'm going to ask her for the second time. I've just begun asking, Claude; I'm going to keep it up till she says yes."

"She's not yondah!" snarled Claude, with the frown and growl of a mastiff. "She's gone to de city."

Mr. Tarbox gazed a moment in blank amazement. Then he slowly lifted his hat from his head, expanded his eyes, drew a long slow groan, turned slowly half around, let the inhalation go in a long keen whistle, and cried:

"Oh! taste! taste! Who's got the taste? What do you take me

for? Who are you talking about? That little monkey? Why, man alive, it's the mother I'm after. Ha, ha, ha!"

If Claude said any thing in reply, I cannot imagine what it was. Mr. Tarbox had a right to his opinion and taste, if taste it could be called, and Claude was helpless to resent it, even in words; but for hours afterward he execrated his offender's stupidity, little guessing that Mr. Tarbox, in a neighboring chamber, alone and in his night-robe, was bending, smiting his thigh in silent merriment, and whispering to himself:

"He thinks I'm an ass! He thinks I'm an ass! He can't see that I was simply investigating him!"

# CHAPTER XI

## HE ASKS HER AGAIN

Claude and his father left the next day,—Saturday. Only the author of the A. of U. I. knew whither they were gone. As they were going he said very privately to Claude:

"I'll be with you day after to-morrow. You can't be ready for me before then, and you and your father can take Sunday to look around, and kind o' see the city. But don't go into the down-town part; you'll not like it; nothing but narrow streets and old buildings with histories to 'em, and gardens hid away inside of 'em, and damp archways, and pagan-looking females who can't talk English, peeping out over balconies that offer to drop down on you, and then don't keep their word; every thing old-timey, and Frenchy, and Spanishy; unprogressive—you wouldn't like it. Go up-town. That's American. It's new and fresh. There you'll find beautiful mansions, mostly frame, it's true, but made to look like stone, you know. There you'll see wealth! There you'll get the broad daylight—

*'The merry, merry sunshine, that makes the heart so gay.'*

See? Yes, and Monday we'll meet at Jones's, 17 Tchoupitoulas Street; all right; I'll be on hand. But to-day and to-morrow— 'Alabama'—'here I rest.' I feel constrained"—he laid his hand upon his heart, closed one eye, and whispered—"to stay. I would fain spend the sabbath in sweet Vermilionville. You get my idea?"

139

The sabbath afternoon, beyond the town, where Mr. Tarbox strolled, was lovelier than can be told. Yet he was troubled. Zoséphine had not thus far given him a moment alone. I suppose, when a hundred generations more have succeeded us on the earth, lovers will still be blind to the fact that women do not do things our way. How can they? That would be capitulation at once, and even we should find the whole business as stupid as shooting barnyard fowls.

Zoséphine had walked out earlier than Tarbox. He had seen her go, but dared not follow. He read "thou shalt not" as plain as print on her back as she walked  quietly away; that same little peremptory back that once in her father's calèche used to hold itself stiff when 'Thanase rode up behind. The occasional townsman that lifted his slouch hat in deep deference to her silent bow, did not read unusual care on her fair brow; yet she, too, was troubled.

Marguerite! she was the trouble. Zoséphine knew her child could never come back to these old surroundings and be content. The mother was not willing she should. She looked at a photograph that her daughter had lately sent her. What a change from the child that had left her! It was like the change from a leaf to a flower. There was but one thing to do: follow her. So Zoséphine had resolved to sell the inn. She was gone, now, to talk with the old ex-governor about finding a purchaser. Her route was not by the avenue of oaks, but around by a northern and then eastern circuit. She knew Mr. Tarbox must have seen her go; had a genuine fear that he would guess whither she was bound, and yet, deeper down in her heart than woman ever lets soliloquy go, was willing he should. For she had another trouble. We shall come to that presently.

Her suitor walked in the avenue of oaks.

"She's gone," he reckoned to himself, "to consult the governor about something, and she'll come back this way." He loitered out across fields, but not too far off or out of sight; and by and by there she came, with just the slightest haste in her walk. She received him with kindly reserve, and they went more slowly, together.

She told where she had been, and that the governor approved a decision she had made.

"Yass; I goin' sell my hotel."

"He's right!" exclaimed her companion, with joy; "and you're right!"

"Well, 'tain't sold yet," she responded. She did not smile as she looked at him. He read trouble; some trouble apart from the subject, in her quiet, intense eyes.

"You know sombodie want buy dat?" she asked.

140

"I'll find some one," he promptly replied. Then they talked a little about the proper price for it, and then were very still until Mr. Tarbox said:

"I walked out here hoping to meet you."

Madame Beausoleil looked slightly startled, and then bowed gravely.

"Yes; I want your advice. It's only business, but it's important, and it's a point where a woman's instinct is better than a man's judgment."

There was some melancholy satire in her responding smile; but it passed away, and Mr. Tarbox went on:

"You never liked my line of business"—

Zoséphine interrupted with kind resentment:

"Ah!"

"No; I know you didn't. You're one of the few women whose subscription I've sought in vain. Till then I loved my business. I've never loved it since. I've decided to sell out and quit. I'm going into another business, one that you'll admire. I don't say any thing about the man going into it,—

'Honor and shame from no condition rise:
Act well your part; there all the honor lies,'—

but I want your advice about the party I think of going in with. It's Claude St. Pierre."

Zoséphine turned upon the speaker a look of steady penetration. He met it with a glance of perfect confiding. "She sees me," he said, at the same time, far within himself.

It was as natural to Mr. Tarbox to spin a web as it is for a spider. To manœuvre was the profoundest instinct of his unprofound nature. Zoséphine felt the slender threads weaving around her. But in her heart of hearts there was a certain pleasure in being snared. It could not, to her, seem wholly bad for Tarbox to play spider, provided he should play the harmless spider. Mr. Tarbox spoke again, and she listened amiably.

"Claude is talented. He has what I haven't; I have what he hasn't, and together we could make each other's fortunes, if he's only the square, high-style fellow I think he is. I'm a student of human nature, and I think I've made him out. I think he'll do to tie to. But will he? You can tell me. You read people by instinct. I ask you just as a matter of business advice and in business confidence. What do you think? Will you trust me and tell me—as my one only trusted friend—freely and fully—as I would tell you?"

Madame Beausoleil felt the odds against her, but she looked

141

into her companion's face with bright, frank eyes and said: "Yass, I t'ink yass; I t'ink 'tis so."

"Thanks!" said her friend, with unnecessary fervor and tenderness. "Then Claude will be my partner, unless—my dear friend, shall you be so kind—I might almost say confiding—to me, and me not tell you something I think you'd ought to know? For I hope we are always to be friends; don't you?"

"Yass," she said, very sadly and sweetly.

"Thanks! And if Claude and I become partners that will naturally bring him into our circle, as it were; see?"

The little madame looked up with a sudden austere exaltation of frame and intensity of face, but her companion rushed on with— "And I'm going to tell you, let the risk to me be what it may, that it may result in great unhappiness to Claude; for he loves your daughter, who, I know, you must think too good for him!"

Madame Beausoleil blushed as though she herself were Marguerite and Tarbox were Claude.

"Ah! love Marguerite! Naw, naw! He dawn't love noboddie but hees papa! Hees papa tell me dat! Ah! naw, 'tis not so!"

Mr. Tarbox stopped still; and when Zoséphine saw they were in the shadow of the trees while all about them was brightened by the momentary Southern twilight, she, too, stopped, and he spoke.

"What brought Claude back here when by right he should have gone straight to the city? You might have guessed it when you saw him." He paused to let her revolve the thought, and added in his own mind—"If you had disliked the idea, you'd 'a' suspected him quick enough"—and was pleased. He spoke again. "But I didn't stop with guessing."

Zoséphine looked up to his face from the little foot that edgewise was writing nothings in the dust.

"No," continued her companion: "I walked with him two evenings ago in this avenue, and right where we stand now, without his ever knowing it—then or now—he as good as told me. Yes, Josephine, he dares to love your beautiful and accomplished daughter! The thought may offend you, but—was I not right to tell you?"

She nodded and began to move slowly on, he following.

"I'm not betraying anyone's confidence," persisted he; "and I can't help but have a care for you. Not that you need it, or anybody's. You can take care of yourself if any man or woman can. Every time your foot touches the ground it says so as plain as words. That's what first caught my fancy. You haven't got to have somebody to take care of you. O Josephine! that's just why I want to take care of you so bad! I can take care of myself, and I used to like to do it; I was just that selfish and small; but love's widened me. I can take care of myself; but, oh! what satisfaction is there in it? Is there any? Now, I ask you! It may do for you, for you're worth taking care of; but I want to take care of something I needn't be ashamed to love!" He softly stole her hand as they went. She let it stay, yet looked away from him, up through the darkling branches, and distressfully shook her head.

"Don't, Josephine!—don't do that. I want you to take care of me. You could do better, I know, if love wasn't the count; but when it comes to loving you, I'm the edition deloox! I know you've an aspiring nature, but so have I; and I believe with you to love and you loving me, and counselling and guiding me, I could climb high. O Josephine! it isn't this poor Tarbox I'm asking you to give yourself to; it's the Tarbox that is to be; it's the coming Tarbox! Why, it's even a good business move! If it wasn't I wouldn't say a word! You know I can, and will take the very best care of every thing you've got; and I know you'll take the same of mine. It's a good move, every way. Why, here's every thing just fixed for it! Listen to the mocking-bird! See him yonder, just at the right of the stile. See! O Josephine! don't you see he isn't

*'Still singing where the weeping willow waves'?*

he's on the myrtle; the myrtle, Josephine, and the crape-myrtle at that!—widowhood unwidowed!—Now he's on the fence—but he'll not stay there,—and you mustn't either!" The suitor smiled at his own ludicrousness, yet for all that looked beseechingly in earnest. He stood still again, continuing to hold her hand. She stole a furtive glance here and there for possible spectators. He smiled again.

"You don't see anybody; the world waives its claim." But there was such distress in her face that his smile passed away, and he made a new effort to accommodate his suit to her mood. "Josephine, there's no eye on us except it's overhead. Tell me this; if he that was yours until ten years ago was looking down now and could speak to us, don't you believe he'd say yes?"

"Oh! I dunno. Not to-day! Not dis day!" The widow's eyes met his gaze of tender inquiry and then sank to the ground. She shook her head mournfully. "Naw, naw; not dis day. 'Tis to-day 'Thanase was kill'!"

Mr. Tarbox relaxed his grasp and Zoséphine's hand escaped. She never had betrayed to him so much distress as filled her face now. "De man what kill' him git away! You t'ink I git marrie' while dat man alive? Ho-o-o! You t'ink I let Marguerite see me do dat! Ah! naw!" She waved him away and turned to leave the spot, but he

143

pressed after, and she paused once more. A new possibility lighted his eyes. He said eagerly:

"Describe the man to me. Describe him. How tall was he? How old would he be now? Did they try to catch him? Did you hear me talking yesterday about a man? Is there any picture of him? Have you got one? Yes, you have; it's in your pocket now with your hand on it. Let me see it."

"Ah! I di'n' want you to see dat!"

"No, I don't suppose, as far as you know yourself, you did." He received it from her, and with his eyes still on her, continued: "No, but you knew that if I got a ghost of a chance, I'd see you alone. You knew what I'd ask you;—yes, you did, Josephine, and you put this thing into your pocket to make it easier to say no."

"Hah! easier! Hah! easier! I need somethin' to help me do dat? Hah! 'Tis not so!" But the weakness of the wordy denial was itself almost a confession.

They moved on. A few steps brought them into better light. Mr. Tarbox looked at the picture. Zoséphine saw a slight flash of recognition. He handed it back in silence, and they walked on, saying not a word until they reached the stile. But there, putting his foot upon it to bar the way, he said:

"Josephine, the devil never bid so high for me before in his life as he's bidding for me now. And there's only one thing in the way; he's bid too late."

Her eyes flashed with injured resentment. "Ah, you! you dawn't know not'n'—" But he interrupted:

"Stop, I don't mean more than just what I say. Six years ago— six and a half—I met a man of a kind I'd never met, to know it, before. You know who' I mean, don't you?"

"Bonaventure?"

"Yes. That meeting made a turning-point in my life. You've told me that whatever is best in you, you owe to him. Well, knowing him as I do, I can believe it; and if it's true, then it's the same with me; for first he, and then you, have made another man out of me."

"Ah, naw! Bonaventure, maybe; but not me; ah, naw!"

"But I tell you, yes! you, Josephine! I'm poor sort enough yet; but I could have done things once that I can't do now. There was a time when if some miserable outlaw stood, or even seemed, maybe, to stand between me and my chances for happiness, I could have handed him over to human justice, so called, as easy as wink; but now? No, never any more! Josephine, I know that man whose picture I've just looked at. I could see you avenged. I could lay my hands, and the hands of the law, on him inside of twenty-four

144

hours. You say you can't marry till the law has laid its penalties on him, or at least while he lives and escapes them. Is that right?"

Zoséphine had set her face to oppose his words only with unyielding silence, but the answer escaped her:

"Yass, 'tis so. 'Tis ri-ght!"

"No, Josephine. I know you feel as if it were; but you don't think so. No, you don't; I know you better in this matter than you know yourself, and you don't think it's right. You know justice belongs to the State, and that when you talk to yourself about what you owe to justice, it means something else that you're too sweet and good to give the right name to, and still want it. You don't want it; you don't want revenge, and here's the proof; for, Josephine, you know, and I know, that if I—even without speaking—with no more than one look of the eye—should offer to buy your favor at that price, even ever so lawfully, you'd thank me for one minute, and then loathe me to the end of your days."

Zoséphine's face had lost its hardness. It was drawn with distress. With a gesture of repulsion and pain she exclaimed:

"I di'n' mean—I di'n' mean—Ah!"

"What? private revenge? No, of course you didn't! But what else would it be? O Josephine! don't I know you didn't mean it? Didn't I tell you so? But I want you to go farther. I want you to put away forever the feeling. I want to move and stand between you and it, and say—whatever it costs me to say it—'God forbid!' I do say it; I say it now. I can't say more; I can't say less; and somehow,—I don't know how—wherever you learned it—I've learned it from you."

Zoséphine opened her lips to refuse; but they closed and tightened upon each other, her narrowed eyes sent short flashes out upon his, and her breath came and went long and deep without sound. But at his last words she saw—the strangest thing—to be where she saw it—a tear—tears—standing in his eyes; saw them a moment, and then could see them no more for her own. Her lips relaxed, her form drooped, she lifted her face to reply, but her mouth twitched; she could not speak.

"I'm not so foolish as I look," he said, trying to smile away his emotion. "If the State chooses to hunt him out and put him to trial and punishment, I don't say I'd stand in the way; that's the State's business; that's for the public safety. But it's too late—you and Bonnyventure have made it too late—for me to help any one, least of all the one I love, to be revenged." He saw his words were prevailing and followed them up. "Oh! you don't need it any more than you really want it, Josephine. You mustn't ever look toward it again. I throw myself and my love across the path. Don't walk over us. Take my hand; give me yours; come another way; and if you'll let such a

145

poor excuse for a teacher and guide help you, I'll help you all I can, to learn to say 'forgive us our trespasses.' You can begin, now, by forgiving me. I may have thrown away my last chance with you, but I can't help it; it's my love that spoke. And if I have spoiled all and if I've got to pay for the tears you're shedding with the greatest disappointment of my life, still I've had the glory and the sanctification of loving you. If I must say, I can say,

> 'Tis better to have loved and lost
> Than never to have loved at all.'

Must I? Are you going to make me say that?"

Zoséphine, still in tears, silently and with drooping head pushed her way across the stile and left him standing on the other side. He sent one pleading word after her:

"Isn't it most too late to go the rest of the way alone?"

She turned, lifted her eyes to his for an instant, and nodded. In a twinkling he was at her side. She glanced at him again and said quite contentedly:

"Yass; 'tis so," and they went the short remnant of the way together.

# CHAPTER XII

## THE BEAUSOLEILS AND ST. PIERRES

You think of going to New Orleans in the spring. Certainly, the spring is the time to go. When you find yourself there go some day for luncheon—if they haven't moved it, there is talk of that,—go to the Christian Women's Exchange, already mentioned, in the Rue Bourbon,—French Quarter. You step immediately from the sidewalk into the former drawing-room of a house built early in the century as a fashionable residence. That at least is its aspect. Notice, for instance, in the back parlor, crowded now, like the front one, with eating-tables, a really interesting old wooden mantelpiece. Of course this is not the way persons used to go in old times. They entered by the porte-cochère and open carriage-way upon which these drawing-rooms still open by several glass doors on your right. Step out there. You find a veranda crowded with neat white-clothed

146

tables. Before some late alterations there was a great trellis full of green sunshine and broken breezes entangled among vines of trumpet-creeper and the Scuppernong grape. Here you will be waited on, by small, blue-calico-robed damsels of Methodist unsophistication and Presbyterian propriety, to excellent refreshment; only, if you know your soul's true interest, eschew their fresh bread and insist on having yesterday's.

However, that is a matter of taste there, and no matter at all here. All I need to add is that there are good apartments overhead to be rented to women too good for this world, and that in the latter end of April, 1884, Zoséphine and Marguerite Beausoleil here made their home.

The tavern was sold. The old life was left far behind. They had done that dreadful thing that everybody deprecates and everybody likes to do—left the country and come to live in the city. And Zoséphine was well pleased. A man who had tried and failed to be a merchant in the city, he and his wife, took the tavern; so Zoséphine had not reduced the rural population—had not sinned against "stastistics."

Besides, she had the good conscience of having fled from Mr. Tarbox—put U. and I. apart, as it were—and yet without being so hid but a suitor's proper persistency could find her. Just now he was far away prosecuting the commercial interests of Claude's one or two inventions; but he was having great success; he wrote once or twice—but got no reply—and hoped to be back within a month.

When Marguerite, after her mother's receipt of each of these letters, thought she saw a cloud on her brow, Zoséphine explained, with a revival of that old look of sweet self-command which the daughter so loved to see, that they contained matters of business not at all to be called troubles. But the little mother did not show the letters. She could not; Marguerite did not even know their writer had changed his business. As to Claude, his name was never mentioned. Each supposed the other was ignorant that he was in the city, and because he was never mentioned each one knew the other was thinking of him.

Ah, Claude! what are you thinking of? Has not your new partner in business told you they are here? No, not a word of it. "That'll keep till I get back," Mr. Tarbox had said to himself; and such shrewdness was probably not so ungenerous, after all. "If you want a thing done well, do it yourself," he said one evening to a man who could not make out what he was driving at; and later Mr. Tarbox added to himself, "The man that flies the kite must hold the thread." And so he kept his counsel.

But that does not explain. For we remember that Claude

already knew that Marguerite was in the city, at least had her own mother's word for it. Here, weeks had passed. New Orleans is not so large; its active centre is very small. Even by accident, on the street, Canal Street especially, he should have seen her time and again.

And he did not; at any rate not to know it. She really kept very busy indoors; and in other doors so did he. More than that, there was his father. When the two first came to the city St. Pierre endured the town for a week. But it was martyrdom, doing it. Claude saw this. Mr. Tarbox was with him the latter part of the week. He saw it. He gave his suggestive mind to it for one night. The next day St. Pierre and he wandered off in street-cars and on foot, and by the time the sun went down again a new provision had been made. At about ninety minutes' jaunt from the city's centre, up the river, and on its farther shore, near where the old "Company Canal" runs from a lock in the river bank, back through the swamps and into the Baratarian lakes, St. Pierre had bought with his lifetime savings a neat house and fair-sized orangery. No fields? None:

"You see, bom-bye [by-and-by] Claude git doze new mash-in' all right, he go to ingineerin' agin, and him and you [Tarbox] be takin' some cawntrac' for buil' levee or break up old steamboat, or raise somet'in' what been sunk, or somet'in' dat way. And den he certain' want somboddie to boss gang o' fellows. And den he say, 'Papa, I want you.' And den I say how I got fifty arpent' [42 acres] rice in field. And den he say, 'How I goin' do widout you?' And den dare be fifty arpent' rice gone!" No, no fields.

Better: here with the vast wet forest at his back; the river at his feet; the canal, the key to all Barataria, Lafourche, and Terrebonne, full of Acadian fishermen, hunters, timber-cutters, moss-gatherers, and the like; the great city in sight from yonder neighbor's balustraded house-top; and Claude there to rally to his side or he to Claude's at a moment's warning; he would be an operator—think of that!—not of the telegraph; an operator in the wild products of the swamp, the prairies tremblantes, the lakes, and in the small harvests of the pointes and bayou margins: moss, saw-logs, venison, wild-duck, fish, crabs, shrimp, melons, garlic, oranges, Périque tobacco. "Knowledge is power;" he knew wood, water, and sky by heart, spoke two languages, could read and write, and understood the ways and tastes of two or three odd sorts of lowly human kind. Self-command is dominion; I do not say the bottle went never to his lips, but it never was lifted high. And now to the blessed maxim gotten from Bonaventure he added one given him by Tarbox: "In h-union ees strank!" Not mere union of hands alone; but of counsels! There were Claude and Tarbox and he!

For instance; at Mr. Tarbox's suggestion Claude brought to his father from the city every evening, now the "Picayune" and now the "Times-Democrat." From European and national news he modestly turned aside. Whether he read the book-notices I do not know; I hope not. But when he had served supper—he was a capital camp cook—and he and Claude had eaten, and their pipes were lighted, you should have seen him scanning the latest quotations and debating the fluctuations of the moss market, the shrimp market, and the garlic market.

Thus Claude was rarely in the city save in the busy hours of the day. Much oftener than otherwise, he saw the crimson sunsets, and the cool purple sunrises as he and St. Pierre pulled in the father's skiff diagonally to or fro across the Mississippi, between their cottage and the sleepy outposts of city street-cars, just under the levee at the edge of that green oak-dotted plain where a certain man, as gentle, shy, and unworldly as our engineer friend thought Claude to be, was raising the vast buildings of the next year's Universal Exposition.

But all this explains only why Claude did not, to his knowledge, see Marguerite by accident. Yet by intention! Why not by intention? First, there was his fear of sinning against his father's love. That alone might have failed to hold him back; but, second, there was his helplessness. Love made Tarbox, if any thing were needed to make him, brave; it made Claude a coward. And third, there was that helpless terror of society in general, of which we have heard his friend talk. I have seen a strong horse sink trembling to the earth at the beating of an empty drum. Claude looked with amazed despair at a man's ability to overtake a pretty girl acquaintance in Canal Street, and walk and talk with her. He often asked himself how he had ever been a moment at his ease those November evenings in the tavern's back-parlor at Vermilionville. It was because he had a task there; sociality was not the business of the hour.

And now I have something else to confess about Claude; something mortifying in the extreme. For you see the poverty of all these explanations. Their very multitude makes them weak. "Many fires cannot quench love;" what was the real matter? I will tell.

Claude's love was a deep sentiment. He had never allowed it to assert itself as a passion. The most he would allow it to be was a yearning. It was scarcely personal. While he was with Marguerite, in the inn, his diffidence alone was enough to hide from him the impression she was making on his heart. In all their intercourse he had scarcely twice looked her full in the face. Afterward she had simply become in memory the exponent of an ideal. He found himself often, now, asking himself, why are my eyes always looking for her? Should I actually know her, were I to see her on this sidewalk, or in this street-car? And while still asking himself these silent questions, what does he do one day but fall—to all intents and purposes, at least—fall in love—pell-mell—up to the eyebrows—with another girl!

Do you remember Uncle Remus's story of Brer Rabbit with the bucket of honey inverted on him? It was the same way with Claude. "He wa'n't des only bedobble wid it, he wuz des kiver'd." It happened thus: An artist friend, whose studio was in Carondelet Street just off of Canal, had rented to him for a workroom a little loft above the studio. It had one window looking out over roofs and chimney-pots upon the western sky, and another down into the studio itself. It is right to say friend, although there was no acquaintanceship until it grew out of this arrangement. The artist, a single man, was much Claude's senior; but Claude's taste for design, and love of work, and the artist's grave sincerity, simplicity, and cordiality of character—he was a Spaniard, with a Spaniard's perfect courtesy—made a mutual regard, which only a common diffidence prevented from running into comradeship.

One Saturday afternoon Claude, thirsting for outdoor air, left his eyrie for a short turn in Canal Street. The matinée audiences were just out, and the wide balcony-shaded sidewalks were crowded with young faces and bright attires. Claude was crossing the "neutral ground" toward Bourbon Street, when he saw coming out of Bourbon Street a young man, who might be a Creole, and two young girls in light, and what seemed to him extremely beautiful dresses; especially that of the farther one, who, as the three turned with buoyant step into Canal Street to their left, showed for an instant the profile of her face, and then only her back. Claude's heart beat consciously, and he hurried to lessen the distance between them. He had seen no more than the profile, but for the moment in which he saw it, it seemed to be none other than the face of Marguerite!

# CHAPTER XIII

## THE CHASE

Claude came on close behind. No; now he could see his mistake, it was not she. But he could not regret it. This was Marguerite repeated, yet transcended. The stature was just perceptibly superior. The breadth and grace of these shoulders were better than Marguerite's. The hair, arranged differently and far more effectively than he had ever seen it on Marguerite's head, seemed even more luxurious than hers. There was altogether a finer dignity in this one's carriage than in that of the little maid of the inn. And see, now,—now!—as she turns her head to glance into this shop window! It is, and it isn't, it isn't, and it is, and—no, no, it is not Marguerite! It is like her in profile, singularly like, yet far beyond her; the nose a little too fine, and a certain sad firmness about the mouth and eyes, as well as he could see in the profile, but profiles are so deceptive—that he had never seen in Marguerite.

"But how do I know? What do I know?" he asked himself, still following on. "The Marguerite I know is but a thing of my dreams, and this is not that Marguerite of my actual sight, to whom I never gave a word or smile or glance that calls for redemption. This is the Marguerite of my dreams."

Claude was still following, when without any cause that one could see, the young man of the group looked back. He had an unpleasant face; it showed a small offensive energy that seemed to assert simply him and all his against you and all yours. His eyes were black, piercing, and hostile. They darted their glances straight into Claude's. Guilty Claude! dogging the steps of ladies on the street! He blushed for shame, turned a corner into Exchange Alley, walked a little way down it, came back, saw the great crowd coming and going, vehicles of all sorts hurrying here and there; ranks of street-cars waiting their turns to start to all points of the compass; sellers of peanuts and walking-sticks, buyers of bouquets, acquaintances meeting or overtaking one another, nodding bonnets, lifted hats, faces, faces, faces; but the one face was gone.

Caught, Claude? And by a mere face? The charge is too unkind. Young folly, yes, or old folly, may read goodness rashly into all beauty, or not care to read it in any. But it need not be so. Upon the face of youth the soul within writes its confessions and promises; and when the warm pulses of young nature are sanctified by upward yearnings, and a pure conscience, the soul that seeks its mate will seek that face which, behind and through all excellencies of mere tint and feature, mirrors back the seeker's own faiths and hopes; and when that is found, that to such a one is beauty. Judge not; you never saw this face, fairer than Marguerite's, to say whether its beauty was mere face, or the transparent shrine of an equal nobility within.

Besides, Claude would have fired up and denied the first word of the charge with unpleasant flatness. To be caught means to be in love, to be in love implies a wish and hope to marry, and these were just what Claude could not allow. May not a man, nevertheless, have an ideal of truth and beauty and look worshipfully upon its embodiment? Humph!

His eyes sought her in vain not only on that afternoon, but on many following. The sun was setting every day later and later through the black lace-work of pecan-trees and behind low dark curtains of orange groves, yet he began to be more and more tardy each succeeding day in meeting his father under the riverside oaks of the Exposition grounds. And then, on the seventh day, he saw her again.

Now he was more confident than ever that this vision and he, except in dreams, had never spoken to each other. Yet the likeness was wonderful. But so, too, was the unlikeness. True, this time, she only flashed across his sight—out of a bank, into a carriage where a very "American"-looking lady sat waiting for her and was gone. But the bank; the carriage; that lady; those earlier companions,—no, this could not be Marguerite. Marguerite would have been with her mother. Now, if one could see Madame Beausoleil's daughter with Madame Beausoleil at her side to identify her and distinguish her from this flashing and vanishing apparition it would clear away a trying perplexity. Why not be bold and call upon them where they were dwelling? But where? Their names were not in the directory. Now, inventive talent, do your best.

"Well!" said St. Pierre after a long silence. Claude and he were out on the swollen Mississippi pulling with steady leisure for the home-side shore, their skiff pointed half to and half from the boiling current. The sun was gone; a purple dusk wrapped either low bank; a steamboat that had passed up stream was now, at the turning of the bend, only a cluster of soft red lights; Venus began to make a faint silvery pathway across the waters. St. Pierre had the forward seat, at Claude's back. The father looked with fond perplexity at the strong young shoulders swinging silently with his own, forward and backward in slow, monotonous strokes, and said again:

"Well? Whass matter? Look like cat got yo' tongue. Makin' new mash-in?" Then in a low dissatisfied tone—"I reckon somet'in'

152

mighty curious." He repeated the last three words in the Acadian speech: "Tcheuque-chose bien tchurieux."

"Yass," replied the son, "mighty strange. I tell you when we come at home."

He told all. Recounted all his heart's longings, all his dreams, every least pang of self-reproach, the idealization of Marguerite, and the finding of that ideal incarnated in one who was and yet seemed not to be, or rather seemed to be and yet was not, Marguerite. And then he went on to re-assure his father that this could never mean marriage, never mean the father's supplanting. A man could worship what he could never hope to possess. He would rather worship this than win such kind as he would dare woo.

He said all these things in a very quiet way, with now and then a silent pause, and now and then a calm, self-contained tone in resuming; yet his sentences were often disconnected, and often were half soliloquy. Such were the only betrayals of emotion on either side until Claude began to treat—in the words just given—his father's own heart interests; then the father's eyes stood brimming full. But St. Pierre did not speak. From the first he had listened in silence and he offered no interruption until at length Claude came to that part about the object of his regard being so far, so utterly, beyond his reach. Then—

"Stop! Dass all foolishness! You want her? You kin have her!"

"Ah, papa! you dawn't awnstand! What I am?"

"Ah, bah! What anybody is? What she is? She invanted bigger mash-in dan you? a mo' better corn-stubbl' destroyer and plant-corner?" He meant corn-planter. "She invant a more handier doubl'-action pea-vine rake? What she done mak' her so gran'? Naw, sir! She look fine in de face, yass; and dass all you know. Well, dass all right; dass de 'Cajun way—pick 'em out by face. You begin 'Cajun way, for why you dawn't finish 'Cajun way? All you got do, you git good saddle-hoss and ride. Bom-bye you see her, you ride behind her till you find where her daddy livin' at. Den you ride pas' yondah every day till fo', five days, and den you see de ole man come scrape friend wid you. Den he hass you drop round, and fus' t'ing you know—adjieu la calége!"

Claude did not dispute the point, though he hardly thought this case could be worked that way. He returned in silent thought to the question, how to find Madame Beausoleil. He tried the mail; no response. He thought of advertising; but that would never do. Imagine, "If Madame Beausoleil, late of Vermilionville, will leave her address at this office, she will hear of something not in the least to her advantage." He couldn't advertise.

It was midday following the eve of his confession to his father.

153

For the last eleven or twelve days, ever since he had seen that blessed apparition turn with the two young friends into Canal Street out of Bourbon—he had been venturing daily, for luncheon, just down into Bourbon Street, to the Christian Women's Exchange. Now, by all the laws of fortune he should in that time have seen in there at least once or twice a day already, the face he was ever looking for. But he had not; nor did he to-day. He only saw, or thought he saw, the cashier—I should say the cashieress—glance crosswise at him with eyes that seemed to him to say:

"Fool; sneak; whelp; 'Cajun; our private detectives are watching you."

Both rooms and the veranda were full of ladies and gentlemen whose faces he dared not lift his eyes to look into. And yet even in that frame there suddenly came to him one of those happy thoughts that are supposed to be the inspirations of inventive genius. A pleasant little female voice near him said:

"And apartments up-stairs that they rent to ladies only!" And instantly the thought came that Marguerite and her mother might be living there. One more lump of bread, a final gulp of coffee, a short search for the waiter's check, and he stands at the cashieress's desk. She makes change without looking at him or ceasing to tell a small hunchbacked spinster standing by about somebody's wedding. But suddenly she starts.

"Oh! wasn't that right? You gave me four bits, didn't you? And I gave you back two bits and a picayune, and—sir? Does Madame who? Oh! yes. I didn't understand you; I'm a little deaf on this side; scarlet fever when I was a little girl. I'm not the regular cashier, she's gone to attend the wedding of a lady friend. Just wait a moment, please, while I make change for these ladies. Oh, dear! ma'am, is that the smallest you've got? I don't believe I can change that, ma'am. Yes—no—stop! yes, I can! no, I can't! let's see! yes, yes, yes, I can; I've got it; yes, there! I didn't think I had it." She turned again to Claude with sisterly confidence. "Excuse me for keeping you waiting; haven't I met you at the Y. M. C. A. sociable? Well, you must excuse me, but I was sure I had. Of course I didn't if you was never there; but you know in a big city like this you're always meeting somebody that's ne-e-early somebody else that you know— oh! didn't you ask me—oh, yes! Madame Beausoleil! Yes, she lives here, she and her daughter. But she's not in. Oh! I'm sorry. Neither of them is here. She's not in the city; hasn't been for two weeks. They're coming back; we're expecting them every day. She heard of the death of a relative down in Terrebonne somewhere. I wish they would come back; we miss them here; I judge they're relatives of

154

yours, if I don't mistake the resemblance; you seem to take after the daughter; wait a minute."

Some one coming up to pay looked at Claude to see what the daughter was like, and the young man slipped away, outblushing the night sky when the marshes are afire.

The question was settled; settled the wrong way. He hurried on across Canal Street. Marguerite had not been, as he had construed the inaccurate statement, in the city for two weeks. Resemblances need delude him no longer. He went on into Carondelet Street and was drawing near the door and stairway leading to his friend's studio and his own little workroom above it, when suddenly from that very stairway and door issued she whom, alas! he might now no longer mistake for Marguerite, yet who, none the less for lessening hope, held him captive.

# CHAPTER XIV

# WHO SHE WAS

For a moment somewhat more than her profile shone upon Claude's bewildered gaze.

"I shall see her eye to eye at last!" shouted his heart within: but the next moment she turned away, and with two companions who came across the same threshold, moved up the street, and, at the nearest corner, vanished. Her companions were the American lady and the artist. Claude wheeled, and hurried to pass around the square in the opposite direction, and, as he reached the middle of its third side, saw the artist hand them into the street-car, lift his hat, and return towards the studio. The two men met at the foot of the stairs. The Spaniard's countenance betrayed a restrained elation.

"You goin' see a picture now," he said, in a modestly triumphant tone. "Come in," he added, as Claude would have passed the studio door.

They went in together. The Spaniard talked; Claude scarcely spoke. I cannot repeat the conversation literally, but the facts are these: A few evenings before, the artist had been one of the guests at a musical party given by a lady whose name he did not mention. He happened—he modestly believed it accidental—to be seated beside the hostess, when a young lady—"jung Creole la-thy," he called her—who was spending a few days with her, played the violin. The Spaniard's delicate  propriety left her also nameless; but he explained that, as he understood, she was from the Teche. She played charmingly—"for an amateur," he qualified: but what had struck him more than the music was her beauty, her figure, her picturesque grace. And when he confessed his delight in these, his hostess, seemingly on the inspiration of the moment, said:

"Paint her picture! Paint her just so! I'll give you the order. Not a mere portrait—a picture." And he had agreed, and the "jung" lady had consented. The two had but just now left the studio. To-morrow a servant would bring violin, music-rack, etc.; the ladies would follow, and then—

"You hear music, anyhow," said the artist. That was his gentle way of intimating that Claude was not invited to be a looker-on.

On the next day, Claude, in his nook above, with the studio below shut from view by the curtain of his inner window, heard the ladies come. He knows they are these two, for one voice, the elder, blooms out at once in a gay abundance of words, and the other speaks in soft, low tones that, before they reach his ear, run indistinguishably together.

Soon there comes the sound of tuning the violin, while the older voice is still heard praising one thing and another, and asking careless questions.

"I suppose that cotton cloth covers something that is to have a public unveiling some day, doesn't it?"

Claude cannot hear the answer; the painter drops his voice even below its usual quiet tone. But Claude knows what he must be saying; that the cloth covers  merely a portrait he is finishing of a young man who has sat for it to please a wifeless, and, but for him, childless, and fondly devoted father. And now he can tell by the masculine step, and the lady's one or two lively words, that the artist has drawn away the covering from his (Claude's) own portrait. But the lady's young companion goes on tuning her instrument—"tink, tink, tink;" and now the bow is drawn.

"Why, how singular!" exclaims the elder lady. "Why, my dear, come here and see! Somebody has got your eyes! Why, he's got your whole state of mind, a reduplication of it. And—I declare, he looks almost as good as you do! If—I"—

The voice stops short. There is a moment's silence in which the unseen hearer doubts not the artist is making signs that yonder window and curtain are all that hide the picture's original, and the voice says again,—

"I wish you'd paint my picture," and the violin sounds once more its experimental notes.

But there are other things which Claude can neither hear, nor see, nor guess. He cannot see that the elder lady is already wondering at, and guardedly watching, an agitation betrayed by the younger in a tremor of the hand that fumbles with her music-sheets and music-stand, in the foot that trembles on the floor, in the reddened cheek, and in the bitten lip. He may guess that the painter sits at his easel with kindling eye; but he cannot guess that just as the elder lady is about to say,—

"My dear, if you don't feel"—the tremor vanishes, the lips gently set, and only the color remains. But he hears the first soft moan of the tense string under the bow, and a second, and another; and then, as he rests his elbows upon the table before him, and covers his face in his trembling hands, it seems to him as if his own lost heart had entered into that vibrant medium, and is pouring thence to heaven and her ear its prayer of love.

Paint, artist, paint! Let your brushes fly! None can promise you she shall ever look quite like this again. Catch the lines,—the waving masses and dark coils of that loose-bound hair; the poise of head and neck; the eloquent sway of the form; the folds of garments that no longer hide, but are illumined by, the plenitude of an inner life and grace; the elastic feet; the ethereal energy and discipline of arms and shoulders; the supple wrists; the very fingers quivering on the strings; the rapt face, and the love-inspired eyes.

Claude, Claude! when every bird in forest and field knows the call of its mate, can you not guess the meaning of those strings? Must she open those sealed lips and call your very name—she who would rather die than call it?

He does not understand. Yet, without understanding, he answers. He rises from his seat; he moves to the window; he will not tiptoe or peep; he will be bold and bad. Brazenly he lifts the curtain and looks down; and one, one only—not the artist and not the patroness of art, but that one who would not lift her eyes to that window for all the world's wealth—knows he is standing there, listening and looking down. He counts himself all unseen, yet presently shame drops the curtain. He turns away, yet stands hearkening. The music is about to end. The last note trembles on the air. There is silence. Then someone moves from a chair, and then the single cry of admiration and delight from the player's companion is the player's name,—

"Marguerite Beausoleil!"

Hours afterward there sat Claude in the seat where he had sunk down when he heard that name. The artist's visitors had made

157

a long stay, but at length they were gone. And now Claude, too, rose to go out. His steps were heard below, and presently the painter's voice called persuadingly up:—

"St. Pierre! St. Pierre! Come, see."

They stood side by side before the new work. Claude gazed in silence. At length he said, still gazing:

"I'll buy it when 'tis finish'."

But the artist explained again that it was being painted for Marguerite's friend.

"For what she want it?" demanded Claude. The Spaniard smiled and intimated that the lady probably thought he could paint. "But at any rate," he went on to say, "she seemed to have a hearty affection for the girl herself, whom," he said, "she had described as being as good as she looked." Claude turned and went slowly out.

When at sunset he stood under the honey-locust tree on the levee where he was wont to find his father waiting for him, he found himself alone. But within speaking distance he saw St. Pierre's skiff just being drawn ashore by a ragged negro, who presently turned and came to him, half-lifting the wretched hat that slouched about his dark brows, and smiling.

"Sim like you done fo'got me," he said. "Don't you 'member how I use' live at Belle Alliance? Yes, seh. I's de one what show Bonaventure de road to Gran' Point'. Yes, seh. But I done lef' dah since Mistoo Wallis sole de place. Yes, seh. An' when I meet up wid you papa you nevva see a nigger so glad like I was. No, seh. An' likewise you papa. Yes, seh. An' he ass me is I want to wuck fo' him, an' I see he needin' he'p, an' so I tu'n in an' he'p him. Oh, yes, seh! dass mo' 'n a week, now, since I been wuckin' fo' you papa."

They got into the skiff and pushed off, the negro alone at the oars.

"Pow'ful strong current on udder side," he said, pulling quietly up-stream to offset the loss of way he must make presently in crossing the rapid flood. "Mistoo Claude, I see a gen'leman dis day noon what I ain't see' befo' since 'bout six year' an' mo'. I disremember his name, but——"

"Tarbox?" asked Claude with sudden interest.

"Yes, seh. Dass it! Tah-bawx. Sim like any man ought to 'member dat name. Him an' you papa done gone down de canal. Yes, seh; in a pirogue. He come in a big hurry an' say how dey got a big crevasse up de river on dat side, an' he want make you papa see one man what livin' on Lac Cataouaché. Yes, seh. An you papa say you fine you supper in de pot. An' Mistoo Tah-bawx he say he want you teck one hoss an' ride up till de crevasse an' you fine one frien' of yose yondah, one ingineer; an' he say—Mistoo Tah-bawx—how he

158

'low to meet up wid you at you papa' house to-morrow daylight. Yes, seh; Mistoo Tah-bawx; yes, seh."

## CHAPTER XV

## CAN THEY CLOSE THE BREAK?

The towering cypresses of the far, southern swamps have a great width of base, from which they narrow so rapidly in the first seven or eight feet of their height, and thence upward taper so gradually, that it is almost or quite impossible for an axe-man, standing at their roots, to chop through the great flare that he finds abreast of him, and bring the trees down. But when the swamps are deep in water, the swamper may paddle up to these trees, whose narrowed waists are now within the swing of his axe, and standing up in his canoe, by a marvel of balancing skill, cut and cut, until at length his watchful, up-glancing eye sees the forest giant bow his head. Then a shove, a few backward sweeps of the paddle, and the canoe glides aside, and the great trunk falls, smiting the smooth surface of the water with a roar that, miles away, reaches the ear like the thunder of artillery. The tree falls: but if the woodsman has not known how to judge and choose wisely when the inner wood is laid bare under the first big chip that flies, there are many chances that the fallen tree will instantly sink to the bottom of the water, and cannot be rafted out. One must know his craft, even in Louisiana swamps. "Knowledge is power."

When Zoséphine and Mr. Tarbox finished out that Sunday twilight walk, they talked, after leaving the stile behind, only on business. He told her of having lately been, with a certain expert, in the swamps of Barataria, where he had seen some noble cypress forests tantalizingly near to navigation and market, but practically a great way off, because the levees of the great sugar estates on the Mississippi River shut out all deep overflows. Hence these forests could be bought for, seemingly, a mere tithe of their value. Now, he proposed to buy such a stretch of them along the edge of the shaking prairie north of Lake Cataouaché as would show on his part, he said, "caution, but not temerity."

He invited her to participate. "And why?" For the simple

159

reason that the expert, and engineer, had dropped the remark that, in his opinion, a certain levee could not possibly hold out against the high water of more than two or three more years, and that when it should break it would spread, from three to nine feet of water, over hundreds of square miles of swamp forests, prairies tremblantes, and rice and sugar fields, and many leagues of railway. Zoséphine had consented; and though Mr. Tarbox had soon after gone upon his commercial travels, he had effected the purchase by correspondence, little thinking that the first news he should hear on returning to New Orleans would be that the remotely anticipated "break" had just occurred.

And now, could and would the breach be closed, or must all Barataria soon be turned into, and remain for, months, a navigable yellow sea? This, Claude knew, was what he must hasten to the crevasse to discover, and return as promptly to report upon, let his heart-strings draw as they might towards the studio in Carondelet Street and the Christian Women's Exchange.

# CHAPTER XVI

## THE OUTLAW AND THE FLOOD

What suffering it costs to be a coward! Some days before the crevasse occurred, he whom we know as the pot-hunter stood again on the platform of that same little railway station whence we once saw him vanish at sight of Bonaventure Deschamps. He had never ventured there since, until now. But there was a new station agent.

His Indian squaw was dead. A rattlesnake had given her its fatal sting, and the outcast, dreading all men and the coroner not the least, had, silently and alone, buried her on the prairie.

The train rolled up to the station again as before. Claude's friend, the surveyor, stepped off with a cigar in his mouth, to enjoy in the train's momentary stay the delightful air that came across the open prairie. The pot-hunter, who had got rid of his game, ventured near his former patron. It might be the engineer could give him work whereby to earn a day's ready money. He was not disappointed. The engineer told him to come in a day or two, by the waterways the pot-hunter knew so well, across the swamps and prairies to Bayou Terrebonne and the little court-house town of Houma. And then he added:

"I heard this morning that somebody had been buying the swamp land all around you out on Lake Cataouaché. Is it so?"

The Acadian looked vacant and shook his head.

"Yes," said the other, "a Madame Beausoleil, or somebod— What's the matter?"

"All aboard!" cried the train conductor.

"The fellow turned pale," said the surveyor, as he resumed his seat in the smoking-car and the landscape began again to whirl by.

The pot-hunter stood for a moment, and then slowly, as if he stole away from some sleeping enemy, left the place. Alarm went with him like an attendant ghost. A thousand times that day, in the dark swamp, on the wide prairie, or under his rush-thatch on the lake-side, he tortured himself with one question: Why had she— Zoséphine—reached away out from Carancro to buy the uncultivable and primeval wilderness round about his lonely hiding-place? Hour after hour the inexplicable problem seemed to draw near and nearer to him, a widening, tightening, dreamlike terror, that, as it came, silently pointed its finger of death at him. He was glad enough to leave his cabin next day in his small, swift pirogue— shot-gun, axe, and rifle his only companions—for Terrebonne.

It chanced to be noon of the day following, when he glided up the sunny Terrebonne towards the parish seat. The shores of the stream have many beauties, but the Acadian's eyes were alert to any thing but them. The deep green, waxen-leaved casino hedges; the hedges of Cherokee rose, and sometimes of rose and casino mingled; the fields of corn and sugar-cane; the quaint, railed, floating bridges lying across the lazy bayou; the orange-groves of aged, giant trees, their dark green boughs grown all to a tangle with well-nigh the density of a hedge, and their venerable trunks hairy with green-gray lichens; the orange-trees again in the door-yards, with neat pirogues set upon racks under their deep shade; the indescribable floods of sunlight and caverns of shadow; the clear, brown depths beneath his own canoe; or, at the bottom, the dark, waving, green-brown tresses of water-weeds,—these were naught to him.

But the human presence was much; and once, when just ahead of him he espied a young, sunbonneted woman crouching in the pouring sunshine beyond the sod of the bayou's bank, itself but a few inches above the level of the stream, on a little pier of one plank pushed out among the flags and reeds, pounding her washing with a wooden paddle, he stopped the dip of his canoe-paddle, and gazed with growing trepidation and slackening speed. At the outer end of the plank, the habitual dip of the bucket had driven aside the water-lilies, and made a round, glassy space that reflected all but perfectly to him her busy, young, downcast visage.

"How like"—Just then she lifted her head. He started as though his boat had struck a snag. How like—how terribly like to that young Zoséphine whose ill-concealed scorn he had so often felt in days—in years—long gone, at Carancro! This was not, and could not be, the same—lacked half the necessary years; and yet, in the joy of his relief, he answered her bow with a question, "Whose was yonder house?"

She replied in the same Acadian French in which she was questioned, that there dwelt, or had dwelt, and about two weeks ago had died, "Monsieur Robichaux." The pot-hunter's paddle dipped again, his canoe shot on, and two hours later he walked with dust-covered feet into Houma.

The principal tavern there stands on that corner of the court-house square to which the swamper would naturally come first. Here he was to find the engineer. But, as with slow, diffident step he set one foot upon the corner of the threshold, there passed quickly by him and out towards the court-house, two persons,—one a man of a county court-room look and with a handful of documents, and the other a woman whom he knew at a glance. Her skirts swept his ankles as he shrank in sudden and abject terror against the wall, yet she did not see him.

He turned and retreated the way he had come, nothing doubting that only by the virtue of a voodoo charm which he carried in his pocket he had escaped, for the time being, a plot laid for his capture. For the small, neatly-robed form that you may still see disappearing within the court-house door beside the limping figure of the probate clerk is Zoséphine Beausoleil. She will finish the last pressing matter of the Robichaux succession now in an hour or so, and be off on the little branch railway, whose terminus is here, for New Orleans.

When the pot-hunter approached Lake Cataouaché again, he made on foot, under cover of rushes and reeds taller than he, a wide circuit and reconnoissance of his hut. While still a long way off, he saw, lighted by the sunset rays, what he quickly recognized as a canoe drawn half out of the water almost at his door. He warily drew nearer. Presently he stopped, and stood slowly and softly shifting his footing about on the oozy soil, at a little point of shore only some fifty yards away from his cabin. His eyes, peering from the ambush, descried a man standing by the pirogue and searching with his gaze the wide distances that would soon be hidden in the abrupt fall of the southern night.

162

The pot-hunter knew him. Not by name, but by face. The day the outlaw saw Bonaventure at the little railway station this man was with him. The name the pot-hunter did not know was St. Pierre.

The ambushed man shrank a step backward into his hiding-place. His rifle was in his hand and he noiselessly cocked it. He had not resolved to shoot; but a rifle is of no use until it is cocked. While he so stood, another man came into view and to the first one's side. This one, too, he knew, despite the soft hat that had taken the place of the silk one; for this was Tarbox. The Acadian was confirmed in his conviction that the surveyor's invitation for him to come to Houma was part of a plot to entrap him.

While he still looked the two men got into the canoe and St. Pierre paddled swiftly away. The pot-hunter let down the hammer of his gun, shrank away again, turned and hurried through the tangle, regained his canoe, and paddled off. The men's departure from the cabin was, in his belief, a ruse. But he knew how by circuits and short cuts to follow after them unseen, and this he did until he became convinced that they were fairly in the Company Canal and gliding up its dark colonnade in the direction whence they had evidently come. Then he returned to his cabin and with rifle cocked and with slow, stealthy step entered it, and in headlong haste began to prepare to leave it for a long hiding-out.

He knew every spot of land and water for leagues around, as a bear or a fox would know the region about his den. He had in mind now a bit of dry ground scarce fifty feet long or wide, deeply hidden in the swamp to the north of this lake. How it had ever happened that this dry spot, lifted two or three feet above the low level around it, had been made, whether by some dumb force of nature or by the hand of men yet more untamable than he, had never crossed his thought. It was beyond measure of more value to him to know, by what he had seen growing on it season after season, that for many a long year no waters had overflowed it. In the lake, close to his hut, lay moored his small centerboard lugger, and into this he presently threw his few appliances and supplies, spread sail, and skimmed away, with his pirogue towing after.

His loaded rifle lay within instant reach. By choice he would not have harmed any living creature that men call it wrong to injure; but to save himself, not only from death, but from any risk of death, rightful or wrongful, he would, not through courage, but in the desperation of frantic cowardice, have killed a hundred men, one by one.

By this time it was night; and when first the lugger and, after it was hidden away, the pirogue, had carried him up a slender bayou as near as they could to the point he wished to reach, he had still to drag the loaded pirogue no small distance through the dark, often wet and almost impenetrable woods. He had taken little rest and less sleep in his late journeyings, and when at length he cast himself down before his fire of dead fagots on the raised spot he had chosen, he slept heavily. He felt safe from man's world, at least for the night.

Only one thing gave him concern as he lay down. It was the fact that when, with the old woods-habit strong on him, he had approached his selected camping ground, with such wariness of movement as the dragging pirogue would allow, he had got quite in sight of it before a number of deer on it bounded away. He felt an unpleasant wonder to know what their unwilling boldness might signify.

He did not awake to replenish his fire until there were only a few live embers shining dimly at his feet. He rose to a sitting posture; and in that same moment there came a confusion of sound—a trampling through bushes—that froze his blood, and robbed his open throat of power to cry. The next instant he knew it was but those same deer. But the first intelligent thought brought a new fear. These most timid of creatures had made but a few leaps and stopped. He knew what that meant! As he leaped to his feet the deer started again, and he heard, to his horror,—where the ground had been dry and caked when he lay down,—the plash of their feet in water.

Trembling, he drew his boots on, made and lighted a torch, and in a moment was dragging his canoe after him in the direction of the lugger. Presently his steps, too, were plashing. He stooped, waved the torch low across the water's surface, and followed the gleam with his scrutiny. But he did so not for any doubt that he would see, as he did, the yellow flood of the Mississippi. He believed, as he believed his existence, that his pursuers had let the river in upon the swamp, ruin whom they might, to drive him from cover.

Presently he stepped into the canoe, cast his torch into the water, took his paddle, and glided unerringly through a darkness and a wild tangle of undergrowth, large and small, where you or I could not have gone ten yards without being lost. He emerged successfully from the forest into the open prairie, and, under a sky whose stars told him it would soon be day, glided on down the little bayou lane, between walls of lofty rushes, up which he had come in the evening, and presently found the lugger as he had left her, with her light mast down, hidden among the brake canes that masked a little cove.

The waters were already in the prairie. As he boarded the little vessel at the stern, a raccoon waddled in noiseless haste over the bow, and splashed into the wet covert of reeds beyond. If only to keep from sharing his quarters with all the refuge-hunting vermin of the noisome wilderness, the one human must move on. He turned the lugger's prow towards the lake, and spread her sails to the faint, cool breeze. But when day broke, the sail was gone.

Far and wide lay the pale green leagues of reeds and bulrushes, with only here and there a low willow or two beside some unseen lagoon, or a sinuous band of darker green, where round rushes and myrtle bushes followed the shore of some hidden bayou. The waters of the lake were gleaming and crinkling in tints of lilac and silver stolen from the air; and away to the right, and yet farther to the left, stood the dark phalanxes of cypress woods.

Thus had a thousand mornings risen on the scene in the sight of the outlaw. Numberless birds fluttered from place to place, snatching their prey, carolling, feeding their young, chattering, croaking, warbling, and swinging on the bending rush. But if you looked again, strange signs of nature's mute anguish began to show. On every log or bit of smaller drift that rain-swollen bayous had ever brought from the forest and thrown upon their banks some wild tenant of the jungle, hare or weasel, cat, otter, or raccoon, had taken refuge, sometimes alone, but oftener sharing it, in common misery and silent truce, with deadly foes. For under all that expanse of green beauty, the water, always abundant, was no longer here and there, but everywhere.

See yonder reed but a few yards away. What singular dark enlargement of stem is that near its top, that curious spiral growth?—growth! It is a great serpent that has climbed and twined himself there, and is holding on for the life he loves as we love ours. And see! On a reed near by him, another; and a little farther off, another; and another—and another! Where were our eyes until now? The surface of the vast brake, as far as one can see such small things, is dotted with like horrid burdens. And somewhere in this wild desolation, in this green prospect of a million deaths waiting in silence alike for harmful and harmless creatures, one man is hiding from all mankind.

# CHAPTER XVII

## WELL HIDDEN

Of all the teeming multitudes of the human world, the pot-hunter knows not one soul who is on his side; not one whom he dare let see his face or come between him and a hiding-place. The water is rising fast. He dare not guess how high it will come; but rise as it may, linger at its height as it may, he will not be driven out. In his belief a hundred men are ready, at every possible point where his foot could overstep the line of this vast inundation, to seize him and drag him to the gallows. Ah, the gallows! Not being dead—not God's anger—not eternal burnings; but simply facing death! The gallows! The tree above his head—the rope around his neck—the signal about to be spoken—the one wild moment after it! These keep him here.

He has taken down sail and mast. The rushes are twelve feet high. They hide him well. With oars, mast, and the like, he has contrived something by which he can look out over their tops. He has powder and shot, coffee, salt, and rice; he will not be driven out! At night he spreads his sail and seeks the open waters of the lake, where he can sleep, by littles, without being overrun by serpents; but when day breaks, there is no visible sign of his presence. Yet he is where he can see his cabin. It is now deep in the water, and the flood is still rising. He is quite sure no one has entered it since he left it. But—the strain of perpetual watching!

When at dawn of the fifth day he again looked for cover in the prairie, the water was too high to allow him concealment, and he sought the screen of some willows that fringed the edge of the swamp forest, anchoring in a few rods' width of open water between them and the woods. He did not fear to make, on the small hearth of mud and ashes he had improvised in his lugger, the meagre fire needed to prepare his food. Its slender smoke quickly mingled with the hazy vapors and shadows of the swamp. As he cast his eye abroad, he found nowhere any sign of human approach. Here and there the tops of the round rushes still stood three feet above the water, but their slender needles were scarcely noticeable. Far and near, over prairie as over lake, lay the unbroken yellow flood. There was no flutter of wings, no whistle of feathered mate to mate, no call of nestlings from the ruined nests. Except the hawk and vulture, the birds were gone. Untold thousands of dumb creatures had clung to life for a time, but now were devoured by birds of prey and by alligators, or were drowned. Thousands still lived on. Behind him in the swamp the wood-birds remained, the gray squirrel still barked and leaped from tree to tree, the raccoon came down to fish, the plundering owl still hid himself through the bright hours, and the chilled snake curled close in the warm folds of the hanging moss. Nine feet of water below. In earlier days, to the northward through the forest, many old timbers rejected in railway construction or repair, with dead logs and limbs, had been drifted together by heavy rains, and had gathered a covering of soil; canebrake, luxurious willow-bushes, and tough grasses had sprung up on them and bound them with their roots. These floating islands the flood, now covering the dense underbrush of the swamp, lifted on its free surface, and, in its slow creep southward, bore through the pillared arcades of the cypress wood and out over the submerged prairies. Many a cowering deer in those last few days that had made some one of these green fragments of the drowned land a haven of despair, the human castaway left unharmed.

Of all sentient creatures in that deluge he was suffering most. He was gaunt and haggard with watching. The thought of pursuit bursting suddenly around him now fastened permanently upon his imagination. He feared to sleep. From the direction of the open water surprise seemed impossible; but from the forest! what instant might it not ring with the whoop of discovery, the many-voiced halting challenge, and the glint of loaded Winchester? And another fear had come. Many a man not a coward, and as used to the sight of serpents as this man, has never been able to be other than a coward concerning them. The pot-hunter held them in terror. It was from fear of them that he had lighted his torch the night of his bivouac in the swamp. Only a knowledge of their ordinary haunts and habits and the art of avoiding them had made the swamp and prairie life bearable. Now all was changed. They were driven from their dens. In the forest one dared not stretch forth the hand to lay it upon any tangible thing until a searching glance had failed to find the glittering eye and forked tongue that meant "Beware!" In the flooded prairie the willow-trees were loaded with the knotted folds of the moccasin, the rattlesnake, and I know not how many other sorts of deadly or only loathsome serpents. Some little creatures at the bottom of the water, feeding on the soft white part of the round rush near its root, every now and then cut a stem free from its base, and let it spring to the surface and float away. Often a snake had wrapped himself about the end above the water, and when this refuge gave way and drifted abroad he would cling for a time, until some less forlorn hope came in sight, and then swim for it. Thus scarce a minute of the day passed, it seemed, but one, two, or three of these creatures, making for their fellow-castaway's boat, were

167

turned away by nervous waving of arms. The nights had proved that they could not climb the lugger's side, and when he was in her the canoe was laid athwart her gunwales; but at night he had to drop the bit of old iron that served for an anchor, and the very first night a large moccasin—not of the dusky kind described in books, but of that yet deadlier black sort, an ell in length, which the swampers call the Congo—came up the anchor-rope. The castaway killed it with an oar; but after that who would have slept?

About sunset of the fifth day, though it was bright and beautiful, the hunter's cunning detected the first subtle signs of a coming storm. He looked about him to see what provision was needed to meet and weather its onset. On the swamp side the loftiest cypresses, should the wind bring any of them down, would not more than cast the spray of their fall as far as his anchorage. The mass of willows on the prairie side was nearer, but its trees stood low,—already here and there the branches touched the water; the hurricane might tear away some boughs, but could do no more. He shortened the anchor-rope, and tried the hold of the anchor on the bottom to make sure the lugger might not swing into the willows, for in every fork of every bough was a huge dark mass of serpents plaited and piled one upon another, and ready at any moment to glide apart towards any new shelter that might be reached.

While eye and hand were thus engaged, the hunter's ear was attentive to sounds that he had been hearing for more than an hour. These were the puff of 'scape-pipes and plash of a paddle-wheel, evidently from a small steamer in the Company Canal. She was coming down it; that is, from the direction of the river and the city.

Whither was she bound? To some one of the hundred or more plantations and plantation homes that the far-reaching crevasse had desolated? Likely enough. In such event she would not come into view, although for some time now he had seen faint shreds of smoke in the sky over a distant line of woods. But it filled him with inward tremors to know that if she chose to leave the usual haunts of navigation on her left, and steam out over the submerged prairies and the lake, and into the very shadow of these cypresses, she could do it without fear of a snag or a shallow. He watched anxiously as the faint smoke reached a certain point. If the next thin curl should rise farther on, it would mean safety. But when it came it seemed to be in the same place as the last; and another the same, and yet another the same: she was making almost a straight line for the spot where he stood. Only a small low point of forest broke the line, and presently, far away, she slowly came out from behind it.

# CHAPTER XVIII

# THE TORNADO

The Acadian stooped at once and with a quick splash launched his canoe. A minute later he was in it, gliding along and just within the edge of the forest where it swept around nearly at right angles to the direction in which the steamboat was coming. Thus he could watch the approaching steamer unseen, while every moment putting distance between himself and the lugger.

The strange visitor came on. How many men there were on her lower deck! Were they really negroes, or had they blackened their faces, as men sometimes do when they are going to hang a poor devil in the woods? On the upper deck are two others whose faces do not seem to be blackened. But a moment later they are the most fearful sight of all; for only too plainly does the fugitive see that they are the same two men who stood before the doorway of his hut six days before. And see how many canoes on the lower deck!

While the steamer is yet half a mile away from the hidden lugger, her lamps and fires and their attendant images in the water beneath glow softly in the fast deepening twilight, and the night comes swiftly down. The air is motionless. Across the silent waste an engine bell jangles; the puff of steam ceases; the one plashing paddle-wheel at the stern is still; the lights glide more and more slowly; with a great crash and rumble, that is answered by the echoing woods, the anchor-chain runs out its short measure, and the steamer stops.

Gently the pot-hunter's paddle dipped again, and the pirogue moved back towards the lugger. It may be that the flood was at last numbing his fear, as it had so soon done that of all the brute-life around him; it was in his mind to do something calling for more courage than he had ever before commanded in his life, save on that one day in Carancro, when, stung to madness by the taunts of a brave man, and driven to the wall, he had grappled and slain his tormentor. He had the thought now to return, and under cover of the swamp's deep outer margin of shadow, silently lift into the canoe the bit of iron that anchored the lugger, and as noiselessly draw her miles away to another covert; or if the storm still held back, even at length to step the mast, spread the sail, and put the horizon between him and the steamer before daybreak. This he had now started to do, and would do, if only courage would hold on and the storm hold off.

169

For a time his canoe moved swiftly; but as he drew near the lugger his speed grew less and less, and eye and ear watched and hearkened with their intensest might. He could hear talking on the steamer. There was a dead calm. He had come to a spot just inside the wood, abreast of the lugger. His canoe slowly turned and pointed towards her, and then stood still. He sat there with his paddle in the water, longing like a dumb brute; longing, and, without a motion, struggling for courage enough to move forward. It would not come. His heart jarred his frame with its beating. He could not stir.

As he looked out upon the sky a soft, faint tremor of light glimmered for a moment over it, without disturbing a shadow below. The paddle stirred gently, and the canoe slowly drew back; the storm was coming to betray him with its lightnings. In the black forest's edge the pot-hunter lingered trembling. Oh for the nerve to take a brave man's chances! A little courage would have saved his life. He wiped the dew from his brow with his sleeve; every nerve had let go. Again there came across the water the very words of those who talked together on the steamer. They were saying that the felling of trees would begin in the morning; but they spoke in a tongue which Acadians of late years had learned to understand, though many hated it, but of which he had never known twenty words, and what he had known were now forgotten—the English tongue. Even without courage, to have known a little English would have made the difference between life and death. Another glimmer spread dimly across the sky, and a faint murmur of far-off thunder came to the ear. He turned the pirogue and fled.

Soon the stars are hidden. A light breeze seems rather to tremble and hang poised than to blow. The rolling clouds, the dark wilderness, and the watery waste shine out every moment in the wide gleam of lightnings still hidden by the wood, and are wrapped again in ever-thickening darkness over which thunders roll and jar, and answer one another across the sky. Then, like a charge of ten thousand lancers, come the wind and the rain, their onset covered by all the artillery of heaven. The lightnings leap, hiss, and blaze; the thunders crack and roar; the rain lashes; the waters writhe; the wind smites and howls. For five, for ten, for twenty minutes,—for an hour, for two hours,—the sky and the flood are never for an instant wholly dark, or the thunder for one moment silent; but while the universal roar sinks and swells, and the wide, vibrant illumination shows all things in ghostly half-concealment, fresh floods of lightning every moment rend the dim curtain and leap forth; the glare of day falls upon the swaying wood, the reeling, bowing, tossing willows, the seething waters, the whirling rain, and in the midst the small form of the distressed steamer, her revolving paddle-wheels toiling behind to lighten the strain upon her anchor-chains; then all are dim ghosts again, while a peal, as if the heavens were rent, rolls off around the sky, comes back in shocks and throbs, and sinks in a long roar that before it can die is swallowed up in the next flash and peal.

The deserted lugger is riding out the tornado. Whirled one moment this way and another that, now and again taking in water, her forest-shelter breaks the force of many a gust that would have destroyed her out in the open. But in the height of the storm her poor substitute for an anchor lets go its defective hold on the rushy bottom and drags, and the little vessel backs, backs, into the willows. She escapes such entanglement as would capsize her, and by and by, when the wind lulls for a moment and then comes with all its wrath from the opposite direction, she swings clear again and drags back nearly to her first mooring and lies there, swinging, tossing, and surviving still,—a den of snakes.

The tempest was still fierce, though abating, and the lightning still flashed, but less constantly, when at a point near the lugger the pirogue came out of the forest, laboring against the wind and half-filled with water. On the face of the storm-beaten man in it each gleam of the lightning showed the pallid confession of mortal terror. Where that frail shell had been, or how often it had cast its occupant out, no one can ever know. He was bareheaded and barefooted. One cannot swim in boots; without them, even one who has never dared learn how may hope to swim a little.

In the darkness he drew alongside the lugger, rose, balanced skilfully, seized his moment, and stepped safely across her gunwale. A slight lurch caused him to throw his arms out to regain his poise; the line by which he still held the canoe straightened out its length and slipped from his grasp. In an instant the pirogue was gone. A glimmer of lightning showed her driving off sidewise before the wind. But it revealed another sight also. It was dark again, black; but the outcast stood freezing with horror and fright, gazing just in advance of his feet and waiting for the next gleam. It came, brighter than the last; and scarcely a step before him he saw three great serpents moving towards the spot that gave him already such slender footing. He recoiled a step—another; but instantly as he made the second a cold, living form was under his foot, its folds flew round his ankle, and once! twice! it struck! With a frantic effort he spurned it from him; all in the same instant a blaze of lightning discovered the maimed form and black and red markings of a "bastard hornsnake," and with one piercing wail of despair, that was drowned in the shriek of the wind and roar of the thunder, he fell.

A few hours later the winds were still, the stars were out, a sweet silence had fallen upon water and wood, and from her deck the watchmen on the steamer could see in the north-eastern sky a broad, soft, illumination, and knew it was the lights of slumbering New Orleans, eighteen miles away.

By and by, farther to the east, another brightness began to grow and gather this light into its outstretched wings. In the nearest wood a soft twitter came from a single tiny bird. Another voice answered it. A different note came from a third quarter; there were three or four replies; the sky turned to blue, and began to flush; a mocking-bird flew out of the woods on her earliest quest for family provision; a thrush began to sing; and in a moment more the whole forest was one choir.

What wonderful purity was in the fragrant air; what color was on the calm waters and in the deep sky; how beautiful, how gentle was Nature after her transport of passion! Shall we ever subdue her and make her always submissive and compliant? Who knows? Who knows what man may do with her when once he has got self, the universal self, under perfect mastery? See yonder huge bull-alligator swimming hitherward out of the swamp. Even as you point he turns again in alarm and is gone. Once he was man's terror, Leviathan. The very lions of Africa and the grizzlies of the Rockies, so they tell us, are no longer the bold enemies of man they once were. "Subdue the earth"—it is being done. Science and art, commerce and exploration, are but parts of religion. Help us, brothers all, with every possible discovery and invention to complete the conquest begun in that lost garden whence man and woman first came forth, not for vengeance but for love, to bruise the serpent's head. But as yet, both within us and without us, what terrible revolts doth Nature make! what awful victories doth she have over us, and then turn and bless and serve us again!

As the sun was rising, one of the timber-cutters from the steamer stood up in his canoe about half a mile away, near the wood and beside some willows, and halloed and beckoned. And when those on the steamer hearkened he called again, bidding them tell "de boss" that he had found a canoe adrift, an anchored boat, and a white man in her, dead.

Tarbox and St. Pierre came in a skiff.

"Is he drowned?" asked Mr. Tarbox, while still some distance off.

"Been struck by lightnin' sim like," replied the negro who had found the body.—"Watch out, Mistoo Tah-bawx!" he added, as the skiff drew near; "dat boat dess lousy wid snake'!"

172

Tarbox stood up in the skiff and looked sadly upon the dead face. "It's our man," he said to St. Pierre.

"Dass what I say!" exclaimed the negro. "Yes, seh, so soon I see him I say, mos' sholy dass de same man what Mistoo Tah-bawx lookin' faw to show him 'roun' 'bout de swamp! Yes, seh, not-instandin' I never see him befo'! No, seh.—Lawd! look yondeh! look dat big bahsta'd hawn-snake! He kyant git away: he's hu't! Lawd! dass what kill dat man! Dat man trawmp on him in de dark, and he strack him wid his hawny tail! Look at dem fo' li'l' spot' on de man' foot! Now, Mistoo Tah-bawx! You been talk' 'bout dem ah bahsta'd hawn-snake not pizen! Well, mos' sholy dey bite ain't pizen; but if dat hawn on de een of his tail dess on'y tetch you, you' gone! Look at dat man! Kill' him so quick dey wa'n't time for de place to swell whah he was hit!" But Tarbox quietly pointed out to St. Pierre that the tiny wounds were made by the reptile's teeth.

"The coroner's verdict will probably be 'privation and exposure,'" said he softly; "but it ought to be, 'killed by fright and the bite of a harmless snake.'"

On his murmured suggestion, St. Pierre gave orders that, with one exception, every woodsman go to his tree-felling, and that the lugger and canoe, with the dead man lying untouched, be towed by skiff and a single pair of oars to the head of the canal for inquest and burial.

"I'll go with him," said Tarbox softly to St. Pierre. "We owe him all we're going to get out of these woods, and I owe him a great deal more." When a little later he was left for a moment without a hearer, he said to the prostrate form, "Poor fellow! And to think I had her message to you to come out of this swamp and begin to live the life of a live man!"

The rude funeral moved away, and soon the woods were ringing with the blow of axes and the shout and song of black timber-men as gayly as though there never had been or was to be a storm or a death.

# CHAPTER XIX

## "TEARS AND SUCH THINGS"

Marguerite and her friend had no sooner taken their seats to drive home from the studio the day the sketch was made than Marguerite began a perfect prattle. Her eyes still shone exaltedly, and leaped and fell and darkened and brightened with more than the swift variety of a fountain in the moonlight, while she kept trying in vain to meet her companion's looks with a moment's steady regard.

Claude was found! and she trembled with delight. But, alas! he had heard her passionate call and yet stood still; had looked down upon her in silence, and drawn again the curtain between them. She had thought until the last moment, "He will come; he will confront us as we pass out the door—will overtake us at the foot of the stairs—on the sidewalk—at the carriage window." But it had not been so; and now they were gone from the place; and here sat this friend, this gay, cynical knower of men's and women's ways, answering her chatter in short, smiling responses, with a steady eye fixed on her, and reading, Marguerite believed, as plainly as if it were any of the sign-boards along the rattling street, the writing on her fluttering heart. And so, even while she trembled with strange delight, pain, shame, and alarm pleaded through her dancing glances, now by turns and now in confusion together, for mercy and concealment. But in fact, as this friend sat glancing upon the young face beside her with secret sympathy and admiration, it was only this wild fear of betrayal that at length betrayed.

Reaching the house, the street door was hardly shut behind them when Marguerite would have darted up to her chamber; but her friend caught her hands across the balustrade, and said, with roguery in her own eyes:

"Marguerite, you sweet rowdy—"

"W'at?"

"Yes, what. There's something up; what is it?"

The girl tried to put on surprise; but her eyes failed her again. She leaned on the rail and looked down, meanwhile trying softly to draw away up-stairs; but her friend held on to one hand and murmured:

"Just one question, dearie, just one. I'll not ask another: I'll die first. You'll probably find me in articulo mortis when you come down-stairs. Just one question, lovie."

"W'at it is?"

"It's nothing but this; I ask for information." The voice dropped to a whisper,—"Is he as handsome as his portrait?"

The victim rallied all her poor powers of face, and turned feebly upon the questioner:

"Po'trait? Who?" Her voice was low, and she glanced furtively at the nearest door. "I dawn't awnstan you." Her hand pulled softly for its freedom, and she turned to go, repeating, with averted face, "I dawn't awnstan you 't all."

"Well, never mind then, dear, if you don't understand," responded the tease, with mock tenderness. "But, ma belle Créole—"

"Je suis Acadienne."

"You're an angel, faintly disguised. Only—look around here—only, Angelica, don't try to practise woman's humbug on a woman. At least, not on this old one. It doesn't work. I'll tell you whom I mean." She pulled, but Marguerite held off. "I mean," she hoarsely whispered,—"I mean the young inventor that engineer told us about. Remember?"

Marguerite, with her head bowed low, slowly dragged her hand free, and moved with growing speed up the stairs, saying:

"I dawn't know what is dat. I dawn't awnstan you 't all." Her last words trembled as if nigh to tears. At the top of the stairs the searching murmur of her friend's voice came up, and she turned and looked back.

"Forgive me!" said the figure below. The girl stood a moment, sending down a re-assuring smile.

"You young rogue!" murmured the lady, looking up with ravished eyes. Then she lifted herself on tiptoe, made a trumpet of both little hands, and whispered:

"Don't—worry! We'll bring it out—all right!"

Whereat Marguerite blushed from temple to throat, and vanished.

The same day word came from her mother of her return from Terrebonne, and she hastened to rejoin her in their snug rooms over the Women's Exchange. When she snatched Zoséphine into her arms and shed tears, the mother merely wiped and kissed them away, and asked no explanation.

The two were soon apart. For Marguerite hungered unceasingly for solitude. Only in solitude could she, or dared she, give herself up to the constant recapitulation of every minutest incident of the morning. And that was ample employment. They seemed the happenings of a month ago. She felt as if it were imperative to fix them in her memory now, or lose them in confusion and oblivion forever. Over them all again and again she went, sometimes quickening memory with half-spoken words, sometimes halting in long reverie at some intense juncture: now with tingling pleasure at the unveiling of the portrait, the painter's cautionary revelation of the personal presence above, or Claude's appearance at the window; now with burnings of self-abasement at the passionate but ineffectual beseechings of her violin; and always ending with her face in her hands, as though to hide her face even from herself for shame that with all her calling—her barefaced, as it seemed to her, her abject calling—he had not come.

"Marguerite, my child, it is time for bed."

She obeyed. It was all one, the bed or the window. Her mother, weary with travel, fell asleep; but she—she heard the clock down-stairs strike, and a clock next door attest, twelve—one—two—three—four, and another day began to shine in at the window. As it brightened, her spirits rose. She had been lying long in reverie; now she began once more the oft-repeated rehearsal. But the new day shone into it also. When the silent recital again reached its end, the old distress was no longer there, but in its place was a new, sweet shame near of kin to joy. The face, unhidden, looked straight into the growing light. Whatever else had happened, this remained,— that Claude was found. She silently formed the name on her parted lips—"Claude! Claude! Claude! Claude!" and could not stop though it gave her pain, the pain was so sweet. She ceased only when there rose before her again the picture of him drawing the curtain and disappearing; but even then she remembered the words, "Don't worry; we'll bring it out all right," and smiled.

When Zoséphine, as the first sunbeam struck the window-pane, turned upon her elbow and looked into the fair face beside her, the eyes were closed in sleep. She arose, darkened the room, and left it.

# CHAPTER XX

## LOVE, ANGER, AND MISUNDERSTANDING

The city bells had sounded for noon when the sleeper opened her eyes. While she slept, Claude had arrived again at his father's cottage from the scene of the crevasse, and reported to Tarbox the decision of himself and the engineer, that the gap would not be closed for months to come. While he told it, they sat down with St. Pierre to breakfast. Claude, who had had no chance even to seek sleep, ate like a starved horse. Tarbox watched him closely, with hidden and growing amusement. Presently their eyes fastened on each other steadily. Tarbox broke the silence.

"You don't care how the crevasse turns out. I've asked you a question now twice, and you don't even hear."

"Why you don't ass ag'in?" responded the younger man, reaching over to the meat-dish and rubbing his bread in the last of the gravy. Some small care called St. Pierre away from the board. Tarbox leaned forward on his elbows, and, not knowing he quoted, said softly,—

"There's something up. What is it?"

"Op?" asked Claude, in his full voice, frowning. "Op where?— w'at, w'at is?"

"Ah, yes!" said Tarbox, with affected sadness. "Yes, that's it; I thought so.

'Oh-hon for somebody, oh hey for somebody.'"

Claude stopped with a morsel half-way to his mouth, glared at him several seconds, and then resumed his eating; not like a horse now, but like a bad dog gnawing an old bone. He glanced again angrily at the embodiment of irreverence opposite. Mr. Tarbox smiled. Claude let slip, not intending it, an audible growl, with his eyes in the plate. Mr. Tarbox's smile increased to a noiseless laugh, and grew and grew until it took hopeless possession of him. His nerves relaxed, he trembled, the table trembled with him, his eyes filled with tears, his brows lifted laboriously, he covered his lips with one hand, and his abdomen shrank until it pained him. And Claude knew, and showed he knew it all; that was what made it impossible to stop. At length, with tottering knees, Mr. Tarbox rose and started silently for the door. He knew Claude's eyes were following. He heard him rise to his feet. He felt as though he would have given a thousand dollars if his legs would but last him through the doorway. But to crown all, St. Pierre met him just on the threshold, breaking, with unintelligent sympathy, into a broad, simple smile. Tarbox laid one hand upon the door for support, and at that moment there was a hurtling sound; something whizzed by Tarbox's ear, and the meat-dish crashed against the door-post, and flew into a hundred pieces.

The book-agent ran like a deer for a hundred yards and fell grovelling upon the turf, the laugh still griping him with the energy of a panther's jaws, while Claude, who, in blind pursuit, had come

177

threshing into his father's arms, pulled his hat over his eyes and strode away towards the skiff ferry. As Mr. Tarbox returned towards the cottage, St. Pierre met him, looking very grave, if not displeased. The swamper spoke first.

"Dass mighty good for you I was yondah to stop dat boy. He would 'a' half-kill' you."

"He'd have served me ex-actly right," said the other, and laughed again. St. Pierre shook his head, as though this confession were poor satisfaction, and said,—

"Dass not safe—make a 'Cajun mad. He dawn't git mad easy, but when he git mad it bre'k out all ove' him, yass. He goin' feel bad all day now; I see tear' in his eye when he walk off."

"I'm sorry," said Tarbox sincerely, and presently added, "Now, while you look up a picked gang of timber-men, I'll see if I can charter a little stern-wheel steamer, get that written permission from Madame Beausoleil to cut trees on her land, and so forth, and so forth. You'll hardly see me before bedtime again."

It was the first hour of the afternoon when Claude left his little workroom and walked slowly down to, and across, Canal Street and into Bourbon. He had spent the intervening hours seated at his work-table with his face in his hands. He was in great bitterness. His late transport of anger gave him no burdensome concern. Indeed, there was consolation in the thought that he should, by and by, stand erect before one who was so largely to blame, and make that full confession and apology which he believed his old-time Grande Pointe schoolmaster would have offered could Bonaventure ever have so shamefully forgotten himself. Yet the chagrin of having at once so violently and so impotently belittled himself added one sting more to his fate. He was in despair. An escaped balloon, a burst bubble, could hardly have seemed more utterly beyond his reach than now did Marguerite. And he could not blame her. She was right, he said sternly to himself—right to treat his portrait as something that reminded her of nothing, whether it did so or not; to play on with undisturbed inspiration; to lift never a glance to his window; and to go away without a word, a look, a sign, to any one, when the least breath or motion would have brought him instantly into her sacred presence. She was right. She was not for him. There is a fitness of things, and there was no fitness—he said—of him for her. And yet she must and would ever be more to him than any one else. He would glory in going through life unloved, while his soul lived in and on the phantom companionship of that vision of delight which she was and should ever be. The midday bells sounded softly here and there. He would walk.

As I say, he went slowly down the old rue Bourbon. He had no hunger; he would pass by the Women's Exchange. There was nothing to stop there for; was not Madame Beausoleil in Terrebonne, and Marguerite the guest of that chattering woman in silk and laces? But when he reached the Exchange doors he drifted in as silently and supinely as any drift-log would float into the new crevasse.

The same cashier was still on duty. She lighted up joyously as he entered, and, when he had hung his hat near the door, leaned forward to address him; but with a faint pain in his face, and loathing in his heart, he passed on and out into the veranda. The place was well filled, and he had to look about to find a seat. The bare possibility that she might be there was overpowering. There was a total suspension of every sort of emotion. He felt, as he took his chair and essayed to glance casually around, as light and unreal as any one who ever walked the tight-rope in a dream. The blood leaped in torrents through his veins, and yet his movements, as he fumbled aimlessly with his knife, fork, and glass, were slow and languid.

A slender young waitress came, rested her knuckles on the table, and leaned on them, let her opposite arm hang limply along the sidewise curve of her form, and bending a smile of angelic affection upon the young Acadian, said in a confidential undertone:

"The cashier told me to tell you those ladies have come."

Claude rose quickly and stood looking upon the face before him, speechless. It was to him exactly as if a man in uniform had laid a hand upon his shoulder and said, "You're my prisoner." Then, still gazing, and aware of others looking at him, he slowly sank again into his seat.

"She just told me to tell you," said the damsel. "Yes, sir. Have you ordered?"

"Humph?" He was still looking at her.

"I say, have you given your order?"

"Yass."

She paused awkwardly, for she knew he had not, and saw that he was trying vainly to make her words mean something in his mind.

"Sha'n't I get you some coffee and rolls—same as day before yesterday?"

"Yass." He did not know what she said. His heart had stopped beating; now it began again at a gallop. He turned red. He could see the handkerchief that was wadded into his outer breast-pocket jar in time with the heavy thump, thump, thump beneath it. The waitress staid an awful time. At last she came.

"I waited," she sweetly said, "to get hot ones." He drew the

179

refreshments towards him mechanically. The mere smell of food made him sick. It seemed impossible that he should eat it. She leaned over him lovingly and asked, as if referring to the attitude, "Would you like any thing more?—something sweet?" His flesh crawled. He bent over his plate, shook his head, and stirred his coffee without having put any thing into it.

She tripped away, and he drew a breath of momentary relief, leaned back in his chair, and warily passed his eyes around to see if there was anybody who was not looking at him and waiting for him to begin to eat.

Ages afterward—to speak with Claude's feelings—he rose, took up his check, and went to the desk. The cashier leaned forward and said with soft blitheness:

"They're here. They're up-stairs now."

Claude answered never a word. He paid his check. As he waited for change, he cast another glance over the various groups at the tables. All were strangers. Then he went out. On the single sidewalk step he halted, and red and blind with mortification, turned again into the place; he had left his hat. With one magnificent effort at dignity and unconcern he went to the rack, took down the hat, and as he lowered it towards his head cast a last look down the room, and—there stood Marguerite. She had entered just in time, it seemed to him, but just too late, in fact, to see and understand the blunder. Oh, agony! They bowed to each other with majestic faintness, and then each from each was gone. The girl at the desk saw it and was dumb.

# CHAPTER XXI

## LOVE AND LUCK BY ELECTRIC LIGHT

Mr. Tarbox was really a very brave man. For, had he not been, how could he have ventured, something after the middle of that afternoon, in his best attire, up into Claude's workroom? He came to apologize. But Claude was not there.

He waited, but the young man did not return. The air was hot and still. Mr. Tarbox looked at his watch—it was a quarter of five. He rose and descended to the street, looked up and down it, and then moved briskly down to, and across, Canal Street and into Bourbon. He had an appointment.

Claude had not gone back to his loft at all. He was wandering up and down the streets. About four he was in Bienville Street, where the pleasure-trains run through it on their way out to Spanish Fort, a beautiful pleasure-ground some six miles away from the city's centre, on the margin of Lake Pontchartrain. He was listlessly crossing the way as a train came along, and it was easy for the habit of the aforetime brakeman to move him. As the last platform passed the crossing, he reached out mechanically and swung aboard.

Spanish Fort is at the mouth of Bayou St. John. A draw-bridge spans the bayou. On the farther, the eastern, side, Claude stood leaning against a pile, looking off far beyond West End to where the sun was setting in the swamps about Lake Maurepas. There— there—not seen save by memory's eye, yet there not the less, was Bayou des Acadiens. Ah me! there was Grande Pointe.

"O Bonaventure! Do I owe you"—Claude's thought was in the old Acadian tongue—"Do I owe you malice for this? No, no, no! Better this than less." And then he recalled a writing-book copy that Bonaventure had set for him, of the schoolmaster's own devising: Better Great Sorrow than Small Delight. His throat tightened and his eyes swam.

A pretty schooner, with green hull and new sails, came down the bayou. As he turned to gaze on her, the bridge, just beyond his feet, began to swing open. He stepped upon it and moved towards its centre, his eyes still on the beautiful silent advance of the vessel. With a number of persons who had gathered from both ends of the bridge, he paused and leaned over the rail as the schooner, with her crew looking up into the faces of the throng, glided close by. A female form came beside him, looking down with the rest and shedding upon the air the soft sweetness of perfumed robes. A masculine voice, just beyond, said:

*"A thing of beauty is a joy forever."*

Claude started and looked up, and behold, Marguerite on the arm of Tarbox!

His movement drew their glance, and the next instant Mr. Tarbox, beaming apology and pouring out glad greetings, had him by the hand. Burning, choking, stammering, Claude heard and answered, he knew not how, the voice of the queen of all her kind. Another pair pressed forward to add their salutations. They were Zoséphine and the surveyor.

Because the facilities for entertaining a male visitor were slender at the Women's Exchange, because there was hope of more and cooler air at the lake-side, because Spanish Fort was a pretty and romantic spot and not so apt to be thronged as West End, and because Marguerite, as she described it, was tired of houses and streets, and also because he had something to say to Zoséphine, Mr. Tarbox had brought the pretty mother and daughter out here. The engineer had met the three by chance only a few minutes before, and now as the bridge closed again he passed Zoséphine over to Claude, walked only a little way with them down a path among the shrubbery, and then lifted his hat and withdrew.

For once in his life Mr. G. W. Tarbox, as he walked with Marguerite in advance of Claude and her mother, was at a loss what to say. The drollness of the situation was in danger of overcoming him again. Behind him was Claude, his mind tossed on a wild sea of doubts and suspicions.

"I told him," thought Tarbox, while the girl on his arm talked on in pretty, broken English and sprightly haste about something he had lost the drift of—"I told him I was courting Josephine. But I never proved it to him. And now just look at this! Look at the whole sweet mess! Something has got to be done." He did not mean something direct and openhanded; that would never have occurred to him. He stopped, and with Marguerite faced the other pair. One glance into Claude's face, darkened with perplexity, anger, and a distressful effort to look amiable and comfortable, was one too many; Tarbox burst into a laugh.

"Pardon!" he exclaimed, checking himself until he was red; "I just happened to think of something very funny that happened last week in Arkansas—Madame Beausoleil, I know it must look odd,"—his voice still trembled a little, but he kept a sober face—"and yet I must take just a moment for business. Claude, can I see you?"

They went a step aside. Mr. Tarbox put on a business frown, and said to Claude in a low voice,—

"Hi! diddle, diddle, the cat and the fiddle, the cow jumped over the moon the little dog laughed to see the sport and the dish ran away with the spoon you understand I'm simply talking for talk's sake as we resume our walk we'll inadvertently change partners—a kind of Women's Exchange as it were old Mother Hubbard she went to the cupboard to get her poor dog a bone but when she got there the cupboard—don't smile so broadly—was bare and so the poor dog had none will that be satisfactory?"

Claude nodded, and as they turned again to their companions the exchange was made with the grace, silence, and calm unconsciousness of pure oversight,—or of general complicity. Very soon it suited Zoséphine and Tarbox to sit down upon a little bench beside a bed of heart's-ease and listen to the orchestra. But

182

Marguerite preferred to walk in and out among the leafy shadows of the electric lamps.

And so, side by side, as he had once seen Bonaventure and Sidonie go, they went, Claude and Marguerite, away from all windings of disappointment, all shadows of doubt, all shoals of misapprehension, out upon the open sea of mutual love. Not that the great word of words—affirmative or interrogative—was spoken then or there. They came no nearer to it than this,—

"I wish," murmured Claude,—they had gone over all the delicious "And-I-thought-that-you's" and the sweetly reproachful "Did-you-think-that-I's," and had covered the past down to the meeting on the bridge,—"I wish," he murmured, dropping into the old Acadian French, which he had never spoken to her before,—"I wish"—

"What?" she replied, softly and in the same tongue.

"I wish," he responded, "that this path might never end." He wondered at his courage, and feared that now he had ruined all; for she made no answer. But when he looked down upon her she looked up and smiled. A little farther on she dropped her fan. He stooped and picked it up, and, in restoring it, somehow their hands touched,—touched and lingered; and then—and then—through one brief unspeakable moment, a maiden's hand, for the first time in his life, lay willingly in his. Then, as glad as she was frightened, Marguerite said she must go back to her mother, and they went.

# CHAPTER XXII

## A DOUBLE LOVE-KNOT

Spanish Fort—West End—they are well enough; but if I might have one small part of New Orleans to take with me wherever I may wander in this earthly pilgrimage, I should ask for the old Carrollton Gardens.

They lie near the farthest upper limit of the expanded city. I should want, of course, to include the levee, under which runs one side of the gardens' fence; also the opposite shore of the Mississippi, with its just discernible plantation houses behind their levee; and the great bend of the river itself, with the sun setting in unutterable gorgeousness behind the distant, low-lying pecan groves of Nine-mile Point, and the bronzed and purpled waters kissing the very crown of the great turfed levee, down under whose land side the gardens blossom and give forth their hundred perfumes and bird songs to the children and lovers that haunt their winding alleys of oleander, jasmine, laurestine, orange, aloe, and rose, the grove of magnolias and oaks, and come out upon the levee's top as the sun sinks, to catch the gentle breeze and see the twilight change to moonlight on the water.

One evening as I sat on one of the levee benches here, with one whose I am and who is mine beside me, we noticed on the water opposite us, and near the farther shore, a large skiff propelled with two pairs of oars and containing, besides the two rowers, half a dozen passengers.

Then I remembered that I had seen the same craft when it was farther down the stream. The river is of a typical character about here. Coming around the upper bend, the vast current sweeps across to this, the Carrollton side, and strikes it just above the gardens with an incalculable gnawing, tearing power. Hence the very high levee here; the farther back the levee builders are driven by the corroding waters the lower the ground is under them, and the higher they must build to reach the height they reached before. From Carrollton the current rebounds, and swinging over to the other shore strikes it, boiling like a witch's caldron, just above and along the place where you may descry the levee lock of the Company Canal.

I knew the waters all about there, and knew that this skiff full of passengers, some of whom we could see were women, having toiled through the seething current below, was now in a broad eddy, and, if it was about to cross the stream, would do so only after it had gone some hundred yards farther up the river. There it could cross almost with the current.

And so it did. I had forgotten it again, when presently it showed itself with all its freight, silhouetted against the crimson sky. I said quickly:

"I believe Bonaventure Deschamps is in that boat!"

I was right. The skiff landed, and we saw its passengers step ashore. They came along the levee's crown towards us, "by two, by two." Bonaventure was mated with a young Methodist preacher, who had been my playmate in boyhood, and who lived here in Carrollton. Behind him came St. Pierre and Sidonie. Then followed Claude and Marguerite; and, behind all, Zoséphine and Tarbox.

They had come, they explained to us, from a funeral at the head of the canal. They did not say the funeral of a friend, and yet I could see that every one of them, even the preacher, had shed tears. The others had thought it best and pleasantest to accompany the minister thus far towards his home, then take a turn in the gardens, and then take the horse-cars for the city's centre. Bonaventure and Sidonie were to return next day by steamer to Belle Alliance and Grande Pointe. The thoughtful Tarbox had procured Bonaventure's presence at the inquest of the day before as the identifying witness, thus to save Zoséphine that painful office. And yet it was of Zoséphine's own motion, and by her sad insistence, that she and her daughter followed the outcast to his grave.

"Yes," she had said, laying one hand in Bonaventure's and the other in Sidonie's and speaking in the old Acadian tongue, "when I was young and proud I taught 'Thanase to despise and tease him. I did not know then that I was such a coward myself. If I had been a better scholar, Bonaventure, when we used to go to school to the curé together—a better learner—not in the books merely, but in those things that are so much better than the things books teach—how different all might have been! Thank God, Bonaventure, one of us was." She turned to Sidonie to add,—"But that one was Bonaventure. We will all go"—to the funeral—"we will all go and bury vain regrets—with the dead."

The influence of the sad office they had just performed was on the group still, as they paused to give us the words of greeting we coveted. Yet we could see that a certain sense of being very, very rich in happiness was on them all, though differently on every one.

Zoséphine wore the pear-shaped pearl.

The preacher said good-day, and started down the steps that used to lead from the levee down across a pretty fountained court and into the town. But my friend Tarbox—for I must tell you I like to call him my friend, and like it better every day; we can't all be one sort; you'd like him if you knew him as I do—my friend Tarbox beckoned me to detain him.

"Christian!" I called—that is the preacher's real name. He turned back and met Tarbox just where I stood. They laid their arms across each other's shoulders in a very Methodist way, and I heard Tarbox say:

"I want to thank you once more. We've put you to a good deal of trouble. You gave us the best you had: I'll never forget what you said about 'them who through fear of death are all their life-time subject to bondage.' I wish you were a Catholic priest."

"Why?"

"So we could pay you for your trouble. I don't think you ought to take it hard if you get a check in to-morrow's mail."

"Thy money survive with thee," said the preacher. "Is that all

185

you want me to be a priest for? Isn't there another reason?" His eyes twinkled. "Isn't there something else I could do for you—you or Claude—if I should turn priest?"

"Yes," said Tarbox, with grave lips, but merry eyes; "we've both got to have one."

In fact they had two. Yet I have it from her husband himself, that Madame Tarbox insists to this day, always with the same sweet dignity, that she never did say yes.

On the other hand, when Claude and Marguerite were kneeling at the altar the proud St. Pierre, senior, spoke an audible and joyously impatient affirmative every time either of them was asked a question. When the time came for kissing, Sidonie, turning from both brides, kissed St. Pierre the more for that she kissed not Claude, then turned again and gave a tear with the kiss she gave to Zoséphine. But the deepest, gladdest tears at those nuptials were shed by Bonaventure Deschamps.

www.ingramcontent.com/pod-product-compliance
Lightning Source LLC
Chambersburg PA
CBHW011504170626
46812CB00008B/2970